DAUGHTER OF
GODS AND SHADOWS

ACKNOWLEDGMENTS

I will tell you that writing this story was more than a labor of love. It was labor fueled by determination, apprehension, confusion, fear, and finally desperation. And I loved every minute of it.

"We're not going to release it until it's ready."

My editor, Monique Patterson, said those words to me four years and six versions ago and that's when I knew that she was on my side and that the two of us were in this together. I couldn't have been more grateful. Thank you, M.P., for your patience, and your guidance, and thank you for caring.

Alex Sehulster jumped into this project bringing along a pair of fresh eyes and a new perspective when I needed them most. I am so happy for the time you took to read my story and for your insightful observations. Your perspective was more valuable than you probably realized and I look forward to working with you going forward.

Sara Camilli, I don't know how many times or how many more ways that I can thank you, so I'll just keep it simple. You are not only a wonderful agent but a dear friend as well. You've supported every crazy idea I've ever had for stories, and believe me when I say that you are irreplaceable.

And finally to those who pick up this book and take a chance on this story, my hope is that you will find it as entertaining to read as I did to write.

DAUGHTER OF
GODS AND SHADOWS

PECULIAR

This wasn't Brooklyn. Eden had taken the subway home from work and stepped out onto the platform, but she wasn't standing in the subway station. Her feet sank into a bed of sand. Hot desert winds whipped her locks across her face. The weighted gray sky bore down on her like an anvil. In the distance were sand dunes as tall as the New York City skyline. She shouldn't be here!

Eden turned to go back through the doors of the subway, but it was gone. Even the tracks were gone, and it was as if the train had never been there.

"Peeeeee-cuuuule-leeeeee-aaaaaarrrrr!"

Eden jerked around to the source of the whisper being carried on the wind, but there was no one. She scanned the terrain as far as she could see, and there was nothing but sand and wind, dead space, a dead place! *Ara!* The word just came to her. Ara was the name of this place. How did she know that?

It was wrong. Everything about this world was wrong. It felt cursed and angry, even evil. A bitter film coated her tongue and the back of her throat. Eden was lost here, and she was frightened and alone—so very, very alone. She wanted desperately to cry, but the tears wouldn't come. She wanted to leave, but there was nowhere to run.

All of a sudden she looked down and noticed a trail of footprints in the sand that were unaffected by the wind. Without understanding why, she felt compelled to follow them. A warning snaked up her spine, but every instinct in her drove her to follow those steps, which vanished behind her as she walked. Each print fit her perfectly, as if she'd been the one to make them. But how? How could she have done that?

The heat quickly became unbearable, and with each step, Eden stripped off more and more of her clothing until all she had on were her panties. She was thirstier than she'd ever been, and the dismal realization that she might not ever leave this place began to sink in, filling her with a hopelessness and despair that weighed her down even more.

Nothing could live here. Nothing could thrive or exist in a place like this, and it was killing her, slowly, deliberately killing her. The hot, unyielding wind began to wear away her flesh, making it crack and then bleed, until wounds hardened and scabbed over her body. There was no sun on Ara, but the heat was unforgiving, rising up from inside the planet, burning the soles of her feet. For a time they were raw, but then the soft, vulnerable skin burned off completely until she hobbled on bone.

Liquid dripped from her eyes, as her vision slowly began to deteriorate. At first Eden believed that she was finally crying, but then she realized the terrible truth, that the gels of her eyes were melting.

"Peeeeee-cuuuule-leeeeee-aaaaaarrrrr!"

She followed the sound of the voice, whispering to her again. Peculiar. It called to her. Eden raised her head to peer with what remained of her vision off into the distance and saw her, the one calling to her—a woman, naked. As Eden approached her, she noticed the woman's skin was even more petrified than Eden's, burnt red and leathered. Her hair was a twisted and tangled mass of twigs and thorns, and her breasts were sagging and desiccated. She was tall, taller than anyone Eden had ever seen before, and she was so emaciated that her body looked like painted bones. She stood defiantly, looking up at the sky with her mouth gaping. Her arms and legs were heavily shackled with chains buried deep into the sand.

Eden should've been afraid—and she was—but she was also drawn to her in an unexplainable way that confused her. She cautiously approached the woman, but she still seemed to be miles away from her.

Confusion enveloped Eden. She knew things about this place, about the woman, that she shouldn't have known.

Mkombozi, she said in her head. The Redeemer and the destroyer of Theia.

It was as if the woman heard her and noticed her for the

first time. She closed her mouth and slowly lowered her head and appeared to *look* at Eden standing across the desert. Eden's heart jumped into her throat, and the fear she felt left her breathless. She had made a mistake coming here. She realized that now, but it was too late. Mkombozi pulled so hard against one of the chains that she snatched the end of it out of the ground, stretched out her shackled arm, and reached miles and miles across the desert to wrap long bony fingers around Eden's neck and raise her high up off the ground. Eden kicked, scratched, and struggled to break free of her grasp, but Mkombozi was too strong.

She drew Eden to her and held her at face level. The terror of being this close to her, to Mkombozi, was overwhelming, and Eden felt as if her heart would burst through her chest.

Mkombozi carefully studied Eden, tilting her large head from one side and then to the other. The gels of the woman's eyes were gone, probably melted away the same way Eden's were melting now.

"What Peeeeee-cuuuule-leeeeee-aaaaaarrrrr—tttthhhhh-iiiingggg—arrrrrrre—youuuuuuu?" Her voice was ragged and deep, but her inquisitive demeanor reminded Eden of a child.

Eden prayed for tears. She prayed for a voice to scream, but she had been without water for so long that she doubted she could even speak anymore. The more she struggled, kicking and clawing at the woman's hand, the more Mkombozi tightened her grip around Eden's neck. It was only a matter of time before she killed Eden. So why was she fighting? Eden had no strength left to fight, and she wilted in Mkombozi's grasp, closed her eyes, and waited to die.

All of a sudden she was floating. It was over. It was finally . . . Eden suddenly felt the ground rise up to meet her.

"What Peeeeee-cuuuule-leeeeee-aaaaaarrrrr—tttthhhhhiiiin-gggg—arrrrrrre—youuuuuuu?" Mkombozi repeated, staring down at Eden, who lay crumpled on the ground at her feet.

Eden coughed, cleared her throat, and finally attempted to speak in a language she wasn't even aware that she knew. "I—am—us!"

Stunned by her own response, Eden stared terrified and confused at Mkombozi. Why had she said that? It made no sense. What would make her say that? She didn't understand why or how, but she knew instinctively that she had spoken the truth to the powerful creature towering over her.

Mkombozi tilted her head, quizzically. "Youuuuu—have—the—Omennnnnsssssss?"

She shook her head quickly. "No!" she managed to say, swallowing. "No! I don't have them, and I don't want them!"

Mkombozi needed to know this. She needed to understand that Eden had no intention of ever bonding with the Omens.

"I don't want them!" She cleared her throat and said it again. "I don't want the Omens! I never wanted them!"

Mkombozi cringed and Eden felt her pain, her torment, and her rage. She felt her yearning and her desire. She was engulfed in Mkombozi's desperation.

"IIIII—ammmmm—ussssss!" Mkombozi pointed a long, crooked finger in Eden's face. "Youuuuuu—arrrrrrrre!"

Eden shook her head and then she nodded and then she

shook it again. "I am, but—I don't have the Omens! I don't want them!"

This time, Mkombozi reached down and grabbed Eden by the hair and dangled her in the air. *"Thennnnn—youuuuuuu—arrrrrre—nothingggggg—tooooo—meeeeee!"*

Eden felt her hair begin to tear away from her scalp. "That's not true, Mkombozi!" she screamed, closing her eyes. "I am your salvation!"

Mkombozi dropped her again, reared back, and glared at her. Doubt, disbelief furrowed her brow.

It was true. Eden didn't know how it was true or why she'd even said it, because it sounded ridiculous! How could she be Mkombozi's salvation, when Mkombozi had had the power of the Omens and the strength to destroy the Demon and Theia? Who was Eden that she should believe that she could save anyone, when it was painfully obvious that she wasn't even capable of saving herself? How could she save Mkombozi if she was terrified to make the bond with the Omens, which had been the source of Mkombozi's power when she lived?

"Mmmmyyyyyyyy—ssssssalvationnnnnnn?" Mkombozi questioned.

Eden managed to struggle and stand. "We are destined, Mkombozi!" she shouted. "We are prophesied and we are one!"

Those words cut into her like a blade. Never had Eden dreamed she'd ever say them out loud. Never had she wanted to believe that they were true, but they were. Eden had been told these things since she was a child. Rose, the woman who'd raised her, had told them to her. Khale née

Khale had said them as well, and Eden had always rejected them. In this moment, those words rang true. Eden and Mkombozi were one.

Mkombozi bent at the waist to look directly into Eden's face. "*Thennnnnn—bringgggg—meeeeee—mmmmyyyyyyy—Omensssssss,*" she said sternly.

Eden became small again, and afraid. "I . . . can't," she murmured, fearfully.

Mkombozi stood up. "*Thennnnnnn—diiiiiieeeeeee!*"

She drew back her long shackled arm.

"You need me!" Eden blurted out in her panic.

Mkombozi paused, looked down her nose at Eden, and curled one corner of her mouth in a half smile. "*IIIIIII—doubt—that!*"

Eden would never forget the sound Mkombozi's shackle made as it whipped through the air and landed against the side of Eden's head. She heard the sound of splitting wood, felt her body travel across sand, time, and space. Eden was beyond pain now, and thirst, and fear. It was over. She was over—finally. As her eyes began to close, a dark shadow cast over her—a bird, a man. The darkness cloaked her and held her.

"*Beloved,*" he whispered.

Eden tried to take a breath, but she was suffocating.

"Eden!"

Rose couldn't believe what she was seeing. She stood in the doorway of Eden's bedroom, clutching the inside door frame with both hands to keep from being thrown backward and out into the hallway. The force pushing against her was overwhelming, hot, and stifling. Rose could barely breathe against the air swirling in that room.

Eden hovered six feet above her bed, her arms and legs dangling, her back arched and her face raised toward the ceiling. Eden's eyes were wide, her mouth gaped open, her clothes drenched. Eden's body suddenly convulsed violently in midair, until finally she went limp and fell onto the bed again.

Rose rushed over to her. "Eden!" she gasped desperately, lifting one of her arms and both legs back onto the bed.

The nightmares were getting worse. They were getting so much worse.

Rose cried and cradled Eden's head in her lap. "Oh, sweetheart."

A normal mother would've called an ambulance to rush her daughter to the hospital; maybe she'd have called a priest. But there was nothing normal about the kind of mother Rose was. And there was nothing normal about Eden. Rose just held her. She held her until the sun came up, and waited.

Eden had spent most of the following two days in her room. Rose understood that she needed time to sort through the nightmares after they happened. Eden needed to sort through so many things happening to her now.

"You should eat," Rose said, setting a plate down in front

of Eden, who had finally come out of her room and sat at the kitchen table and stared out of the window.

Eden wrapped her robe tightly around her. She hadn't looked at Rose or even acknowledged that she was in the same room with her, as if she somehow blamed Rose for how her life was unfolding.

Rose sat across from her. "It's important that you keep up your strength, Eden," she said helplessly.

Eden drew her robe even tighter around her and ran her hand through her locks.

"I'm just trying to help," Rose said.

"Help with what, Rose?" Eden finally asked, turning to look at her.

Dark half-moon circles cradled her eyes. Eden tried to cover the bruises around her neck with the collar of her robe.

"You gonna tell me more stories about Theia? Mkombozi and the Omens? About how she used them to save their world or how they used her to destroy it?"

Eden was a lonely and frightened young woman, and it broke Rose's heart.

"No," Rose said, forcing a smile. "I suppose not."

Eden pushed her plate away, stood up, and left Rose sitting in the kitchen. Rose was so tired. Tired from not being able to sleep for the last two nights, and tired of not knowing what was going to happen next to Eden. She had tried to prepare her from such a young age, mostly by telling Eden stories, but there were no stories that could've prepared anyone for the fate that awaited this young woman. There were no stories to prepare her for the things that were happening to her now or that would happen.

"She'll resist," Khale née Khale had told Rose years ago, when Eden was a toddler. "I can tell you now that she will not embrace her fate, but will fight it."

"Maybe she won't, Khale," Rose had said, sensing the dread that Khale felt. "Maybe she will welcome it."

But there was a knowing in Khale's eyes that warned Rose otherwise. "Teach her, Rose. Tell her those things that will help her to understand and to accept."

"You know I will," Rose said, anxiously. "You can trust me, Khale."

"It's not you that I don't trust." Khale turned to her and smiled. "It's her fear that I distrust. It runs deep inside her. I see it when she looks at me."

"It'll be easier as she grows," Rose tried assuring her, but once again, Khale knew better.

"Fear is her greatest enemy," Khale said, staring admiringly at the child as she slept. "But the will of the Ancient inside her is determined, Rose. The fear and the Ancient will war until one wins, and Eden will pay the ultimate price," she said, sadly.

Eden's nightmares were becoming more and more violent as she grew older. Rose worried that if she weren't diligent, if she didn't watch over Eden to assure her safety, that one of them might actually kill her. Wars were waged in Eden's dreams, wars that transversed the laws of physics, time, and space. She'd wake from them bruised, exhausted, and once she'd even fractured her wrist.

But the other night had taught Rose a valuable lesson. It had taught her that she was helpless to save Eden from herself now. And that if Eden didn't step up and accept her fate, and save herself, she would ultimately be responsible for her own destruction.

SAKARABRU

As Sakarabru gradually became aware of his surroundings, confusion and disorientation overwhelmed him. Was he standing? Was he lying down? He could not get his bearings. Shadows crossed in front of his eyes, fleeting and haunting. Smoke and haze distorted his vision. Where was he? What was this place? He fixed his gaze on an image, a form across the room from him. Familiar? Yes—vaguely. He knew it! He remembered that face, the face of the Djinn, Kifo.

"W-where am I?" He peered at Kifo demanding answers.

Sakarabru reached for Kifo, but his hand—what should have been his hand—passed through air. The Demon drew his hand to his face and stared into it, through it, almost as if it were not there, but he felt it!

"Kifo!" He stumbled toward the Djinn. "What have you done to me?" he yelled, terrified.

"I've done as I've promised, Sakarabru," Kifo said unemotionally. "I've brought you back."

He held his hands up to his face and looked down at the gray smoke that was his body. "As what? A ghost?" he asked, terrified.

The Demon saw a mirror on the wall across the room, made his way over to it, and stared at his reflection.

Sakarabru's body was shadow. He tried to clasp his hands together, but they would not touch. He attempted to sweep long strands of hair from his face, but his fingers passed through it.

Frightened and confused green eyes stared back at him through cascading strands of stark white hair. His hair and eyes were solid, but his body was liquid smoke, holding together in the shape of what used to be his physical body.

He turned again to the Djinn in a rage. "What have you done to me?" his voice bellowed as he looked down at Kifo, suddenly realizing how small the mystic appeared to be.

This was a trick. This one had the face of Sakarabru's loyal mystic, Kifo, but he was too small to have been him. His head was clean-shaven, his skin as dark as a night, but his clothes were different, strange and something otherworldly.

Sakarabru reached again for this imposter, but again, he could not touch him. "What have you done with my mystic?" he asked, suspiciously.

This imposter smiled. It was Kifo's smile. "You should sit." He held out his hand and motioned toward a large chair that seemed to have appeared out of thin air. The Demon was weary. He needed to sit, and so reluctantly he lumbered over to the chair and hovered slightly above it.

Kifo, or whoever this being was, strolled casually to the center of the room, his hands clasped behind his back. He had Kifo's eyes, dark and unreadable. And the strange garment he wore was in Kifo's signature white color. If his intention was to torture the Demon, then Sakarabru would be too weak to stop him.

"Your condition is only temporary, Sakarabru," Kifo said, matter-of-factly. "You have to understand that the amount of power, time, and energy it has taken me to bring you back is immeasurable. You have been gone for a very long time, but I didn't forget my promise."

"Promise? What promise?"

Sakarabru's mind was still shrouded in darkness. He recalled images, glimpses of things, of moments that had been his life, but there was no single continuous stream of thought; no clear perspective of time or place would form to help him understand what was happening to him now.

"Why am I like this?" he asked, glaring at the imposter.

"You are literally a shadow of your former self now, Lord Sakarabru," he explained. "But as you grow stronger, your form will solidify, and soon you will fully regain everything you lost in that battle against the Redeemer."

"The Redeemer?" The mention of her name shed some light on his memory, a moment—a horrendous and painful incident that could not have possibly been real.

"The war," Sakarabru murmured absently. He closed his eyes and listened to the echoes of screams rising up from the surface meeting him in the air. Beyond the echoes he could hear the song of the Troll Seers, a chorus of lamenting and sorrow. Sakarabru had been fighting too long and hard to get to that one moment that would solidify his place as the ultimate ruler of Theia.

He slowly opened his eyes and looked at the small version of the Djinn. "I was to rule them. All of them," he stated quietly.

Kifo nodded.

Sakarabru and his Brood Army had all but destroyed Khale's Ancient forces. The Great Shifter had lost her territories to Sakarabru. She had been the most powerful Ancient in their world and the most determined. Khale shifted into her most dangerous form, that of a dragon with wings as expansive as the horizon, but she was still weak.

"Give up, Shifter! It is not necessary for you to die!"

She had been his once, only once for an evening. Khale née Khale had let herself be taken by him, seduced and loved by him, the Demon. She could be his again.

He had never felt more in control, more formidable than he was in that moment. Sakarabru controlled the most destructive army that had ever existed. Her forces were depleted until there was only a handful of them left. She had lost.

"It is over, Khale! You have nothing left!"

He surveyed the debris of wounded and dead bodies that littered the ground around him.

"If you want what's left of my territories," Khale shouted, "you'll have to kill me for them!"

It was a shame. "So be it, Shifter!"

"It's been more than four thousand of this world's years since that battle, Demon," the imposter continued. "Theia was lost that night with you. Those of us who survived have come to live in this new world."

These things that Kifo was saying confused Sakarabru. What was he talking about? Four thousand years? This world? Panic began to overwhelm the Demon, and he tried to stand but he was too weak.

"This world? What are you telling me? The battle with the Redeemer was just . . ."

"Four thousand years ago, Sakarabru. And Theia is no more."

If this was an imposter, then he was an imposter who took liberties with Sakarabru's patience. "Lies! You lie to me. You deceive me."

Again, his memories sprung to life.

He looked at the imposter. "She was legend. A child's fairy tale. A myth."

The imposter stared back at him but said nothing.

Sakarabru had been wrong. The Redeemer, Mkombozi, was no character from a child's story.

Thick tresses of black hair swirled in a twisted, chaotic mass around her head, hiding her face from him. She ran toward him, her chest lowered with her arms stretched behind her, fingers splayed wide on one hand, and in the other, she held her weapon, the kpinga, *his weapon of choice. She had taken it from him. Strange markings shined on her arms and chest.*

The symbols glowed a fiery blue bursting from her body. There were three of them, one on each arm, and one in the center of her chest, just above her heart. The symbol on her left arm was of a starburst with a small circle in the center. The second, on her right arm, was reversed, consisting of a circle with a small starburst at its core. The last symbol was a starburst surrounded by a circle, with a bolt of lightning crossing through it from top to bottom.

She wasn't like the other soldiers. This Redeemer rushed at him without fear or hesitation, and as she drew closer, she let out a yell, powerful enough to shake the ground, and swung the weapon through the air at his throat, missing him by a hair.

"The Redeemer! She is here!" Someone shouted from the survivors. "Mkombozi will save us! She will destroy the Demon!"

Their words infuriated Sakarabru, and he reared back, lowered his head with its massive horns, charged toward the Redeemer, Mkombozi, and impaled her through her stomach. Mkombozi, she did not scream, and she did not die. Whoosh! Whoosh! Whoosh!

The Guardian was heard before he was seen.

"Tukufu!" Khale called out, panicked, searching for him all around her. "Free her! She will defeat him if you free her!"

The black, expansive wings of the Guardian blended with the dark skies until it was impossible to tell where one began and the other ended.

"Touch her and die, Guardian!" Sakarabru threatened.

"Only you will die this day, beast!" the Guardian growled.

The Guardian, Tukufu, swooped down from the sky in a blur and snatched the female from the Demon's horns before Sakarabru could stop him. But the Guardian left himself vulnerable.

Sakarabru swung a mighty fist at Tukufu and landed it on his chin. The Guardian flew backward but stopped himself and changed direction toward the Demon, and leading with his feet, planted both of them hard in Sakarabru's chest, caving it in until he lost his breath. The Guardian had hurt him. Until this moment, no one had ever hurt Sakarabru before.

Sakarabru charged at Tukufu, but Mkombozi rushed past the Guardian, caught the Demon by those same horns that had stabbed into her, raised him high above her head, and tore each of them off at his skull with her bare hands.

Sakarabru cried out in agony, writhing in pain. Tukufu caught the Demon, held him from behind, and locked his gaze on her.

The sound of thunder rumbled throughout the heavens. The sun in the center of this universe, which had had its light blocked by the darkness of Sakarabru, began to burn brighter, its heat scorching, and it blazed furiously in the distance.

The blackness blinding Khale was gone, but the heat from the sun was unbearable. "Mkombozi!" she called out.

The whites of Mkombozi's eyes filled with blood. Mkombozi stretched her arms out at her sides and slowly closed them together, facing her palms toward the Demon. Slowly, the three of them lifted off the ground and rose higher and higher into the air.

Sakarabru began to twist and scream. Tukufu's wings began to burn, and he released his hold on the Demon and flew away. "Mkombozi! Too much! Pull it back! Control it!" The Guardian called out to her.

Her chest heaved, she balled her fists, the symbols glowed with the power of the sun. Blinding white light from the symbols on her arms and chest seemed to swallow her whole.

"No!" Khale gasped, rushing to Mkombozi from behind. "The Omens have taken her!" Khale reached for her, but the heat com-

ing from the Omens burned her flesh to the bone, and she fell back screaming. "The Omens have taken her!"

Sakarabru felt himself burning. He watched in horror as layers of his own skin began to melt and fall to the ground.

A strange look of something akin to regret shadowed the imposter's face. "You are starting to remember. Aren't you?"

The Djinn took a deep breath, conjured a chair behind himself, and sat down across the room from Sakarabru. "Our world was destroyed when you were," he explained. "The Redeemer, with the power of the Omens, obliterated you, and after that, the influence of those damn things was so powerful, she couldn't pull back on the devastating rage they filled her with. She destroyed Theia, some say by hurling it into the sun. Most of us managed to escape to this world, but those that didn't . . ."

Sakarabru still wanted to believe that the smaller Kifo was an imposter, but he knew that he was wrong.

"I took the rumors of the Omens for granted," he admitted wearily. "Stories of the Redeemer had never been more than bedtime stories to me."

Kifo simply watched him.

"Theia is gone?"

"It is."

"And the Redeemer?"

"Khale destroyed her using the Spell of Dissolution." The Demon could not believe what he was hearing.

"The Spell of Dissolution?" She was a Shifter, not a mystic. "How did she come to know that spell?"

It was a spell that had not been used in his lifetime. It was one that was thought to have been dead and buried with Ancients, generations before their time.

"I believe she learned it from Andromeda, but no one knows for sure. Who else but Andromeda could know it?"

She was the Troll Seer of the Ages. Andromeda had unlimited sight into the past, present, future, even the afterlife all at once. It was said that she had seen the rise of Sakarabru and that he would ultimately rule Theia. But it was also said that she had created the Omens, which would be his destruction.

"What is this new world, Magician?" He glared at Kifo and watched, satisfied, as the Djinn grimaced at the word "magician." It was a test, a small one, but enough of one to confirm that this Kifo was no imposter. Even in his smaller form, wearing his strange garments, the word "magician" still offended him.

"Earth. Smaller than Theia. The atmosphere is much heavier, and it's colder than Theia, but over time, we have adapted."

"We?" he asked. "Who survives?"

"Many of the lesser Ancient races," he said, shrugging. "Pixies, Imps, and Vampyres."

Sakarabru would've laughed if he had the strength. The mystic had been generous in referring to these creatures as lesser Ancients. They were pests.

Kifo continued. "Some Guardians survived, Shifters, Were and Mer Nations."

Now the Demon was interested in what he had to say.

"And what of Khale?" he probed. The Demon gathered enough strength to sit up straight and lean toward the mystic.

Kifo drew a deep breath. "She lives."

"She still rules?"

"This world is different from Theia, Sakarabru. The Ancients do not play the same roles here. I'm sad to say that, like you, we are mere shadows of our former selves. Humans rule here."

"Humans? Are they strong? Good fighters?"

Kifo laughed. "They are . . . different. Warriors of another sort. They have numbers on their side, weapons and technology—satellites and cell phones."

Kifo was speaking in a language the Demon did not understand.

"We have learned to co-exist, Demon. Ancients seem to prefer it that way."

Sakarabru stared back suspiciously. "My army does not co-exist, Kifo."

"Your army is dead, Sakarabru."

Dead? How could an army comprised of so many be dead?

"You brought me back to *co-exist*?"

"I brought you back to prove to you that I could. What you do next is up to you."

The Djinn stood up, and as he did, the chair behind him vanished. "You are tired, Sakarabru, and you need to rest."

The Demon shot an angry glare at him. "You have no idea what I need, Magician!"

Kifo bowed his head slightly. "I trust that you will find this dwelling suitable."

As he slowly spun around the empty space, it began to fill with furnishings and artifacts from Sakarabru's Theian castle.

"It's not as magnificent as you're used to, but it's the best that I can recall from memory," he said, smiling.

Sakarabru was too exhausted to care. Kifo was right. He was weak and he desperately needed his rest, but there was one last statement that he needed to make.

"I will need my army, Kifo," he said gravely. Sakarabru wanted to believe that the loyalty of this mystic was as true and steadfast now as it had been when Sakarabru ruled half of the Theian world. Did bringing the Demon back after so much time had passed confirm that the mystic's intentions were as pronounced now as they were then? And if so, then just how willing was the mystic determined to prove this to the Demon.

"You created my Theian Army," Sakarabru stated under the weight of fatigue.

Kifo nodded. "From the bones of fallen Ancients," he confirmed.

"You have bought me back, but a lord without an army . . ."

Kifo visibly swallowed. "There are no fallen Ancients here, Sakarabru. Only humans, as I have said, and their bodies aren't as strong as those of Theian warriors."

"You go, Kifo," he said, dismissively. "But in this or any other world, I am Lord Sakarabru, and it is impossible for me to co-exist."

Kifo's form gradually faded away as Sakarabru's eyes slowly began to close, and he fell into a deep sleep.

SPECIAL GIRL

Eden lived a paralyzed life. She'd tried leaving Brooklyn several times, only to come running back to the brownstone and Rose's arms with her tail tucked between her legs. She couldn't escape the things that scared her most because those things were everywhere, even here and now on the Staten Island Ferry.

On the surface they looked like people. To everyone around them, that's exactly what they were, but to Eden, the tall, thin man reading the *Post* across from her revealed a mouthful of razor-sharp teeth and had eyes like an owl's. The pretty woman standing at the bow of the ferry, wearing the Donna Karan knit dress and red-bottom pumps, had the face of a cat. And out of the corner of her eye, Eden could've sworn she'd seen a shadowed thing squeeze into a seat next to a window. The old woman sitting in the aisle seat nodded and smiled at it.

Most kids were afraid of the bogeyman under the bed or the monster in the closet, but most kids outgrew those fears when parents said the magic words "You're too old to believe in monsters."

The difference between Eden and those kids was that her mother never told her that.

Lately, it seemed that the Staten Island Ferry was as far away from home as she would go now when she "ran away." She could waste away an entire day and well into the evening riding this thing, pretending she had set sail on an ocean liner headed to the South Pacific. Eden stared out into the water, wishing away the rest of the world, listening to music on her iPhone and trying not to think about what was really going on.

Rose wanted to talk. She always wanted to talk. Rose was scared. She didn't have to say it for Eden to know it, but anytime you find somebody in your house floating above her bed with fresh bruises around her neck, then that's a pretty good reason to be afraid. The bruises were real, and if they were real, then that probably meant that the monster in her dream, Mkombozi had been real, too, which meant—what, exactly?

Eden saw things she didn't want to see. Dreamed things she didn't want to dream, and was living a life she didn't want to live. Eden glanced down at the scars inside her wrists that reminded her how powerless she'd been to even take her own life.

How old was she then? Eighteen. She'd been eighteen when she'd left home for the first time, rented a room in a cheap motel in Jersey, and tried to kill herself. It was as tragically romantic a suicide scene as a girl could come up with: candles, a tub full of water, and a naked and vulnerable teenager, crying, cutting horizontally instead of vertically to make sure she got the job done right.

She'd woken up to Rose and Khale standing over her.

"Silly, silly girl!" Khale fussed, lifting Eden out of the water as if she were a wet puppy.

Eden cursed under her breath. "Damn! And I was nearly in a coma, too."

When they got her home, Dr. Rose expertly sutured her wounds, bandaged them up, and Eden was as good as new.

"Someone is watching, Eden," Khale told her. "Someone is always watching."

Rose had sent Eden a text announcing that Khale was on her way to the brownstone, as if she were the Queen of England, and Eden should rush home to bow to her as she entered the house. She was the Shifter—the *Great* Shifter, Rose called her, but Eden had never seen her shift into anything.

Khale was a mousy-looking woman around Eden's age with oversize glasses and a fetish for coffee. Maybe she assumed that Eden would find her more relatable if she were just an awkward young woman, like Eden. Khale talked cool, was up on all the latest video games and music and clubs.

Eden could see through the disguises of other Ancients, but seeing Khale's true form was impossible for some reason. The Shifter made sure that Eden saw only what she wanted her to see. Maybe that's why she was called the "Great" Shifter, because she was really great at being fake.

She'd been trying to encourage Eden to open up about her "feelings," but she immediately shut down when Eden finally told her, "I have no feelings, Khale. Mkombozi does."

The Shifter hadn't visited Eden and Rose in more than a year, so the fact that she was coming now made Eden sick to her stomach.

"Is this where you hide?"

Shit! Eden immediately recognized Khale's voice and visibly cringed. "It's where I try to hide."

Khale sat down next to Eden. She had on a pair of baggy jeans, belted low on her petite hips, rolled into cuffs at the ankles, and a T-shirt with the words KISS ME, I'M MULTIRACIAL on the front.

"You keep trying to insult me, and I keep telling you that you're not capable," Khale said indifferently.

Khale was a big deal among her kind. She was a big deal to Rose. Rose had told Eden that Khale had been Mkombozi's mother and the one who had ultimately destroyed her. So, what did that make her to Eden? Just fuckin' scary, that's all.

"Are you here to remind me again of how proud I should be about my lot in life?"

Khale sipped on her coffee. "I'm afraid we're out of time for all of that."

That sick feeling in Eden's stomach turned into something else, something unexplainable—or maybe it was just plain fear. She didn't want to talk to Khale, or be Mkombozi, or go out and find her Omens. She didn't want any of this, but nobody seemed to give a damn.

"I'm not doing it, Khale," Eden told her. "You're wasting your time."

"He's back, Eden," Khale said, patiently. "The Seer, Apus, has seen it." Apus was the Seer of present times, of things happening now.

Eden could feel the heat from those oversize lenses burn against the side of her face as Khale stared at her, but she refused to look back at the Ancient.

"So what, he's back?" she shot back. "I don't give a damn that he's back," she said under her breath. *He* was a Demon called Sakarabru, the biggest, bad-assed beast who ever existed, according to Rose and Khale.

"I know you're scared."

Again with that condescending, over-the-top, forced "I feel ya girl" kindredness.

"Wow," Eden said, unemotionally. "Ya think? What part of this crap shouldn't be scary, Khale?"

At the mention of Khale's name, the beautiful and stylish cat-faced creature sauntered over to the two of them and bowed her gorgeous head in reverence to the very plain and unimpressive-looking Shifter before strolling off to the lower deck.

"But you have no choice. . . ."

Eden looked at Khale like she wanted to punch her in the face. "Of course I do!" she said with unexpected and angry tears filling her eyes. "You think you can pull me out of the womb and mold me like clay. You and Rose think you can play games with my life and make me somebody I'm not, but it's going to stop, Khale. It stops now." Eden started to get up

and leave, but Khale grabbed hold of her arm with her petite hand, locking her down with a surprisingly powerful grip.

"Fear is your enemy, Eden," Khale said knowingly. "I've
always known it would be, and I understand."

Frustration washed over her. "No, Khale. You don't understand." She stared in disbelief at the woman, wondering
how in the world this crap had fallen in Eden's lap and not
in someone else's. "You can't tell me who I am. You shouldn't
tell me who I am because you never had that right. I was born.
I had a mother. I had a father. I had a soul . . . my own soul."
Other passengers were starting to stare.

"The child that was born that night died, Eden, and all
that was left was a vessel," she said, keeping her voice low.
"It was the vessel I needed." She looked ashamed all of a sudden. It was unnatural to see shame in Khale's eyes, because
she was always so sure of herself.

Eden couldn't believe what she was hearing. "A vessel?"
Is that all she was to these creatures? A fuckin' vessel? "Why
didn't you just—I don't know—go find an empty milk car-
ton or something if all you needed was a vessel, Khale?"

"The Redeemer is precious, Eden. She is special and the
only one of a kind."

"I'm a vessel and she's special. I don't know. I'm not really feeling the love here, Khale," she shot back sarcastically.
Eden was hurt. It was one thing to be the reincarnation of
an Ancient being, and quite another to be called a "vessel."

"You were chosen, specifically by me. I waited so long for
you." Her voice cracked, and she pressed her lips together in

an attempt to hold back her emotions. "The baby born that night, in this body," she looked at Eden, "passed away quietly, Eden, and when she did, I filled what was left with the essence of my Beloved Mkombozi so that she could complete what has been left incomplete."

Rose had painted her stories of her relation to Mkombozi in broad, easy brushstrokes. Khale had sliced through those romanticized pictures with a knife and carved out details Eden would've preferred not to know.

"I'm sorry that you have to find out like this, Eden, but you have to know, because the time is here and it's now," she said with urgency. "The Demon is back, and his army is coming. He will consume this world like a plague, and everything and everyone you know and love will fall victim to his rule if you don't fulfill this purpose."

Eden was disgusted. She was sick. "You know what you can do with your purpose," she said, softly. Eden swallowed. "Why don't you vanquish me or something for insubordination."

Khale's expression hardened, and all of a sudden that pretty little face of hers looked absolutely menacing. "I'm not asking you, Eden. I don't have to, and you don't have to accept this fate you've been given." She shrugged. "It's not up to me or you. I've done what I can to prepare you. Rose has done all she can do to try and get you to understand all that is about to happen. I hope you have kept her teachings and mine close to your heart and your head. What we have taught you will help, if you let it."

The ferry slowed down, pulled into the Manhattan White-hall Terminal, and Khale stood up to leave. Eden sat frozen, numb to everything the Ancient had told her.

"It's the Ancient in you that will ultimately decide what to do and when to do it. My Mkombzi was not a coward," she said, proudly. "She was a fierce warrior who ran toward her destiny, not away from it. And she won't allow you to walk away from this," she finished confidently. Khale smiled one last time and left Eden sitting there more confused than ever. If Mkombozi was this warrior inside her, then who was this coward sitting here trembling like a scared rabbit? Who was that eighteen-year-old who'd tried to kill her self six years ago? Khale and Rose might have wanted to believe that the baby had died that night in the hospital, but Eden wasn't convinced.

GUARDIAN

Mkombozi's obliteration of the Demon was so powerful that the force of it knocked Tukufu from the sky. He landed on his back and watched Sakarabru disintegrate into tiny particles that vanished like dust. She had done it. The Redeemer, his Beloved Mkombozi, had fulfilled her destiny and had done what no other Ancient, including the Great Khale née Khale, had been able to do. She had finally destroyed Sakarabru.

"Stop Mkombozi!" Tukufu heard Khale cry out.

He, like the others, had believed that the Shifter was dead, killed by Sakarabru moments before Mkombozi had appeared.

The dragon lumbered toward him; one of her wings dangled from her shoulder. The Shifter hadn't the strength to even transform back into her natural state.

"Mkombozi!" Khale called out to her daughter, still hovering above them in the sky. "Please! Please listen to me! Stop it now before you kill us all! Mkombozi!"

What was she saying? Mkombozi hadn't killed the Ancients, she'd killed the Demon, destroyed him just as it was prophesied by the Seers. Tukufu struggled to his feet and flexed his wings, checking them for injury. Pain shot up his leg, but he hobbled toward Khale, confused by this strange reaction she had to the Demon's destruction.

"Khale!" *he called to her.* "It is done, Khale! She destroyed him! The Demon is dead! She saved us!"

Khale stared down at him with tears in her golden eyes. "She's killing us, Guardian," *she said, sorrowfully.*

No, Mkombozi was not killing them. She had killed the Demon. She had saved them from Sakarabru's rule. He was a tyrant, an oppressor, and a tormentor. Tukufu had seen what he was capable of. He had seen the tortured and maimed bodies of Sakarabru's victims, some left for dead, others not fortunate enough to die, and she had saved them from him.

"Mkombozi! You have to stop now! You have to!" *Khale said.*

Tukufu looked up at the sky for his Beloved, but the light emanating from her blinded him. He had sworn his Guardian's Oath to her when he was a child. He had loved her from the moment he first laid eyes on her, held tight in Khale's arms, an infant, barely hours old, and he had known even then that his destiny was to live and ultimately die for her.

He had been with her on the journey to collect and find the Omens, and with each collection, she had come close to losing her life. Tukufu had watched over her. He had protected her from whatever dangers they had encountered in their journeys, and he had helped her to recover after each bond. He was the only other be-

ing on Theia, besides their creator and Mkombozi, who had ever seen the Omens.

She had been afraid of her destiny, but he had been there to let her know that she wasn't alone. Each bonding had taken its toll on her, changed her, one by one, making her more solemn and brooding. She had paid a price each time, which no one, not even Khale, would ever understand, but he understood. And now it was over.

He flew up to meet her in the air, but the light from her was too hot and too powerful for him to get close or to even see her.

"It is over, Beloved," he said to her, wanting to reach out to her and carry her away in his arms. "You have done it! You can rest now, Mkombozi."

"Get away from her, Tukufu!" Khale called out to him. "It is not safe!"

Khale was foolish.

"Beloved." He reached for her, ignoring the heat burning his arm. "Let me take you where you can rest."

She was still here. He felt her presence. Mkombozi was not lost. She was here and she was his.

"Tukufu!" Khale shouted.

The light coming from Mkombozi's eyes burned so hot that it boiled the skin on his chest and felt as if it came out of him on the other side.

"Aaaaaagh!" he yelled, as he fell back to the ground.

Khale hovered over him in dragon form. He stared up at her and watched her lips move soundlessly, as she focused her gaze on Mkombozi. The ground rumbled underneath them before it began to split open and swallow the bodies of other Ancients.

"What's happening? Khale?"

The glow of the Omens' markings seemed to burn even brighter than they had before. Mighty trees were uprooted from the ground. Mountains crumbled. He could hear the screams coming from those around him, and still, Khale remained steadfast, murmuring words that only she could hear.

And then he heard her.

"Mother! Khale! What are you doing?" Mkombozi cried out.

Tukufu looked up and saw Mkombozi glaring down at Khale. The same heat that had radiated from her and that she had used against Sakarabru, she turned on the dragon. Khale's scales began to melt and fall off of her. If she had changed back to her regular form, Mkombozi could've easily killed her. The Shifter held her shape.

"Stop it!" Mkombozi screamed at Khale. "Stop what you are doing!"

Khale raised her voice so that all could hear her chant. And the louder she spoke, the more powerful it became. Tukufu looked up and saw Mkombozi begin to writhe in pain.

"Khale!" He stood next to her. "What are you doing?"

"Do not do this to me!" Mkombozi cried. "Khale! Stop! Mother!"

The glow from Mkombozi's eyes faded as she looked down at Tukufu. "Beloved," she mouthed, and in an instant, she was gone.

He leapt off the ground, balled his fists, and began pummeling the dragon in the head. "What did you do?" he asked in utter disbelief. "Where is she, Khale?"

The dragon collapsed on the ground. "She was going to kill us all, Guardian," she struggled to say. "I did the only thing I could do."

He had always been tethered to Mkombozi. No matter where she was, he had always been able to sense her and to find her, until now. His Beloved was gone.

It was impossible for the Guardian to "blend in." Even in a city as diverse as New York, he stood out like a sore thumb. People stared. They crossed the street when they saw him coming. They took pictures with their camera phones. Tukufu, or Prophet as he was called now. His new name had come as a result of too much wine and a very loose tongue. Loneliness sometimes drove him to talk too much, telling things about his world that made no sense to those who lived in this one. Prophet had spoken of unusual things; of beings who looked a lot like humans, but who could shift into the forms of animal. He'd spoken of wings that materialized when he willed them to, and of mystics, demons, and ghosts.

"What the hell are you?" a lovely young Latin woman asked, sitting on his lap. "A prophet or something?"

"Or a devil," another one stated, biting down on her bottom lip.

He preferred prophet. He liked the word and so he decided to keep it as his new name better suited for his new life. Prophet stood six feet seven and weighed 280. His skin was the color of copper, his silver eyes were kept hidden behind a pair of Ray-Bans, and his thick black dreadlocks hung to the center of his back. The only part of him that wasn't visible to human eyes were his wings. A Guardian's connection to his wings was spiritual. They appeared when he needed them most, when he conjured them. Ink-black wings unfolded from a space hidden just underneath his shoulder blades and spread fourteen feet across when fully expanded.

She is here. Prophet walked through the streets of New York, ignoring the strange looks and whispers he got as he passed people. He could feel her. For the first time since before their world fell, he could feel the familiar essence of the Redeemer reaching out to him. In all this time, he'd never felt so sure that it was she. He'd never been more convinced than he was now. Finally! His patience had paid off. He had clung to hope for so long, suckling on it like mother's milk, waiting and searching for the one who would be Mkombozi, the reborn, like Khale had promised, centuries ago.

"It's not over." Khale had found him fighting in a Moorish Army in the Iberian Peninsula in Earth's eighth century. Tukufu was lost then. He was a Guardian with no purpose. Mkombozi had been his purpose, his reason for being, and after The Fall, he had nothing.

Khale had shown up in his tent, shifted into the form of a man with a long dark beard, turban, and robes. Tukufu was inconvenienced when she suggested that he dismiss several lovely and very accommodating women in exchange for her company. He did so reluctantly.

"Did you hear me, Guardian?" she asked, with that old authority she had once had as his general. "I said, it's not over."

He was tired and dirty, and the last thing he wanted to do was to converse with Khale, who he hadn't seen in many of Earth's centuries.

"What's not over, Khale?" he asked irritably.

She seemed impervious to his impatience. "I have just come from seeing Larcerta," she began to explain.

Larcerta was a Troll Seer, one of six sisters from Theia who had the gift of sight. Larcerta had the gift of being able to see the future, which was why she made herself so scarce. An Ancient could search for Larcerta but would not find her unless she wanted to be found, because she would see into the future and know exactly when to leave.

"The Demon will return, Tukufu."

Khale's turban must have been wrapped too tightly on her head, because he had seen Sakarabru die with his own eyes.

"The Demon is no more, Khale. We both saw him die."

"Larcerta is never wrong, and she is not a liar."

He studied the Shifter to see if she were the one lying. He had learned long ago that Khale was selective in what she chose to share of the truth she knew. Rumor among Ancients was that she had known what the bond with the Omens would ultimately do to Mkombozi and she had warned no one. So what was she keeping to herself now, he wondered?

"How can he return?" *he probed.*

She shrugged. "A spell will bring him back."

"Whose?" *he challenged.*

"Does it matter? The Demon will return and he will try to do to this world what he tried to do on Theia."

"And he'll succeed," *Tukufu offered.* "After all, there is no one to stop him."

His words were cutting on purpose.

"I have found a way to bring her back, Guardian," *she murmured, almost shamefully.*

What did she mean? "What are you saying, Khale? Bring who back?"

"You know who. When the Demon returns, she is the only one who will be able to stop him."

All of a sudden he was livid and bolted to his feet. "You have had the power to bring her back all this time and you haven't?"

"Watch your tone with me, Guardian!" Khale stood up, too, and the two of them faced off in the center of the tent. "I am still your leader!"

He turned his back to her. "You have not been my leader since our world fell from the sky."

Turning your back on Khale was always a mistake. The Shifter suddenly became a cobra wrapped around his neck, and she squeezed and fanned her hood as she stared into his eyes.

"Do not get so full of yourself, Tukufu, that you forget. Do not fool yourself into thinking that I am weak. I will bring her back, and you will wait for her!" She hissed. "You will be the Guardian to her that you swore yourself to be because she will need you, Tukufu."

And just like that, the snake dropped to the ground and slithered out of his tent.

Waiting was an art form that he had mastered long ago. And finally it had paid off. Feelings that had been dormant for four thousand years had been awakened. Prophet had tried ignoring them, believing that that old sense of duty had risen up in him again because of guilt or regret, which happened sometimes. But those feelings were more persistent than ever and as strong as the day he'd first made his oath to her. His Beloved was somewhere in this city, and he wouldn't rest until he found her.

ANDROMEDA

S he could walk freely here. No one noticed an old woman in rags. No one cared who she was or that her face was constantly changing, taking one form and then another, because no one noticed an old woman in rags.

New York City. Was that where she was? Had she been here already, or was she just thinking about going there? It was hard to say. Andromeda tried not to think about such things. That girl would be in New York City. The girl who cried all the time. The one pretending that she wasn't who she really was. The Shifter had called her Eden.

Andromeda cringed at the memory of the Shifter. She didn't like that one. Didn't trust her as far as she could . . . could . . . could what? That one was full of deception and lies and half-truths. Khale née Khale, she called herself. The Forever and Ever, but she wasn't forever. Andromeda had seen and walked in a time when she wasn't, and so even her name was a lie.

"Tell me of the Omens, Andromeda. Tell me where they are?" Khale had asked long ago after Theia had been destroyed by the first Redeemer.

That Shifter was a sneaky one, and she had asked Andromeda to reveal the secrets of the Omens time and time again, but the Seer was just as great as Khale was great, and she had refused to tell her.

Khale knew that the Omens were never meant for her. She knew and yet she still demanded to know where they were.

"I cannot tell you about such things, Khale," Andromeda had told her. "It is not for you to know."

"But I am the leader of my people, Andromeda. What's left of us. And I have to know where they are so that when she is reborn, I will know where to send her to get them and to bond with them."

Andromeda laughed. How arrogant that one was. How full of shit she is. "As if you ever had to tell the Redeemer how to find what belongs to her. You are so in love with yourself."

"The reborn will not be like Mkombozi." Khale was angry, but then she was always angry when she could not get her way. "She will be afraid and she will be uncertain. She will not be a warrior, Andromeda. She will be human."

Andromeda nodded. "She will be. Yes. Khale. She is human."

"Then she will need my help more than Mkombozi ever did."

"What about the Guardian?" Andromeda was asking. "I thought that he was her help?"

Khale lied. Andromeda had already seen her do it. "He is not receptive to this reborn."

Andromeda laughed. "You are a fool again and again, Ancient, if you think that you can tell me such things. I may look and act crazy, Shifter, but I ain't nobody's fool."

Khale didn't need to know where the Omens were, because when it was time the reborn would know, and like Mkombozi, she'd find them. She'd found them all because they had been made for the Redeemer and no one else.

Andromeda lived here, there, and everywhere all at once. In her mind at this very moment, she was at Coors Field in Denver watching a baseball game, breaking bread with Jesus at the Last Supper, flying in a spaceship past one of Jupiter's moons, and was about to kill a fellow in the Roman Colosseum. But she had presence of mind enough to be here now. New York City. Eden was here, and her Guardian was here, and Khale was here. That girl would be crying again soon. Her Omens were growing impatient as the Demon was growing stronger.

These good people rushing past her in New York City, dropping coins into the box on her shopping cart and shoving half-eaten sandwiches into her hand, would be dead soon, or wishing that they were. Their world would change quickly; for some, it had already begun. She glanced at a man sitting on a bench, coughing into his hand. He'd be dead in a few days, but then he'd be back—changed—forever. New York City was about to go to war.

In other places, in other times, the Omens spoke and were speaking to Andromeda now as if they were alive and they were.

Does she look like me?

"Of course she does," Andromeda responded, smiling. The person passing looked at her as if she were crazy.

Does she miss me?

"No. I don't think so. I think she's afraid of you. Doubly so."

She should fear me. I am frightening.

"Yes, you are. You all are."

It had taken a Demon and a Great Shifter to come together in a moment of passion to make the first Redeemer, Mkombozi. It was the only way that the Redeemer could be made. And it had taken a magic spell from a healer to bring this Redeemer into the world, and it had taken her love to keep her here. Rose was her name. And she was like a mother to the Redeemer of this world.

"I knew he wasn't dead," Andromeda said out loud, talking about Sakarabru. "And I knew he'd be back. And I knew when too."

People crossed the street quickly as she spoke.

"This bitch is crazy," someone said to the person they were talking to over the phone.

Eden had been born to bond with the Omens, and she would. And she would spend a lot of time crying and learning and becoming who she was meant to be. Andromeda's heart broke for her, but it was necessary—all of it was.

The Omens were made only for the Redeemer because Andromeda had seen to it. She had traveled through space and time and lives and dimensions, gathering all of the attributes specific to the one who would bond with them, the only one who could. The Omens were more of the attributes of what the Redeemer already possessed, but amplified. They had been created by and of Mkombozi's DNA, her life experiences, all of them. They were everything that was exceptional about her and everything that was terrifying about her. Traits inherently inbred in her by her father, the Demon. They were what was right with her and what was wrong. Eden was chosen for the same reasons Mkombozi had been chosen. She was exceptional and was so much more than what she knew. The Omens would show her that, but Andromeda had made them too powerful. After they empowered Eden, they would ultimately destroy her. And if Khale failed to do her part at the exact time necessary, Eden would devastate this world as Mkombozi had done to Theia.

KATIE SMITH

White chocolate mocha, double white chocolate, low fat, with whip." Katie Smith rang the small bell on the counter. "Up! Upside-down caramel frappé blanco, double shot vanilla, skinny—up!" The place was packed, but she moved like a well-oiled machine, fueled by three triple-shot espressos all before sunrise and her morning donut. "Peppermint white chocolate nonfat, no whip and no foam, half shot, lukewarm mocha—up!"

She was a coffee-shop barista, and Katie Smith loved her job. She loved it so much that there was nothing else that she wanted to do. And she loved her boss, Chad, who told her time and time again how much of an asset she was and that her enthusiasm and drive was infectious and that he wished he had more employees just like her. If it weren't for Chad, Katie Smith would miss taking her breaks, and she'd work every night until closing because she loved what she did.

"You sure you don't need me to close tonight, Chad?" she asked again, and Chad shook his head.

"Not tonight, Katie. Luke is closing tonight."

"Luke, do you need me to stay and help out?" she called out to him over her shoulder as Chad was ushering her out the door.

"No thanks," he said unemotionally.

"Good night, Katie." Chad sort of shoved her and then quickly shut the door behind her.

Katie stood there for a few minutes, wondering what there was for her to do now. Fries. Her stomach growled, and she realized that she hadn't eaten anything all day except for the glazed donut and coffee.

"I'll take three large orders of fries, please," she told the clerk at the fast-food restaurant. "And coffee."

"Cream and sugar?"

"No, thanks. And ketchup. Lots of ketchup."

She sat at the window shoving French fries into her mouth, watching Manhattan pass by. Every now and then, another Shifter, Were, or even a rare sighting of a Guardian would pass by her. The once-great alliances were all but shattered now, and the races—what was left of them—had dispersed into lives overshadowed by humans. She believed in her heart, though, that they would all join together again to fight against the Demon. The truth was that all she could do was hope.

The Fall had changed everything for Ancients. When her beloved Theia was destroyed, some Ancients fell to this world;

others had jumped, believing that they were leaping to their deaths. She, like so many of them, came here believing that she'd meet her end as well, but that didn't happen. Nothing was the same for any of them, though.

Humankind didn't know it, but much of their history and many of their legends had been born of Ancients. Egyptian hieroglyphics, Native American symbols, even their democratic systems were based on practices that Ancients brought with them from Theia. Metalsmithing was an Ancient art form, mastered by the Valkyrie races and introduced to human culture, as was mining.

Human legends of werewolves and phantoms were born from early human interaction with Ancients before the few mystics who were left created the spell of glamour to hide the Ancients true form from human eyes.

The dominant race on Theia was that of Shifters. There were many different types of Shifters, some limited by size or shape, others capable of shifting into one form of creature. Weres were Shifters, though they hated being called by that name. Khale was the Great Shifter because she was the only one without limits.

Humans were easily frightened by the things that couldn't be explained. They panicked when coming into contact with someone different from them, sometimes, even panicking over differences in their own human race: gender, race, sexual orientation. And they judged harshly, which proved to be dangerous for lesser Ancients like the Pixies and Vampyrs. Humans killed when they judged, when they panicked. Katie, of course, was never in any danger, but she understood why the lesser Theians chose to remain closeted.

She finished up the last of her fries and decided that it was time to go back to her apartment on the Upper East Side.

"Miss Smith," Ron, the doorman, said pleasantly, tipping his hat and holding the door open for her.

Katie smiled back. "Thank you, Ron. You look very handsome today."

He blushed. "And you look lovely yourself."

Of course she did. She was twenty-five. Katie Smith had determined some time ago that twenty-five was the age she wanted to be for now. Humans had a thing about age. Telling people she was twenty-five garnered plenty of appreciative nods and smiles and remarkes of "Oh, I remember when," so she made up her mind that she'd stay twenty-five until she discovered some other age-driven experience she was interested in trying.

Katie owned every apartment on the twenty-first floor, because she liked the views and could live in any of them depending on her moods. The one she lived in now was on the end with a beautiful skyline that took her breath away at night. Actually, it didn't literally take her breath away, but she liked using that metaphor because humans used it all the time and it sounded dramatic.

She was considered wealthy. Most Ancients lived the way she did, unless they chose not to. Because they lived longer than humans, they had the benefit of time to collect things humans considered valuable: land, art, gemstones, and precious metals. When this world was young, it was full of treasures that could easily be found on mountainsides or in rivers. They stored such things, and as time passed, the value in them increased, allowing them to afford the comforts this world had to offer.

She stopped at the door next to her apartment. Most times, she walked right past it, almost forgetting that it was even there—that *she* was there. Katie had found it difficult to be too far away from her, even now, after The Fall had changed so much of her life. She had grown to love this world, almost as much as she'd loved Theia. But it was one thing to rule a world, and another to actually live in it like everyone else. Behind that door, though, was a part of her, a part of her past that she held close to her heart, unable to let it go, no matter how much she knew she should.

Katie looked at the doorknob and watched it turn to open at her will. The door creaked open, and slowly she walked into what had been a small apartment but now was a portal to a vast wasteland, a prison in limbo between time and space. The hot desert wind whipped against the side of her face, nearly blowing off her large framed glasses and toppling over her petite frame. Sand gave way to each step she took toward the moaning and wailing coming from the distance miles away from where she entered. Katie peeled out of her sweater and let it fall to the ground behind her. The oppressive heat weighed down on her like bricks, and thirst scratched the back of her throat. In the apartment, she'd only walked a few feet before finally seeing her. But in this arid land, she'd walked for many miles to get to her Beloved daughter, Mkombozi, or what was left of her.

This place wasn't real, but it was a reflection of a world and of a time far removed from the one she lived in now. The place had been made at Khale's request, using a collection of spells from the Pixies. For reasons even she didn't understand, Khale had needed this, a painful reminder of her love, loss, and sacrifice.

Khale-Katie stood far enough away to see her, but to still be safe from the rage spewing from her body in a poisonous gas that would kill anyone who stood too close, even an Ancient as old as she was. Ara had not been like this before Khale had exiled her to this place. Ara had been to Ancients what humans imagined heaven to be: beautiful, serene, and peaceful. It had been a place to rest.

The merciless heat instantly dried her eyes of any tears threatening to form in them at the sight before her—Mkombozi, with shackles around her wrists and ankles anchored deep into the ground. Her skin, dry and cracked, made her unrecognizable as the beautiful young female she'd once been. Her hair was a mass of thorns and twigs. This creature was a hull of the Mkombozi she'd known. She was what was left after Katie Smith—Khale—came to accept that her Beloved child was overrun with rage to the point that there was no getting her back.

Khale had waited and hoped that the essence of Mkombozi

would somehow break through the destruction and rage of the Omens to become herself again. Theia had fallen because of Mkombozi. She had succumbed to the Omens. Omens, that at one time had been the salvation of their world, had led to the devastation of it. The Omens had destroyed Mkombozi until there was nothing left of her except everything that had been evil in them.

Mkombozi had been a warrior, and she had been Khale's heart and soul. And Mkombozi had been the keeper of the Theian Omens that would have destroyed Sakarabru once and for all.

Mkombozi wailed like a banshee in the distance, breaking Khale's heart. She'd have stayed here forever with her if she could. But Katie Smith had to go back to her apartment and take a shower. She had to watch the *American Idol* finale and get ready for work in the morning. She blew a kiss to her Beloved, then turned and started the long trek back toward the front door to that apartment. The time had come. It was here now. Eden would finally finish what the Redeemer had been called to do, and Eden would succeed where Mkombozi had failed. She had no choice.

SILLY GIRL

T*he beginning is always followed by the end. . . . When did I become a ghost?*
    Kid Cudi had a surprising way of keeping things in perspective. Maybe he was like her, a shadow of who he thought he was, and just as confused as Eden.

Eden walked with her head lowered, her arms folded across her chest, angry. It seemed like she was always angry and guarded, prepared to fight, ready to explode. It was not a good way to live but it was easier with her head down. She didn't have to look at them, and they were everywhere—creatures that looked like they were straight out of a horror movie, or aliens, only nobody else seemed to notice but her.

Eden walked down into the subway station replaying Rose's words back from memory.

"You're starting to see them." The knowing look in Rose's eyes

years ago, when Eden was just a child, caught Eden by surprise. "I know you are," the beautiful and ageless olive-skinned Rose had said, taking hold of Eden's hands in hers. "You don't have to tell me. I know what you see."

"Who are they, MyRose? Are they aliens?"

She laughed. "They are just different, Eden. And only very special people are allowed to see them."

That's how Rose spun things to her that couldn't be explained. She called Eden special. Rose did the best she could under the circumstances. Eden didn't always tell her how much she loved her. She wasn't Eden's birth mother, but she had raised her, taken care of her, and loved her.

When Eden was a child, Rose was her refuge and her teacher. As Eden grew older, Rose became her anchor in a life that seemed to become more confusing with each passing year. Rose had tried to make Eden understand what was happening to her. She'd hoped that Eden would somehow embrace her so-called destiny, but she might as well have asked Eden to take a running leap over the moon.

They only wanted the pretty ones. This one was pretty. Very pretty. Tall and shapely; she wore her hair long. Both of them liked long hair on a woman. She wore her jeans tight. Nice. She was young too, with smooth skin, soft-looking and brown. And she had a beautiful mouth. It was hard not to be impressed by the shape of it, with lips that looked pillow-soft. One of them liked to kiss and would kiss her. The other didn't care for kissing at all, but still . . . she had a nice mouth.

All the girls were careless. That's one of the things they all had in common. They felt safe in their own skin, believed that nothing or no one could hurt them. It was obvious in how they walked and carried themselves, confidently and without concern or worry. They all knew how beautiful they were, but none of them believed that their beauty could be that thing that trapped them and condemned them.

Neither man—brothers—ever had to talk about the things they did. They never had to plan or discuss their intentions with the women. They were twins, after all, and knew each other's thoughts and needs intimately. When they spotted a woman, if they were together, they'd both fall into their roles quite naturally to make the magic happen.

This woman caught the train at three o'clock in the morning into Brooklyn after leaving the bar where she worked. She walked the same path to the same subway station and stood in the same spot on the platform waiting for the same train, and when it came, she'd get on and sit in the same seat. One of the brothers followed her down into that train station; the other was already there, waiting. Except for the three of them, the platform was empty.

The anticipation was nearly as gratifying as the act itself. It was about more than just the sex. It was about the element of surprise, of catching the cocky bitch off guard and proving to her once and for all that she wasn't invincible or too damn beautiful to be touched. It was as much about the power, the control of taking what they wanted without having to wait for permission. It was about the adrenaline coursing through the three of them, the woman in fighting for her virtue and even her life, and the two brothers, fighting back, knowing that they were stronger and that they outnumbered her and that they could have her simply because.

Like so many of the others, she paid more attention to that damn iPhone than she did to her surroundings, and before she could brace herself, the brother who'd followed her in from the street wrapped one muscled arm around her small waist and cupped her mouth with his other hand a split second before she could scream. The other brother grabbed her feet, and together, while she struggled, they carried her kicking and squirming into the janitorial closet. *Broom handles!* One of them imagined the things that could be done to a woman with broom handles, and he salivated.

They were so much alike and yet so different. One of the brothers, the one cupping her mouth, loved to cause them pain. How many different ways could he make her cry, suffer, bleed. But the other was the opposite. He was the one who hated to see them cry, the one who loved them and wanted to make love to them to make them forget about the pain and the suffering. He wanted them to want him, to need him, and to be thankful for him.

"Be still!" the one covering her mouth growled, backing into that small closet with her. "Stop it, or I'll snap your fuckin' neck!"

He pressed his hard cock, thickened, against her spine, letting her know what was waiting for her. The other brother let go of her legs but pushed himself close to her and squeezed between her thighs before she could kick at him.

"Shhhhh," he said, stroking her lovely face. Tears and fear filled her eyes. It broke his heart.

"Do it!" his brother commanded from over her shoulder. "Get her jeans off!"

The one in front of her nodded. His hands raked down her shirt and over firm breasts. Nipples tickled his palms. They were rock hard. She was afraid. They were hard because she was afraid, but he would lick them and taste them and make her forget how afraid she was.

"It's all right," he said, soothingly, but she was getting to be too much. Waiting for her was getting to be too much, and he had to have her. That was the rule. He'd get to have her first, and make love to her while his brother watched. And then, when he finished, he'd hand her over to him. "It's all right, sweetheart. I won't hurt you. I promise."

"Hurry up!" his brother growled.

He unbuttoned and unzipped his jeans and then started to undo hers.

This wasn't happening! It wasn't real!

"I won't hurt you." The man stepped away from her and began to unzip her jeans.

"Hurry the fuck up, man!" The other one holding her from behind demanded.

She was being raped. This was really happening! Eden squeezed her eyes shut.

Stop them! Her voice commanded in her head. Her fear was

overwhelmed by anger. How dare they put their filthy hands on her! And anger became swallowed by blood, red rage!

Fuckin' punish them!

Their ignorance will be their death!

Eden reached for the hand covering her mouth and relished the satisfying sensation of bones crushing in her grasp. The man holding her from behind screamed in agony, but Eden shut him up quickly with a jerk of her head, slamming it so hard into his mouth that she heard his jaw break. He released his grip on her, and Eden dropped hard to the floor on her back.

Movements clicked away in her mind like seconds on a clock, deliberate and methodical, coming to her so naturally that she felt as if she were putting on a performance.

"Hold her! Dammit!" The other man had no choice but to let her go, too, and when he did, Eden kicked him hard in his groin with the heel of her shoe and met him in the face with another kick when he doubled over in pain.

She stood up and looked down at both of them, one gushing blood from his nose and mouth, the other with tears in his eyes, cupping his balls in both hands, and writhing on the floor, glaring up at her.

They looked small and weak. Eden opened the door and stepped over the one sobbing on the floor.

"No!" He reached out and grabbed her by the ankle.

"*Mashbah!*" she growled, jerking away from him and kicking him in the face. The word meant something along the same lines as "fucker."

She grabbed him by the hair and dragged him out of the

small room and into the open, then dropped him like the sack of shit he was on the concrete floor. Eden knelt down next to him to get a closer look at how helpless this *mashbah*— "fucker"—really was.

"You're so fuckin' small," she said, awed by how frail and helpless he truly was. He was inferior to her on so many levels that it was almost painful to look at him. He was an insect, something to be crushed underfoot and not even worth the effort of consideration, no matter how slight.

She was so focused on this one that she forgot about the other one, creeping up behind her, until she heard the sound of him gasping. Eden stood up and turned around. The other man was fighting for air as his feet dangled at least a foot off the ground. An Ancient, one unlike any she had ever seen before, held him by the throat and stared past the gasping would-be rapist at her with eyes the color of mercury.

Eden's heart pounded. She had never seen— But he was familiar! Oh God! She knew this one! How?

His lips parted to say something, but the one on the floor screamed out. "Let my brother go!"

She turned to look at him, and in her mind's eye an image began to take shape. It was . . . dust. Simple dust. And his skin gradually began to turn red. "What's happening?" he cried. What are you— Fuck! Oh . . . fuck!" Piercing screams erupted from him as he watched in horror; his hands begin to wither, his fingernails melted like wax, and the skin on his hands and arms peeled away from muscles and tendons. Even his clothes began to fall away as he looked up at her, screaming in agony and horror as it happened, until finally his screams faded and there was nothing left but bone and ash. In seconds, he was gone.

Eden swallowed the lump in her throat, and a wave of nausea overwhelmed her. She blinked at what was left of that man lying on the ground and stumbled backward knowing that she had done this, only . . . she had no idea how.

"Mkombozi?"

That word, the sound of the Ancient's voice forced her to turn back to him. The other man, the brother of the one she'd turned to ash, lay crumpled on the floor at the giant's feet.

"It is you," he said, taking a step toward her.

It was . . . her! It is her!

"Oh!" She gagged, and covered her mouth with her hand to keep from vomiting.

Eden took a step toward him too, but then . . . she wasn't ready!

"No!" she shouted, holding up her hand to him. "I can't!"

She ran toward the exit and up the stairs out into the street and gulped in buckets of air. Is this how it was going to be? Is this what it meant to be Mkombozi? "*She was a warrior*," Khale had told her. Mkombozi was a telepath who could kill with a thought.

"One day you'll see for yourself what she was capable of, Eden," Khale had said. "Even without the Omens, the Redeemer was dangerous."

Mkombozi was no warrior. She was a killer. Eden had just . . . killed.

SOMEONE TO
WATCH OVER ME

It was not Mkombozi's body, but it was her essence. It was her, and he was not going to let this one deny him. Prophet, the Guardian, chased her out into the city and saw her running half a block from the subway entrance. He chased her down and grabbed hold of her arm.

"It is you!" he said, turning her to look into his eyes.

But fear stared back at him, fear and confusion.

"Let go of me!" she demanded, jerking out of his grasp.

She was crying. It was her—Mkombozi. It had to be, because no human could do what she had just done to the man in the station.

"Don't you know me?" he asked angrily. "If you are her, then you should know me."

The human shook her head and started to run again. Just as he had started to run after her, a small woman with large glasses stepped in front of him.

"Not now, Guardian." It was Khale.

He shoved her out of his way and went after Mkombozi. Seconds later, a bull appeared in front of him. Again, it was Khale.

"I won't let you stop me," he warned her.

"They see you, Guardian, and they see you talking to yourself."

She was referring to the humans who had stopped and stared quizzically at him. Their eyes were masked to the form of the talking animal, but they couldn't deny the images of him.

"I don't give a damn," he snapped, charging toward the bull.

Khale lowered her massive head, charged toward him, and in mid-stride changed her form into a condor, grabbing him with her talons and carrying him away. He tried to will his own wings to extend, but she held him so that he couldn't get them to release.

They flew for miles before she finally dropped him into a wide open field in the middle of nowhere and shifted back into the form of the small woman.

"You're a fucking idiot!" she shouted, stalking around him.

"You have no right to keep me from her, Shifter!" he growled. "I'm her Guardian."

"You *were* Mkombozi's Guardian, yes. But this one— Eden—doesn't know you, Tukufu. She is afraid of you."

"If she is the reborn, then there's no way in hell she can be afraid of me. She knows me the way I know her."

"Did she look as if she knew you?" Khale challenged.

He'd waited too long for this. She was there, right there, in his grasp, his purpose, the one he had been waiting for all these many, many years, and Khale was blocking him.

"She will know me, Khale," he said, forcing his anger to subside. "But she can't if you keep her from me."

The Shifter reigned in her frustration. "She is not one of us, Guardian," she explained. "Yes, she is Mkombozi in essence, but even that is something she still hasn't come to accept yet. We frighten her. I've tried to prepare her as best I could, but there is something about her that resists her destiny. She can't, or won't, accept who she is, and because of that, she won't accept any of us."

He raked his hands through his hair in frustration. "So, what's that supposed to fuckin' mean? That we wait another four thousand years for her to come around?"

"None of us has that long, Tukufu," she said gravely. "The Demon is back. And this war has started already even though no one seems to know it. This world is changing because he's changing it. Humans go on living their lives, while he slowly destroys them. They can't see it."

Prophet studied her. "How do you know this?"

"This mysterious disease infecting humans," she began to explain, "this flu that they've been reporting, isn't what they think it is."

He shrugged. "Humans get the flu. They get sick."

"Not like this," she said gravely. "A doctor, an Ancient, told me that this is unlike anything he's ever seen in human history. People have been on the brink of death with this disease, only to miraculously recover. In some cases, some have even died and come back to life."

He had heard that Sakarabru was back. Ancients everywhere seemed to be preparing for the worst, gathering together again into their colonies, reaching out to one another again to reform old alliances.

"Then we're wasting time," he told Khale. "We can't wait for her to accept me, or any of us. Which is why you need to let me go after her. I can tell her what she needs to know, teach her the things she needs to learn."

"It's not that easy," Khale reasoned. "She's not willing to accept any part of this, not the fact that she is Mkombozi, not you or even me. And she wants nothing to do with the Omens. The bonds have to be made, or this time Sakarabru will succeed."

"So what are you saying? I should back off and let her come into her own when she's ready? If what I'm hearing is true, then she has to be made ready."

Khale wanted to believe that Mkombozi was so brave and fearless, but nothing could've been farther from the truth. How many times had Mkombozi admitted to Tukufu when the two of them had been alone that she just wanted to leave the Omens and the Demon behind and live out her life with him? Mkombozi had never been fearless, but she was devoted to her mother and her destiny. The Ancients needed her and were counting on her to do what no one else could do. Without her, Sakarabru would rule Theia, and her people would suffer a fate that would make them welcome death if he did.

"I can do that. I've done it before."

"And you will again," Khale said, coming over to him and placing a comforting hand on his arm. "The Omens destroyed my daughter, Guardian," she admitted sadly. "I watched them consume her and erase every good and wonderful thing about her and was powerless to stop it."

"We both were," he said.

Khale was thoughtful before continuing, but he could almost read her mind and knew where this was going. "I don't know what they will do to Eden."

Eden. Her name was Eden.

"Truthfully, I don't even know if she'll survive the bonding process. She is not as strong as we are, physically. And she wants nothing to do with them or us. But I would hate to see them do to her what they did to Mkombozi."

The truth was, Mkombozi/Eden's sole purpose for being was to bond with the Omens so that the Demon could finally and ultimately be defeated to the point that he couldn't come back. Even Mkombozi had fallen short because Khale was forced to destroy her before the last molecule of the Demon could be obliterated. As long as any part of him survived, the possibility remained that he could return. If Eden survived the bonds, she would have to survive her battle with the Demon and then her battle with the Omens, which became more powerful the longer they were bonded to the Redeemer.

"Andromeda should tell us how to destroy them after the Redeemer-Eden kills Sakarabru," he said, stating the obvious. "The Seer was the one who created them."

"The Redeemer must destroy the Demon." Khale smiled. "And the last of the Demon must die."

He looked confused. "What the hell is that supposed to mean?"

"That no part of him shall remain," Khale said. "But you know how Ancients are. Full of drama and fuckin' riddles."

The last of the Demon were the Omens. Eden was born to die. She had to destroy a Demon, hopefully not a world, but when she had done what she was born to do, somehow, someway, she was going to die. So why the hell was he so anxious to get to her, if she was nothing more than a sacrificial lamb? Because lamb or not, she was his—his Purpose. She was his reason for breathing. If death was her fate, then it was his as well.

"I'll give you a week, Shifter," he suddenly said. "One week to let her know I'm coming, and then not even you will be able to keep me from her."

Prophet willed his wings to expand, spread them wide, and disappeared into the dark sky.

FREE FALLING

Two men were dead because of her. Eden had literally killed one of them with her thought, and the surveillance footage of the attempted sexual assault against her was all over the news. Eden walked into Patmos, the bar where she worked as a bartender. Ben, the bartender who had been waiting on Eden to take the next shift, was already there, and he glared at her when he saw her coming through the front door. She was late—again.

"Excuse me," she said, winding her way through the crowd. It was just after eight on a Thursday, and the place was packed already. She happened to glance up at one of the televisions mounted behind the bar—and stopped dead in her tracks as she watched the grainy footage on the news from a surveillance camera in the subway station where those men died. Her face couldn't be seen in that footage. The camera was behind her, but there was no mistaking the dark blue jacket she wore, her walk, or her locks.

The blurred images showed a woman being picked up and carried into a broom closet, and then moments later, that same woman dragged a man across the floor.

Eden stood there in shock, watching that woman—watching her—do things that couldn't possibly be done.

"Eden!" her boss, Tawny, stomped toward her. "You're late again!" she said, angrily. "Put your things away and relieve Ben. His shift ended half an hour ago."

Eden couldn't speak. Tawny's hard stare left Eden and trailed to the television screen. She stared at it, confused, and then stared back at Eden. "Eden?"

She knew. That footage had no doubt been played over and over again, and by morning, people would have it memorized, and anyone who knew her would see that she was that woman. Eden jerked away from Tawny and left Patmos knowing that she could never come back.

Snow was just starting to fall when Eden ran out of the bar. She made a mental note to go someplace where it never snowed, someplace with a beach and palm trees and with no Internet or cell phone service.

She had killed a man and *he* had killed the other. The Guardian. Eden knew who he was the moment she saw him, even though she'd never laid eyes on him in her life. She'd felt him and remembered things about him that she couldn't have possibly known. Tukufu was his name. The moment she saw him she could feel what he felt—relief, that he'd finally found her. She was his Beloved and nothing would keep him from her now that he'd found her again. He was real, and she felt things for him that didn't make sense.

"Mkombozi!"

Eden stopped when she heard someone behind her call out that name. A thick lump swelled in her throat, and her heart thumped even harder in her chest.

"That's not what they call you now. Is it?"

Eden turned slowly, dreading the person talking to her. If it knew her by that name, then it was one of them. This one had swamp-water-colored eyes, clay-brown skin, stood about four feet tall, had a wide tree stump for a head, with no neck to speak of. It wore a fashionable, high-end designer coat, had squeezed its massively wide feet into a pair of gold Jimmy Choo stilettos and carried a twenty-five-thousand-dollar Hermès bag on its arm. Diamond earrings dangled from its mangled ear lobes.

People passed right by it without stopping and staring. None of them saw what Eden saw.

"Images of you are on every news channel," it said, stepping toward her. "I don't want to believe it's you, but I know it is."

Eden backed away. "It's not me," she managed to say, shaking her head in disbelief that it was actually speaking to her.

"You're afraid," that thing said, frowning, sounding almost surprised. "Aren't you always?" This thing looked disappointed. "You need to get over it."

The voice coming from it was downright intoxicating. It was comforting, reassuring, seductive, but it looked like a troll and smelled like rotting meat.

"They want you," it said, taking another step toward her. "They won't let you run."

They? The police? "They can't catch me if they can't find me," she said anxiously.

Was it smiling?

"He's bringing one to you now, Redeemer."

"H-he?" Eden stammered. "Who are you talking about? The Guardian?" Was she referring to the Guardian? Is that why he'd appeared?

The creature shook her massive head. "No, not him. He's found you already, but this other one searches for you because the Omen compels him to. She commands him because she has grown impatient. It knows that you won't come to it, so it's coming to you. It doesn't matter what you look like or how far you run. The Omen is coming to find you."

Omen? There was more than one, so why did she just say "Omen"? Eden was practically a story on *America's Most Wanted* and this thing was talking about a fuckin' Omen? She shook her head and turned to walk away.

"You can't deny the truth, Redeemer."

Eden turned to face it. "Stop calling me that! I'm not Mkombozi."

"Liar," it challenged. "And you fail to complete the Prophecy of the Omens." It looked angry, if that were possible. "You fail to destroy Sakarabru, and because you fail, he is back and he is angry."

Fail? Or failed? This thing spoke strangely. Eden shuddered. No one but Rose had ever said that name to her—

Sakarabru. Coming from this thing, it sounded different. It sounded personal.

A couple of guys driving by hung their heads out of the windows of the car, gawking at the troll as if it were filet mignon. "Hey sexy!" one of them called out, licking his lips.

"I think I'm in love," another shouted from the back seat. "Meet us at Patmos! Drinks are on me!"

"And me!" the other shouted from the passenger seat.

That troll thing rolled its eyes in annoyance. "Tiresome," it muttered irritably. It turned its attention back to Eden. "I should be afraid of you." It studied Eden, looking her up and down. The troll smirked. "We all should be afraid of you." Disappointment washed over it as its eyes met and held Eden's gaze. "He's found you."

"Sakarabru?" she asked, hesitantly.

The troll laughed. "Of course not. I'm not talking about him. The other one. He finds you and he's impatient too."

Eden swallowed. "The Guardian," she muttered to herself.

"Your lover." That thing smiled again. "Your Guardian. He is a handsome one and determined. He knows what must be done. Trust him. You need to hurry," it said, before turning and walking away. "Hurry and bond, fulfill the prophecy so that we can all finally be done with this."

Rose stared hypnotized at the video footage being played over and over again on every news station in New York City.

"Authorities are asking anyone who thinks they can identify the woman to contact them immediately."

"It appears that the woman was being attacked by these men, but what happened next . . . well . . . it's just unexplainable."

She had seen so many strange things in all of her years living this life. She had seen Eden do strange things, but nothing like this. The rest of the world could not believe what she'd done, or that things like that were possible. What would they do now that they had seen?

Eden came into the brownstone and blew through the living room, past Rose like a whirlwind, taking the stairs two at a time leading up to her room.

"Eden?" Rose called after her, and followed her upstairs.

Eden had already started packing by the time Rose got there, and she was crying.

"Don't try to stop me, MyRose," she snapped, throwing things into a small suitcase. "I'm no savior. I'm not what these Ancients need. You know it as much as I do."

Eden had tried to be brave, and Rose's heart went out to her. But maybe the girl was right. Mkombozi's essence may have been reborn into this child's body, but it hadn't been reborn to live out its destiny, at least not in this life.

"Stopping you is the last thing I would try and do, My-Eden," she said, sadly, walking over to Eden and taking hold of her hands.

Tears streamed down the girl's face in rivers, and all of a sudden, to Rose, Eden looked like she was six years old again. "It's over," she said, sounding so defeated. "The police are going to be looking for me. I'm all over the news, the Internet . . ." She shrugged. "I killed that guy," she said remorsefully.

"I can't explain how I did it, Rose. I just got so angry and I hated those men for what they were trying to do to me. It's only a matter of time before they find me, MyRose. And what's going to happen when they do? What will I do to the police if they find me?"

The authorities were the least of the challenges facing this young woman, and still, she couldn't see it, but Rose could.

Eden sat down wearily on the side of the bed, pulling Rose down next to her. "I have tried to understand the things you've told me all my life, MyRose," she sobbed. "Believe me, I've tried, but I never wanted to be her. I've never wanted to have to see and do the things she did, because to me, I'm just Eden." She stared helplessly back at Rose. "I'm me."

"And you are, Eden," Rose said, tenderly. "I've always understood that, and I've always tried to do my best to prepare you, but I'm afraid I've failed you." She pressed her hand to Eden's cheek. Rose hadn't realized that she had started crying, too.

"It's all so impossible to believe," Eden said, swallowing, struggling to compose herself. "I'm not—that person, that being. I'm not her, MyRose. I can't be, because . . ."

"Because you're afraid to be," Rose said, finishing her thought for her.

Eden nodded. "Who would want to be that? I killed that man as easily as I'd swat a fly."

"They attacked you, Eden!"

"They fuckin' did!" Eden shot back angrily. But just as quickly, she suppressed it. "They deserved to be punished, but not like that, Rose." Eden grimaced. "I did things to them that . . . I tortured them. No matter how I try to forget that, I can't. I punished them in a way that was cruel and evil. If that's what this Mkombozi is like, then why would I want to be her?"

Rose resisted the urge to tell her that she was trapped into a fate that she couldn't escape. Eden's choices had been taken from her by Khale the moment the Ancient Shifter had decided to reincarnate Mkombozi's essence into that newborn infant.

Defeat washed over Eden's expression as she wiped away her tears with the back of her hand. "I have to go," she said sadly.

Rose nodded and smiled. "Of course you do, MyEden." Rose felt her heart split in two. The world wasn't a big enough place for Eden to run, but Rose couldn't tell her that. It was a lesson she'd have to learn on her own. "Where will you go?"

Eden shrugged again and took a deep breath before responding. "Someplace warm," she quipped, forcing a smile. "Someplace where there are no subways, air pollution, or weird-looking creatures that only I can see."

Rose smiled, too. "I hope you find that place. And I hope that it's all that you dream it should be."

Rose said it but she didn't believe it. There was no place like that in this world for Eden. There never would be.

IN A SMALL TOWN

After a while, Kifo had become numb to the sounds of their screams. It was different than it had been on Theia. Back then, he'd collected the bodies of Ancients who had fallen in battle—Weres, Valkyries, Guardians, and Shifters—and used the spells he'd learned from the mystics and transformed them into soldiers for Sakarabru's Brood Army. Their bodies were strong, even in death, their resolve and discipline unmatched. A Brood soldier who could shift into a beast or who could fly was worth his or her value in treasure.

Kifo's spell not only reanimated the dead, but it made them physically stronger, their muscles and bones as dense as armor, and the beauty of it all was that they all became loyalists to the Demon. They were slaves to his will, and that was what had made the Demon the fierce conqueror that he was on Theia.

Some of the people called out to him in Spanish, *"Reaper! Llévame! ¡Por favor!* Reaper! Take me! Please! Let death relieve me of this torture!"

They weren't the first whom he had turned, and they wouldn't be the last.

The scent of disease, urine, and feces filled the air. Kifo donned another expensive custom suit, which he would later burn because the smell was overwhelming. The mystics knelt over each of the undead humans, performing their rituals that would change them and make them into the Brood soldiers of this world.

He had started with the sick, terminal patients who were close to death already, but the transformation turned sick humans into weak Brood. He needed strong, able bodies for Sakarabru's army. But like forging metal, the strong needed to be broken down before they could be made. The sickness he had released into the world was beginning to spread at an alarming rate, attacking the strong and the weak. The weak would die off. The strong would become soldiers.

Kifo was a Djinn, his mystics were phantoms, and they all had the power to choose whether or not to allow humans to see them. Doctors and nurses rushed through hospital corridors and in and out of rooms tending to the sick who had come to them for help, unaware of the mystics hovering over patients, chanting their spells. There was a sliver of space between life and death, however, where the victims of these rituals could see them. But in the fever of their sickness, their claims of seeing ghosts and spirits fell on deaf ears.

"Wh-what . . . ? Wh-why are you doing this?"

He stopped in the doorway of the room of one patient, a large Latin male going through the transformation, who saw Kifo.

Tears fell from his eyes as he swiped his muscular arm through the mystic at his bedside.

"Calm down, Señor Gomez. Sir, you've got to lie still," the nurse standing on the other side of the bed told him.

He looked at her as if she were the crazy one. "Stop him! Don't let him do this to me!"

"*Declare your allegiance to Sakarabru,*" the mystic chanted. "*Deny your faith. Deny your God. Sakarabru will set you free,*" the mystic muttered over and over again.

"*Medico!*" she called out as the man became more erratic. "*Necesito un doctor aquí!*"

"Why are you doing this? Why?" His cries faded as Kifo walked away.

"*Are you obedient, Kifo?*"

Obedience was important to Sakarabru. More important than power or fighting abilities. It's what he demanded of his Brood Army. It was what he demanded of Kifo.

"*As always, Lord Sakarabru.*"

Why was Kifo doing this? Why had he brought the Demon back from the brink of destruction? Kifo had never known family or where he was from. He had been raised by Sirh Magi in the Northern Territory, and they had taught him the secrets of life and death and the infinite connection between all things.

"*There is no end, Kifo, and there is no beginning. We are all who and what we are at any given moment. And it's the moment that matters. You and I are the same; we are one separate but connected being. If I should die and you live, that bond does not break. We are tethered, as all life is tethered."*

The Sirh were peaceful, spiritual beings who lived quiet and simple lives, neutral to the conflicts brewing between Khale and Sakarabru. It was that neutrality that killed them.

"Run, Kifo! Hide! Go now!"

The Sirh had taught him to respect life and to honor it. They had taught him not to fear the afterlife, but when he lost them, Kifo was a scared and frightened young Djinn, a child who quickly learned that not all Theian Ancients believed as the Sirh had believed that all life was precious, especially his.

He had scavenged for food and a place to sleep at night. He had huddled in caves to avoid being seen or caught up in wars that he wasn't brave enough to fight. Kifo was a mystic, not a soldier, and he was afraid.

He had wandered into the desert and found a Faih, akin to an Earth scorpion. Kifo found it dying and was going to eat it but couldn't bring himself to do it. Did it have the same passion for living as he did? Did it deserve to live? Did he?

Kifo had closed his eyes and repeated a chant he had learned from one of the Sirh magi, and as he chanted, he focused on the bridge that this Faih was traveling to get from life to death. He imagined its fear, its uncertainty, and its regret that it had to leave its life behind too soon. And then, at that crucial moment when he knew that the Faih had accepted its fate, Kifo refused it passage to the other side of that bridge he saw in his mind, and the Faih flipped over on its legs and quickly crawled away.

He had been so caught up in his chanting that it wasn't until he saw the Faih crawl away that he noticed someone standing over him. It was a young general, Sakarabru.

"What did you do?" he asked, towering over Kifo.

Kifo thought long and hard before responding. "I took away its option to cross over," he finally said. "It had no choice but to come back to this life."

Sakarabru had been kind to him. He had been patient and had encouraged his studies in the art of mysticism. It was Sakarabru who convinced him to use his abilities on a fallen Ancient soldier who was near death.

"Remember the Faih?" he asked Kifo, as his soldiers dropped the nearly dead body at Kifo's feet.

Kifo looked confused. "But this is a Shifter, Sakarabru."

"Satisfy my curiosity, Kifo," the Demon had responded.

Kifo lived with the Demon, but in his mind he hadn't chosen a side in the wars. It wasn't until that moment that he realized that the Demon was asking him to choose his side.

It took much longer with the Shifter than it had with the Faih. Kifo had chanted over him for three days before he was finally able to stand. He was alive again, but different. He was angry and almost feral, until Sakarabru spoke to him. The Demon's voice calmed him, and he was obedient to Sakarabru.

"I want you to make me more of these, little mystic."

Sakarabru had taken Kifo in and cared for him when no one else would. In exchange for a home, Kifo gave Sakarabru his loyalty. The opportunity to prove his devotion came at a time when Sakarabru was wounded after a particularly difficult battle. His healers were all around him, suturing his wounds. Sakarabru had summoned Kifo to his room.

"The Shifter, Khale, would have my head if she could, little mystic," he said, cringing when he attempted to laugh. "Today, she nearly did. Fortunately, her aim was off."

"Would you have her head if you could, Sakarabru?" Kifo asked.

Sakarabru stared intently at him. "Yes. Yes, I would."

Had Sakarabru really just called him into his room for small talk? Kifo suspected that that wasn't the case. "Why did you summon me, Lord Sakarabru?"

He grimaced and glared at one of his healers. "Because I thought I was dying," he admitted.

"And you would want me to bring you back?"

The Demon studied him. "Would you bring me back, Kifo?"

He realized right then and there that he was not just Kifo, the little lost Djinn who had been found and thought of as a pet. He was Kifo, the mystic and the maker of soldiers for the Brood Army. He stuck out his chest a little more, drew back his shoulders, and raised his chin. "If I should ever have the opportunity, Lord Sakarabru, yes. I will bring you back."

He had brought Sakarabru back and was rebuilding his army because he was loyal to the Demon, and his loyalty was everything. Sakarabru had saved his life. He had been there for Kifo at a time when he was absolutely alone and afraid. Sakarabru had been like a father to him, and for that, Kifo owed him life, for as long as it was in his power to give it to him.

THIS OLD MAN

One for three. Bring me. Redeem me. Or die the lamb," he repeated in a singsong melody. "I found a trinket! A pretty trinket! But it's not a trinket! Is it?"

Dave Jensen was an archaeologist, or he *had been* an archeologist—a decent one. He shuffled through the streets of Norfolk, stumbling, talking out loud to himself and working hard to keep his balance on the swollen and bloodied stumps that used to be feet. He'd walked them down to nothing.

"Nothing," he grunted to himself.

People crossed the street when they saw him coming, turning up their noses at him or looking down their noses, mumbling things about the way he smelled or complaining about how he looked. But none of them had ever met him.

And none of them knew that Dave Jensen had been a decent archaeologist. But that was a long time ago.

"Too long," he wheezed, disappointed, weighted down by regret and disappointment. If only he hadn't picked it up. If only he hadn't closed it up in his hand. *If only he hadn't wrapped his fingers around it.*

Besh-Ba-Gowah. In Apache, it meant "place of metal," and it was a pueblo, a ruin in a small town just north of Tucson, east of Phoenix, called Globe, Arizona.

"So damn hot," he muttered, shaking his head miserably at the memory.

Dave had been one of the first. Excavation had started in '35—1935. He would never forget that year, even though he'd forgotten most of the others since then. It was his first dig. Four hundred rooms, maybe more. He'd been assigned a room on the ground level.

"Dave," he said the same way it had been told to him, "this is your quadrant. Yours." He nodded in agreement, like he did back then.

It was a proud moment for him. Dave had his own quadrant. The excavation was slow, but it had to be, as they turned up old and rustic tools like stone axes and hoes, obsidian points, minerals, shell jewelry and beads, and wares painted with pictures of birds, animals, and insects.

It looked like it could've belonged there, he supposed. Dave was crouched low in one corner of his room, his quadrant, alone, while everyone else slept. He should've been asleep, too, but he just couldn't . . .

"Sleep," he said, regrettably.

She wouldn't let him sleep. He had heard her calling him for days. But when he looked around at everyone else, they didn't seem to notice. At first he thought he was just crazy. He thought he was dehydrated and needed to drink more water. The heat was getting to him. And so he ignored her. And he dug. The longer he ignored her, though, the louder her calls became. And the more he dug.

"It's late, Dave," one of his colleagues said to him. "You really should get some rest. Whatever's under there has been there a long time. Surely it can wait another night."

She didn't call to him with words, but it was more of a feeling, an anxious, compelling emotion. It was a thought over and over in his head, a warning that he needed to do . . . something. And that he couldn't stop until he was finished. It wasn't until he found her that the feeling went away and that the words finally came to him in a whisper:

One for three
Bring me
Redeem me
Or die the lamb.

"What is that?" the man kneeling next to him asked, staring at the unusual object Dave had dug up from the ground in a corner of the room.

Dave didn't know. It was made of metal, one thick, continuous piece of metal, rust colored and heavy for something so small. It was as old as anything in that pueblo, and it looked like it could've belonged, but it didn't.

It wasn't even as long as his index finger, and it consisted of a star symbol with a small cut-out circle in the center. It was strange, and it was warm, too warm to have been buried nearly a foot underground for years.

"It looks Celtic," his partner said. "But what would it be doing here?" *He reached for it, but Dave jerked it away.*

Dave looked at the man next to him. "Do you hear that?"

The man looked strangely at Dave. No. He hadn't heard anything. He hadn't heard her voice—the trinket's voice.

"It was clear," he blurted out all of a sudden. "Loud and clear! I heard it! I know I did!"

Dave stopped walking abruptly in the middle of a Norfolk street, causing traffic to screech to a halt. Angry drivers honked their horns and yelled profanities at him. He closed his eyes and remembered. "Such a beautiful melody," he said emotionally.

The man kneeling across from Dave the day he found her reached out to touch her. She wasn't meant for him.

"No!" he shouted, shoving his colleague so hard that he fell back onto the ground.

It whispered to him: "Take me to her. She will not come for me."

"What are you?" he asked in disbelief. Was he losing his mind? "Are you . . . alive?"

No! No, Dave wasn't crazy. He was as sane as anybody, a stable and intelligent man, with a PhD. He'd never given in to whims.

"Why me?" And then he realized that he was talking to a piece of metal.

"You are strong and chosen," he heard it say.

Agonizing screams erupted, and a look of sheer and utter shock bulged from his eyes as his fingers lit up like embers and quickly burned like overcooked meat. The man he'd pushed scrambled to his feet, while the others rushed in at the sounds of the commotion. The people around him tried to help him, but the curse leapt from him onto them. The others grabbed Dave by the shoulders.

She punished them for touching him, and he watched in horror as they burned, the whole team, and all that was left were pillars of ashes all around him. He meant to drop her back onto the ground, but she was a part of him, the flesh and bones of his hand protectively cocooned around her. 1935—that was the year he found her, and he had held her ever since.

He wore layers of clothes—shirts, pants, several coats—but still he could never seem to get warm, even in summer. Dave hunched in a doorway at the back of an abandoned warehouse in an alley. She had led him here, Norfolk Virginia, but he still had a long way to go. He drew his old knees to his chest and pulled himself as tight into himself as he could. The dull ache of arthritis throbbed in his knees, but that was nothing. He held his left hand close to his chest. He'd wrapped it in old socks and a couple of T-shirts until it looked like he had a cast. Keeping it wrapped helped with the pain . . . some.

Dave had tried to cut it off. His hand. He'd tried a couple of times, but she would never let him. He had hacked and hacked until his arm was a bloody mess of flesh and tendons splayed out in front of him like a crimson piece of abstract art, and until his screams dulled in his own ears. But each time, she waited until he had sufficiently punished himself, and then she slowly began the equally painful process of weaving his flesh together again.

He carefully unwrapped his hand, realizing that he hadn't looked at it in months. Dave peeled back the filthy and foul-smelling material piece by piece until after several minutes his hand was free. He held it up in front of his face, marveling at its unnatural and misshapen form. It was three times the size of his good hand, swollen and infected from bones that had been too long broken and muscle and flesh that had never healed. She was no more than an inch round. And all those years ago, when he closed her in his fist, she claimed him. She burrowed mercilessly into his skin, digging and grinding until she planted herself deep in the palm of his hand, breaking and spreading his bones to make room for herself.

He had grown used to the pain. His mangled hand and the torture it gave him was as much a part of him now as his eyes, ears, and mouth. It had gotten to the point that he couldn't remember what it was like anymore, not to have it.

"What are you doing? What are you— No! No—please!"

Those people didn't see Dave where he was sitting. His nook was too dark. But he saw them. More and more people were changing, doing things that good people shouldn't do to each other.

The woman's cries became muffled as one of them, the man, covered her mouth with his hand. The other woman watched him suffocate the life out of the one he had in his arms. She didn't even try to stop him. Dave turned his head, disgusted and uncomfortable at what was happening. He wished he were young again. He wished he could help her, to fight them off and save her, but he couldn't. It was not his place to interfere.

"Go ahead!" the man commanded of the woman next to him. "Do it!"

"I . . . I don't think . . . I can't!" the woman sobbed. "You do it! I can't!"

He hit her with the back of his hand. "You're starving, Sasha! We both are! If you don't— I'll feed on both of you if you don't do this!"

She shook her head.

He bent down to the woman lying on the ground barely moving. Her legs shot out straight and stiff like logs. Her body convulsed, and a terrible gurgling sound escaped from her into the air.

He jerked up, slinging blood that spilled across the other woman's face. Dave saw her stick out her tongue and lick what she could from her lips, and then she moaned, raised the other woman's arm to her face, and bit into her, tearing meat from her the way one would tear meat from a drumstick.

Dave wasn't surprised by what they'd done. He'd seen it before. Dave was nearly a hundred years old. He'd traveled from one end of this country to the next and back again, so of course he'd seen change—cars, the way people dressed, the way they spoke, lived, and died. For a while, he truly believed he'd seen it all. But of course no man can see it all,

because no man can truly fathom what another man is capable of.

The man watched the woman feed off of the one lying
on the ground and then shifted his gaze over to the dark doorway where Dave huddled. He slowly stood up and stalked
cautiously to where Dave was sitting. But Dave wasn't afraid.
He knew better than to be afraid, because she wasn't finished
with him yet. He hadn't found the one she'd sent him to find,
but he was close. He could feel it.

The man knelt in front of Dave, grabbed Dave by his
throat, and started to squeeze. Dave slowly raised his left
hand toward the other man's face. The pain of her power
shot down Dave's arm. Her heat glowed like a fire. The man
stared, awed by her at first, but then his eyes bulged as he
released his grip on Dave and shuffled away until his back
pressed up against the wall of the building on the other side
of the alley.

Dave struggled to get to his feet, and he walked over to
the man standing paralyzed with fear and braced against that
brick wall, trembling in terror.

The man shook his head in protest as Dave walked toward him. She made him walk over to that man, to punish
him for threatening Dave. She was so powerful, and Dave felt
sorry for this creature screaming for his life. He pressed his
twisted hand against the side of the man's face. Dave didn't
have to see inside the man to know what was happening to
him. Bones snapped, some breaking through the skin; vital
organs collapsed inside like drying fruit; and blood thickened
and slowed like molasses.

"Oh my God!" Dave heard the woman behind him exclaim, and then the sounds of her footsteps running away from them until she disappeared out of the alley.

This trinket wasn't finished with Dave yet. Until she was, he was invincible.

HER KEEPER

It's pure chaos here in Littleton, Colorado. Can you tell us what happened?" a female reporter asked the frightened mother standing next to her, clutching her young daughter.

"I came home from work. I don't know what's happening. My father—he . . . he tried to . . . Oh my God."

Rose watched with tears in her eyes as the reporter tried to interview a young woman who came home and found her mother dead, killed by her father.

"Did he attack you as well?" the reporter asked, shoving the microphone in the woman's face.

The woman nodded and was immediately collected and gathered up in a man's, presumably her husband's, arms. "She can't do this! Not now!" he said, quickly whisking her away.

Rose had been glued to the television, watching the horror unfold on almost every channel, hour after hour, for the last two days. The sounds of sirens bombarded her from the television and from outside her own window. It was happening everywhere—in her city, in cities across the country and around the world.

She had lived in this world for four thousand of its years, and she had seen the destitution of plagues, wars, even genocide. She had seen entire nations destroyed by volcanoes, cities devastated by earthquakes, floods, and tornados. Rose had lived through everything she thought that this world had to offer, but never had she ever seen anything as horrific, as terrible, or frightening as this.

Humans turned against humans, fathers killed their wives, mothers killed their children, children killed their parents. It started with the sickness, a flu or viral infection of some kind. People died from it, only to come back to life hours later, attacking those around them, feeding on them, like animals, like zombies, only they weren't the mindless creatures she'd seen in movies, these weren't zombies.

They took that young woman's father away in handcuffs, covered in his wife's blood, and he cried like a baby as they dragged him to that police van and shoved him inside.

"I don't know. . . . I don't understand. . . . I'm so—sorry! God! I'm sorry!"

"Rose. Rose?"

She had no idea how many times Khale had called her name before she finally managed to get Rose to peel her gaze from that poor man on the news.

Khale looked like she hadn't slept in days. "We have to go."

Rose stared dumbfounded at her. "Go? Go where, Khale?"

Of course the Shifter knew what was happening, and not just here, but all around the world. There were no safe places left anymore.

"Look," Rose raised a trembling hand toward the television screen. "Look what he's done."

Khale stared blankly at the screen.

Rose turned her attention back to it, too. "I've spent the last four thousand years waiting for this, Khale, always knowing that someday it would come. But deep in my heart, I'd hoped it never would."

"We've been preparing for this, Rose. We've been preparing Eden for this."

"But how could we really?" she questioned. "This task you assigned to me has been an impossible one from the very beginning. There was nothing that I could say or do to get that child ready for what is happening now." The lump in her throat swelled even more.

"We have to go and get Eden and bring her back, Rose. Now is not the time for her to run away."

Rose turned to Khale. "Is that why you're here?"

"You know she won't come home if I ask her. She's closer to you. She listens to you," Khale reminded her. "And she loves you."

All of a sudden Rose was feeling her age. On Theia, she had been Mkombozi's nurse and caregiver, and before that, she had been Khale's. Her kind were healers, known for their tenderness and often sought after by aristocrats of

Theian society to be their physicians or tend to their children.

The term "Ancients" was a misconception. It was a word that construed the theory that their kind lived forever, and that wasn't true. They outlived humans, but their lives ended just as any living creature's life had to end, and Rose was at the end of hers. For the last twenty-four years she'd spent every waking moment of her life taking care of Eden and trying to prepare her for these new times. Rose looked at the screen again, at the chaos and turmoil filling the streets, knowing that she had failed.

"I remember the night she was born," Rose quietly admitted with tears filling her eyes.

She had been a doctor back then and had delivered that child. The mother was a young and frightened teenager.

"She cried, Khale," Rose said sadly, remembering holding the squirming newborn in her hands. "But only for a moment. I'll never forget the sound of it, though, because it was distinctly her cry, her voice. That was Eden."

"Rose," Khale said, woefully. "Rose, we don't have time for this."

Rose ignored her. Maybe Khale didn't have time, but Rose was no longer concerned with the concept of time.

Her mother didn't want her at first, but the young woman cried when that baby died. Her heart was broken. Rose's heart broke for her.

"I was so nervous about performing the ceremony," she admitted with a fragile smile. "I had seen it done before by my elders, but only twice, and I wasn't sure that it would work or even that I wanted it to."

Her memories took her back to that night in her apartment before she left for the morgue.

"You can do this, Rose," Khale had told her all those years ago, long before that child had been born. "The ritual is rooted in Ancient magic, so it will work."

Rose finished packing all the things she needed for the ceremony tonight and had left no traces of herself in that apartment. Rose stood in the middle of the living room, taking deep breaths to calm her nerves. She took an old shoe box from the top shelf of a bookshelf and placed it on the dining room table, opening it and removing its contents, spreading them out in a perfect line next to one another.

The first was a small silver vial, ornate with rubies, diamonds, and emeralds. Inside the vial was water that had been blessed by Ancient Healers in a time before even Khale had existed. Next, Rose pulled out a fragile papyrus scroll that she had been careful to handle, fearing that over time the brittle document would fall apart in her hands. A white candle and lighter and finally a soft angora blanket that she had made with her own hands centuries ago. All lay displayed on the table as she examined them. After taking inventory of these things, she replaced them, carefully packing them away, tucked the box under her arm, and left for the hospital.

Rose's heels clicked lightly against the glossy linoleum of the bottom floor of the building, heading toward the morgue. It was late. Rose flashed her medical credentials to the security guard, who barely glanced in her direction as he buzzed the door open to let her in. Why the dead needed security guards was rather laughable.

The infant looked even smaller than the six pounds, eight ounces she had weighed at birth. Rose laid her on top of the blanket on one of the autopsy tables and stared at her. She didn't look real, and Rose certainly couldn't fathom the idea that somehow the things she was about to do would bring her back to life. But, then again, it wasn't that teenage girl's child who would come to life. That child had passed through this world for a moment before moving on to her next life. This would be Khale's child.

With a finger, Rose pushed down on the tiny chin to open her mouth and, drop by drop, let the water from the jeweled vial fill her mouth until the vial was empty. Rose lit the candle as her Ancestors had done.

"The essence of the individual will follow the light," she had learned. "It is a beacon to those who are lost, whose life journeys have not yet ended, fully. But beware the essence of evil or angry beings, for they should never be allowed to return."

Rose gently unrolled the scroll. Her eyes glistened with tears at the images drawn by her own hand so long ago. A stream of very old symbols filled the page as Rose began to recite the oration to open the gateway between the Ancients and the infant lying on that table.

"Give me the sweet breath that is in your nostrils. I am the guardian of this great being who separates the earth from sky. If I live, she will live; I grow young, I live, I breath the air."

Rose finished her incantation, took a step back away from the table, and held her breath. Had it worked? Had she brought the

Ancient essence of Mkombozi into this world? Out of the corner of her eye she saw movement.

A deep, threatening rumble rose up from the ground. Equipment on the shelves began to shake and fall to the floors. The walls began to crack, and Rose truly feared that the building was about to cave in on her. Then the child started to cry.

"Thank you, Rose." Khale said, stepping out of the darkness, as tall as the ceiling, thin and powerful, with flower petals where lips should be, a stream flowing down her back and onto the floor, filled with all manner of sea creatures, her skin as blue as the sky. "You did it." She smiled. "Mkombozi is here."

"Doc!" the security guard banged hard on the door and tried turning his key into the lock. "Doc, you all right in there? The door's locked! Doctor?"

Rose looked desperately at Khale.

"She is cold, Rose."

Rose snapped out of her hesitation, rushed over to the child, and quickly wrapped the blanket around her.

"I'll get help!" the man said outside of the door.

Rose gathered the child in her arms and held her close to her heart. She looked across the room for Khale, but the Ancient was gone. Several minutes later, the quaking stopped and Rose pulled the door open with little effort. She looked around for the security guard, but he was nowhere to be found. Rose found the stairwell and quickly left with her child.

"Rose? No," Khale said sorrowfully, kneeling down at Rose's feet and taking Rose's hands in hers.

Rose noticed how old her hands looked, and all of a sudden she was so very tired. Rose had unintentionally stepped out of the spell of her glamour, which had kept her looking young all these years, and she felt relieved.

"You can't do this, Rose," Khale pleaded with her. "Not now. She needs us. She needs you to bring her home, Rose. You know she won't come with me."

The Great Shifter was crying.

"I have loved her, Khale, as if she had come from my body. I have done all I can for her. But I will not bring her back. Not this time," she said, surprised by how feeble her voice was.

"Rose, she's not ready to be out there on her own yet. She needs us to guide her and to watch over her on this quest for the Omens."

"I will not lead her to that," Rose said firmly.

"Look! Look at what is happening to this world! Look at what the Demon has started! Rose, she needs to do this, and we have to help her!"

Eden's small and pretty face flashed in Rose's mind. The little girl, so small and afraid, who smiled when she curled up in Rose's lap and laughed until she cried when Rose tickled her. The child who fell asleep in her arms when she sang to her—that was her child. The scared young woman who was out there somewhere, running as far away and as fast as she could from Theian prophecy, was her Eden. And Rose hoped that she would escape it and get as far away from it as she could.

She looked at Khale, gradually fading from her sight, and Rose breathed a sigh of relief as she welcomed her long-awaited rest. "All I've ever wanted was for her to be happy, Khale."

Khale's expression twisted in confusion as if the word "happy" was a foreign concept to her.

They both knew the fate of the Redeemer after the bond with the Omens was completed. The Omens would make her powerful enough to defeat the Demon, and then they would destroy her. There was no other way that it could end. At least if Eden was running, maybe she had a chance. At least running away gave her a choice.

"Rose?" Khale shook her. "Rose!"

The sound of Khale's voice sounded so far away. Weightlessness enveloped Rose and finally she was set free.

BERLINER MORGENPOST
BERLIN OFFICIALS DECLARE A STATE OF EMERGENCY

Military forces have been called in to restore order to Berlin. Scientists have not been able to identify the mysterious plague that has killed thousands. Days later, these same patients, who have been declared legally dead, reanimate or are resurrected, seemingly fully recovered initially, only to attack and appear to feed on other humans. One medical professional interviewed stated the following: "The initial onset of the disease appears as meningitis or influenza, but does not respond to treatment of either. We have no idea what it is."

LAND OF MILK AND HONEY

Three days ago Eden was at the airport trying to buy a one-way plane ticket to Fort Lauderdale. Now she was on a bus heading for Cleveland. All air travel had been suspended until further notice. Eden had been sleeping in a bus terminal for three days before she finally managed to get a ticket out of Brooklyn, and the only bus leaving was headed to Cleveland. The ticket cost her six hundred dollars. She paid it because all that mattered was getting the hell away from this place.

She'd tried calling Rose several times, only to have her calls go straight to voice mail. In the past, Rose, along with Khale, had always found Eden and had always convinced her to go home. This time, Eden had no intention of going back, but it would've been nice to hear Rose's voice and to know that she was okay. Of course she was okay. Rose was an Ancient. For now, at least, Rose had to be safe.

Eden sat huddled beside the window in a seat next to a pregnant woman holding a toddler in her lap. The people on this bus were scared. She was scared. Eden had no idea what was waiting for her in Cleveland or where she'd go after that, but the fact remained that New York had caved in on itself and turned into a nightmare. She'd been checking the news on her smartphone.

People were getting sick and dying and then coming back to life and killing each other. There had even been reports of some people eating other people. It was crazy. Eden had been feeling sick to her stomach for days. She hadn't been able to eat and she'd barely slept. This was it. She knew it. This was what Rose and Khale had been telling her about all these years. It was real. The Demon was real, and this so-called plague was no plague at all. Her gut told her that all of this was a part of the prophecy that had been drilled into her for as long as she could remember.

Eden stared out of the window, blinking back tears. All

of the people on this bus were running, just like her, hoping to find a place to hide until all of this shit blew over.

"When the Demon returns, Eden, his army will rise up and your world will be in jeopardy of falling under his rule, like our world had been," Khale had warned. *"You are the only one who can stop him. You with the power of the Omens can save the human race from annihilation."*

Is that what was happening? Annihilation? Rose and Khale expected her to stop this and to save the world, which had been turned upside down and inside out. People were dying and being resurrected into monsters. No one could fix this, especially not her.

"What's that?" someone in the back of the bus asked. "Did you see that?"

Eden pulled back her hoodie and sat up in her seat, glancing anxiously out of the windows. She felt them before she could see them. But what were they?

"What?" someone else asked.

Her heart raced, and she fought back the urge to scream, to cry. Was it another dream, a nightmare? *Wake up, Eden,* she willed herself.

"What are they doing, man?"

"Mommy?" the toddler sat up in his mother's lap and looked at her.

"Shhhhh, baby," she said, holding on tighter to him.

"Shit!" someone shouted. "Oh shit!"

Eden looked out of the window at the back of the bus and saw a large cargo truck bearing down on them. Moments later, sound closed in on itself and time seemed to almost stand still as Eden felt her body jerk against itself and saw the chaos of other passengers floating in midair. Mouths gaped open, releasing screams into the air. Eyes bulged wide in disbelief. Glass shattered and then fell like rain inside the bus. It wasn't until her body folded and twisted over one of the seats that she realized she'd been airborne. Excruciating pain raked across her back, and loose luggage fell on top of her, pinning her in place.

The scent of smoke and gasoline filled the cabin, and as suddenly as it had begun, it ended, with broken bodies piled on top of each other. The deafening sound of metal scraping against metal and asphalt and screams blended together creating a chorus of terror. Eden smelled blood and tasted it in her mouth.

Everything stopped. She looked for the pregnant woman and her toddler. Eden slowly turned her head to where she believed the driver should be, and through blurred vision saw that the whole front windshield was missing. And then she saw them, people—at least they looked like people, but something about them was different. Their movements were sporadic and unnatural. They were raging, crawling through broken glass and peeling back the door at the front of the bus.

Sakarabru's army. The words came to her all of a sudden: The Brood.

"Noooooo!" The terror in a woman's voice made Eden's skin crawl, and two of them crept through a busted-out window and grabbed her.

Eden watched in horror as they bit into the woman and dragged her back out of window they'd come through. The woman stretched out her arm to the other passengers. "Help meeeeee!"

It didn't take long for others to come in and start to take more passengers. Eden stared frozen in her own fear and disbelief in what was happening—what was actually happening—as passenger after passenger was attacked, torn, and ripped apart by people who looked like them, but didn't—weren't—like them.

Fight! The word kicked her hard in the stomach, nearly taking her breath away. They were killing the passengers on that bus, and if she didn't do something, they would kill her too. Eden willed her body to move but then realized that she was pinned underneath something . . . someone. She fought to turn over and looked into the face of the pregnant woman, lying lifeless on top of her. The baby, the little boy, was pinned underneath Eden.

Eden had to get out. She looked to the back of the bus for a way to escape, but it was blocked by the truck rammed into the rear end. Eden had no choice. There was only one way out of here, and if she wanted to live, she had no choice but to take it. She didn't remember freeing herself, but soon Eden pushed her way past bodies and debris to get to the front of that bus. They were like ants, crawling over each other to get to these people. Eden met them one by one with her fists, breaking faces; she grabbed heads and gauged out eyes.

Fight! Fight or die, Eden! Yes!

Eden was killing, but she had killed before. She climbed

out of that window, stepping on these . . . these cannibals like they were insects, breaking them, stopping them. Eden kicked, breaking knees and forcing these *things* to the ground in agony. *Things.* They weren't human. They were animals, worse than animals. They were monsters. And they deserved to die.

Eden lost herself to the moment. She was drunk on adrenaline, and for the first time in her life, she let go and gave in to the nature of what she was, had always been. Eden was a warrior. But she wasn't fighting alone. Out of the corner of her eye she saw him. A phantom? No. She turned and saw that it was the Guardian. He picked up grown men by their necks and tossed them aside like toys. As he marched toward her, he caved in chests with his fists and twisted heads, leaving bodies with broken necks in the path to get to her. He was coming toward her. He was coming for her. Huge wings, black and wide enough to block out the sun, spread from his back as he ran straight toward Eden; she stumbled back in awe and fear.

"Tukufu," she whispered, closing her eyes and wrapping her arms around him. But there was nothing she could do. The Guardian had her.

FORSAKEN

Kifo walked the streets of Raleigh, North Carolina, with the same disdain and disgust for what he had seen in Turkey, London, Somalia, Mexico. The curse had spread like fire, just like he knew it would, and the undoing of humankind had been at his hands.

The media had called it a flu. A pandemic.

In the Americas: "Tens of thousands have died. . . ."

In Berlin: "*Tausende sind gestorben.* . . ."

In Italy: "*Migliaia sono morti* . . ."

The first so-called resurrections were deemed miracles, and the masses celebrated, doctors were baffled, and common people became overnight celebrities, with microphones shoved under their noses, and cameras in their faces asking them about their experiences.

"What's it like to be clinically dead?"

"Is there an afterlife?"

"How have you changed since you've been born again?"

In the blind excitement to proclaim these miracles, reporters had failed to see the fear and trepidation in the eyes of these miraculously resurrected people. And they certainly didn't see the hunger, a hunger that would make them monsters, an unfortunate side effect of Sakarabru's will. Kifo had warned the Demon that human bodies weren't like the Ancients he'd used to build the Brood Army on Theia. His mystics had performed the same spells on the humans, but the results had not been without consequences.

Bullets whirred past him. Chaos swirled around him. Screams. Sirens echoed through the streets. Confusion. What had happened? Miracles quickly turned into nightmares. A city oblivious to his presence pressed on to try to stop the pandemonium, but Kifo knew that they would fail. They would stop this first wave, but not the second or third or fourth.

"The Seer Larcerta said it would be you."

Kifo recognized the sound of Khale's voice, even though she had never said two words to him. He turned slowly to face her, standing on the other side of the street. She looked ordinary, but still, he should have been afraid. She was Khale née Khale, after all, the Great Shifter and the dragon.

Kifo boldly walked toward her, stopped, leaned down until their noses almost touched, and inhaled.

"I can still smell the sulfur on your breath, Khale," he said bravely.

"Where there is sulfur, there is still fire, Djinn child."

He recognized a warning when he was threatened with one, and Kifo slowly backed away from her.

"You brought the Demon back," she said, stating fact.

Kifo stood back proudly. "Yes. I brought him back."

She looked beyond him at the houses in the neighborhood of suburbia and shook her head. "And you caused all of this." Again, it was a statement, a declaration. "You did this to these people." She turned her attention back to him. "To this world."

Yes. He had.

"All to get back at me, little Djinn."

Of course her intent was to humiliate him. Khale was understandably upset by all the recent events. Even for him, however, old wounds that should've healed long ago were reopened.

"I saw the dragon the day my people were murdered," he said, evenly. "I watched as you flew over our colony, spitting flame out of your mouth until there was nothing left." More than four thousand years later, the images from that day were still crystal clear to Kifo.

"And then I watched as you landed and changed back into your pretty self and walked through the ash examining the charred bodies of the mystics. They were spiritual, peaceful, and had never hurt anyone, and they had taken me in when no one else wanted me."

Tears had the audacity to fill the Shifter's eyes. "It was war, Kifo. And for every one I killed from Sakarabru's territory, he killed ten of mine. It wasn't fair and it wasn't right, but it was war."

"And it is again, Khale," he said coolly.

"You could have left well enough alone, Djinn. We have all found a new home in this world. We have built our lives here. Bringing him back will destroy everything and everyone. You know this. I cannot believe that in your heart you believe that bringing him or his army back is the right thing to do."

"I am obedient," he blurted out, surprising even himself with those words.

Khale frowned. "But you weren't always."

What the hell was she talking about? Of course he had always been obedient to Sakarabru. The Demon had saved Kifo from a life of desolation and starvation after Khale had destroyed everything and everyone who he had ever loved. Kifo owed him his loyalty.

"He tortured you, Kifo," she volunteered.

Kifo couldn't believe the depths to which this liar would go to trick him. "Now is not the time for this, Khale," he said with his own warning. "Don't you have a new Redeemer to play with?"

"He tortured you longer than most, Djinn. I don't even want to try and imagine the kinds of things that Sakarabru did to you, taking you to within an inch of your life, only to bring you back again, saying that he was saving your life, when all he was doing was manipulating you. I have seen him do this. I know what he is capable of."

Gunshots fired in the house behind her, and Khale flinched.

"You've destroyed this world, Kifo. You've destroyed this world. There is no going back for these people. Don't you understand that? He made you do this."

Sakarabru had saved Kifo's life. That's what he understood. And nothing this bitch said would be enough to make Kifo question his loyalty to the Demon.

This place had been his home, too. It wasn't perfect. Humans could sometimes—most times—be their own worst enemies, wallowing in their petty prejudices and selfishness. They were intolerant and ignorant, and war was nothing new to this race. Kifo had started a different kind of war, one that he knew they wouldn't be prepared for. It was the most devastating and heartbreaking thing he'd ever seen, watching entire societies fall apart over what he'd done.

"He will call to them?" she asked. Khale was referring to those who had been turned. "He will gather them and claim them as his army?"

"He's getting stronger," Kifo said. "He'll call them when he's ready."

She visibly swallowed. "She will be ready."

"Your new Redeemer?" he asked smugly.

"Mkombozi reborn," she corrected him.

The Shifter put on a great game face, but something told him that she didn't quite have the same faith in this reborn that she'd had in Mkombozi.

Khale wasn't the only one privy to this so-called prophecy. Kifo had heard his share of the rumors. He had never been one to believe in such things. Kifo had been taught that individuals were born with the gift of choice and selection, and as long as they lived, they could choose. As long as choice allowed, then it was impossible to predict an outcome.

"Didn't you kill the last Redeemer who was prophesied to save our world?" he asked sarcastically. "If prophecy holds true, won't you kill this one?"

She held his gaze with her own. "Perhaps, but not before she destroys your Demon."

"Does this reborn Redeemer possess the Ancient's courage, Khale? Does she have the same conviction?"

Khale's stone-faced expression would've been convincing to someone else. Kifo saw right through it.

"The Demon and his Brood won't stop the bonding, Djinn."

"Then I take it that it hasn't already occurred," he said flippantly. "The advantage is ours, Khale."

She nodded, "For now, but it won't always be so, Djinn."

He watched as the Shifter changed into a small blue bird and flew away. Kifo stood there thinking about the choices he had made, which, consequently, had played well into the Ancient prophecies. He had made them of his own free will.

Bringing the Demon back certainly came with consequences. Sakarabru's ego was too big to settle for merely existing in this world. Kifo understood that by bringing him back, he would bring back the Demon's unquenchable thirst for power and rule.

Ultimately, it was Kifo's ego that had been the deciding factor in bringing Sakarabru back from the brink of destruction. It had taken four thousand years to bring Sakarabru into this world. For all those years, Sakarabru had haunted him, stalked him in his dreams, calling on the Djinn to prove his obedience in the most magnificent test of his abilities he'd ever faced in his life. He'd done it. And in the process, he'd all but destroyed an entire civilization.

LITTLE GIRL BLUE

He pulled a key out of his pocket and unlocked the front door to the massive isolated house that was surrounded by huge trees, as if he were a normal person. The Guardian swung open the front door, grabbed Eden by her wrist, and then pulled her inside, closing the door behind them. Heavy dark wood beams, floors, and windowframes were offset by light-colored walls and picturesque views in every direction that seemed to go on forever.

"Sit," he commanded, leading her to the brown leather sofa in the center of the room. There was nothing in this house that gave her any indication of his personality, no paintings on the walls, sculptures, or even plants.

She had just flown ten thousand feet above ground in the arms of a man with wings. Shit like that didn't just happen. Eden wrapped her arms around herself and sat down on the sofa. Any thought she had to run or to cry or get hysterical was fleeting. Eden had no place to go, and even if she did, leaving wasn't something she necessarily wanted to do right now. She felt safe here with him, protected. Even with Rose, Eden could never remember feeling this secure.

She watched as he shrugged off his long black coat and let it fall to the floor as he made his way over to a bar across the room, his back facing her. She was living this nightmare that she'd always been told would be her life. It was real, and she was as unprepared as ever for how it was all playing out. One very solid revelation stuck in her mind, though. She had just kicked a ton of ass without even breaking a sweat. All this time, Eden had been pretending to be your average girl. The truth was a whole lot different.

She watched him pour himself a drink and finish it in one gulp. He turned his head toward his shoulder, until she could at least see his profile.

"Do you know who I am?" he asked.

The weight of that question bore down on her so heavily that it took everything in her not to run away screaming. She had seen him once before, the night those two men attacked her in the subway station, and she'd run from him, but even back then, she knew him.

Eden swallowed. "You're . . . the Guardian," she murmured. "Her Guardian."

Slowly he turned to face her and then approached her, carrying an empty glass and a carafe filled with whatever it was he had poured in his. He held out the glass to her, and she took it and held it in both hands and waited for him to fill it. Eden swallowed the contents without coming up for air and then coughed and gagged as she held it out for him to pour her some more.

He walked back over to the bar and left her sitting there, glass outstretched.

"Your name is Eden?" he asked, turning to look at her again.

She nodded. "Eden Reid," she said so low, she wondered if he had heard her.

"You can call me Prophet, Eden Reid."

Prophet? "I thought your name was Tukufu?"

God! He was breathtaking! Tall, muscular, and lean, the Guardian's build reminded her of a swimmer. His shoulders were almost as wide as the room. It was his eyes that she found hypnotizing. Eden had locked onto them without even realizing it.

"Eden? Are you all right?" he asked, concerned.

She forced herself to look away. "MyRose told me that the Guardian's name was Tukufu. . . ." Her voice trailed off.

"MyRose?"

She glanced up just long enough to see him smile. Eden desperately craved another drink. She needed to be drunk. She needed to hurry up and get freaking drunk on her ass.

"Well, MyRose was right. That is my name, but only the Ancients call me that now. I go by Prophet."

Like, whatever. Prophet, Tukufu, God of Thunder—it didn't matter what he called himself. He was the Guardian, and he'd brought her here, and what would happen next was anybody's guess.

"Do you understand what's happening, Eden?"

She closed her eyes and concentrated on the sound of him. Her heart raced as she focused on the cadence of his voice, the depth of it, and the tone. It brought memories back to her, but not memories she could see. Memories she could feel. Memories that comforted her, aroused her, and memories that made her want to curl up in his arms and just stay there.

"Eden?" he repeated, stirring her from the trance she'd fallen into. "How much do you know?"

Eden pondered the loaded question before responding. "I know what they told me, Khale and Rose," she murmured. "And I know what I've dreamed. I know that the Demon is the cause of all of this and that everyone's looking to me to stop him."

Basically, she knew more than she wanted to know and way more than any human being should know.

He paused for a moment, giving her a chance to collect herself for his next question. "How much do you remember from before?"

She looked at him and shrugged. "I don't know," she said softly.

"You remember me. Do you remember anything about Theia, what your life was like before?"

Eden frowned. "It's not like that," she snapped, frustrated.

Khale had been notorious for asking her those same questions. Eden was Jonah swallowed up by the whale. Her life lived her, she'd never lived it. And after today, that fact was as clear as day.

"I don't remember things or places," she eventually admitted. "I don't remember people."

"Then tell me how it is," he gently coaxed her.

She stared back at him and saw patience, curiosity, and concern in his expression. He didn't even know her, but she felt like he cared about her as if he did know her.

"I feel things," she started to explain. Feelings are intangible things, so explaining this to him seemed impossible, but he waited.

"The memories I have are of things like the scent of a purple flower growing on the side of a hill where only that flower grows."

He nodded.

"Certain flavors—I crave foods that I try to find but can't."

An image came to mind of bread, but not just any bread. She'd been to every bakery shop in New York City trying to find it, but she never could.

She closed her eyes and inhaled. "That scent," she moaned.

It was intoxicating and perfect, and when she opened her eyes, she realized that it was coming from him.

He smiled.

"Do you know that I am the Guardian because Rose told you that I was?" He approached her carefully and sat down next to her on the sofa.

Eden drew her knees to her chest and tried to disappear into a ball.

"Or do you know that I am the Guardian because you remember me?"

Eden paused before admitting the obvious. "I remember."

No particular image of anything he'd done or said to her

came to mind, but in her heart she knew things about him. "Your strength. Your devotion. You protected her."

"Her? Or you?"

Her. He had been Mkombozi's Guardian. Not Eden's.

"Eden," he said tenderly.

Her stomach fluttered when he said her name, and she knew that she was weak to him. She stared into those silver orbs of his.

Tukufu had always taken Mkombozi's breath away, and now he was trying to take hers too. He had told Mkombozi that he'd loved her from the moment he first saw her in Khale's arms, but the Redeemer had loved him long before that.

"I remember . . ." she murmured, "you."

Prophet raised his arm and extended his hand to her.

She stood up and slowly walked toward him. He was her Guardian, had always been, and would always be.

Eden took hold of his hand and let him gently pull her closer to him.

The minutes passed between them before he finally spoke again. "Do you understand what's happening to this world?" He looked at her.

She nodded. "Doctors are calling it some kind of plague." A plague was easier to digest than the darker thoughts lurking in the back of her mind. If that's all it was, then it could be identified and eventually cured. Humankind was resilient enough to survive a damn outbreak.

He paused again, seeming to search for the right words. Eden studied him, his powerful profile, the long ropes of locks hanging down his back.

He turned to her. "Sakarabru, the Demon, is back, and he's building his army. He's using humans to do it," he explained carefully.

A wave of nausea washed over her.

"He wants to do to Earth what he did to Theia," Prophet explained.

Those people who had attacked the bus weren't humans anymore. Scientists and doctors couldn't explain what they were, but in this moment, she knew.

"Can those people ever be normal again?" she asked, hoping he could tell her what she needed to hear. "Is there a way to stop this? To reverse it?"

Eden was crying, but for probably the first time in her life, it wasn't for herself.

He shook his head. "I honestly don't know."

Eden took her glass and held it in front of him.

Tukufu, Prophet, filled it, she drank, and then he filled it again.

"This is crazy!" And she was finally feeling the effects of the alcohol.

"It is," he said. "It's insane, and I know how hard this is for you."

She resisted the temptation to fall onto his chest and bury herself in him.

"No. You don't." Eden felt helpless. "This is my home. It's my world. Not yours or Khale's or even MyRose's."

"Believe me," he said. "I do. It feels like only yesterday that I lost mine."

"You're still you, Prophet," she said, helplessly. "A week

ago I was a fuckin' bartender who hated my job, but hell, it was a job. The next thing I know, I'm sitting on a bus, people are getting killed and eaten by other people, and then I end up here." How could he possibly know what this all meant, especially the monumental role she was supposed to play in this mess? "What happens next?"

As far as Eden was concerned, she had come to the end of one life and stepped right into the beginning of another one, even worse.

"Have you eaten?" he asked, after she'd calmed down a bit.

Really? After everything she'd just said, that's all he had to say? She shook her head. Eden had left home three days ago, and she couldn't recall the last time she'd eaten or slept.

"I can't eat," she said dismally.

"Then you need to rest," he said, taking hold of her hand and leading her to the staircase.

He took her to one of the bedrooms and, literally, all it had was a bed. He walked over to the closet and pulled out a towel for her and then opened the door that led to a bathroom.

"You can shower in here. The bed's pretty comfortable. There are extra blankets in the closet if you need them."

He closed the door behind him when he left. She pinched herself several times for good measure just to be sure that she was awake. Her hands ached from hitting all those people. At least, that's how she thought of them now, as people, but while Eden was fighting for her life they had been the enemy. Eden had fought those creatures on that bus out of desperation just like she'd fought the men who'd tried to rape her the other night and in both cases, just for a few moments, she had felt liberated. Eden had no idea how long she stood there after he was gone. She barely remembered showering. She seemed to come back to herself as she curled up in that bed, pulled the blankets up to her chin, and eventually drifted off into a restless sleep.

CLEAR A SPACE

She was young, but she was the one he'd sworn his heart and soul to all those years ago in another world, and yet she wasn't. Eden Reid was a confused and frightened woman. She was filled with the essence of Mkombozi, but that didn't mean that she was a carbon copy of the Ancient Redeemer. Bringing her here, watching her as she sat in his home, it became very clear to him that he had to tread lightly with this human woman and resist the natural urges he had to sweep her up in his arms, toss her on the bed, and make love to her until the sun rose. She wasn't ready—and perhaps he wasn't so ready, either.

To anyone else, it was just a blue bird flying toward him as the sun began to set. But he knew better.

"Khale." He muttered her name as she landed on the railing of his balcony overlooking the lake and then transformed into her human form, the young woman with the oversize glasses and stringy brown hair, leggings, and a black T-shirt with oversize, red puckered lips on the front.

"She's here," she said anxiously, jumping down from the railing and starting to rush past him to get inside.

He grabbed her by the arm and stopped her. "She's sleeping."

Of course the Great Shifter was offended that the Guardian would bring it upon himself to actually put his hands on her. But he was offended that she would burst into his home without being invited.

She jerked away from him. "I need to talk to her."

"You can talk to her in the morning," he insisted. "Tonight she rests."

His tone and his demeanor sent a powerful message. The Shifter had been successful at keeping her from him, but Eden was with him now, and his duties as her Guardian took precedence over any authority Khale may have thought she had.

"How is she?" Khale reluctantly asked.

She had warned him that Eden was not ready for him, and she had been right. But the situation had escalated quickly, and Eden needed him now more than ever.

"Scared," he admitted. "Overwhelmed."

Khale looked disappointed. "Because she chooses to be. Eden is stubborn and refuses to accept the truth about her destiny."

"Can you blame her? She's not a Theian, Khale. She knows nothing of our ways, our history."

"Eden has been told the history of Theia from the moment she was old enough to listen, Guardian. She has chosen not to accept the truth. She'd rather be some bitter girl who runs away from her destiny, her responsibilities, rather than stands and faces them."

"You tell her that her world will end if she doesn't step up and become some legendary creature who can save it! You tell her that she's the reincarnation of a being who lived four thousand years before her and who not only destroyed a Demon but her own world in the process, and you expect for her to just accept something like that?"

For all of her so-called fascination with the humans, for all of her efforts in trying to dress and talk like the cool kids, Khale was more out of touch than ever.

"Kifo brought him back," she said, abruptly changing the subject. "I should've destroyed that weasel long ago."

She was right. She should've. But in her grief, Khale had let him live. After The Fall of their world, the Ancients were scattered, afraid, and the differences that had divided them seemed petty in light of losing their entire world. Kifo had done what they all had done. He'd stumbled along, looking for his place in this world, coming to terms with losing everything he'd known, and building a life for himself here.

"Have you seen Sakarabru?" he asked.

The last time he'd laid eyes on Sakarabru, Mkombozi had sent his ashes flying across space.

She shook her head. "But I can feel him. His power—everything that's happening now to these people—is so familiar." She frowned. "Only it's worse for them for some reason.

Kifo had built Sakarabru's army on Theia from the bodies of
fallen Ancients. The transition for them wasn't as devastating as it has been for humans."

She was right. Humans transitioning from human to
Brood had left behind rabid and vicious beasts instead of dis-
ciplined warriors. Humans had turned on other humans and
fed off them, like wild animals. It was a side effect that no
one could've seen coming.

"There isn't much time left, Guardian," Khale said, looking at him. "I know that Eden isn't ready for this. Believe me,
I know more than you realize how frightened and unprepared
she is, but we're out of time. As Sakarabru grows stronger,
this world will grow weaker. Soon he'll be ready to call his
army to him, and he will turn Eden's world upside down even
more than it already is. You know this as much as I do."

Humans all over the world were affected, and those that
weren't, were fodder.

"I may be able to slow him down," she said, concerned.
"But our forces aren't as strong as they once were."

"Our forces aren't anything, Khale," he corrected her.

It pissed him off that the Ancients had grown so indif-
ferent, so weak, even knowing that the day would come when
the Demon would return. They'd grown comfortable in their
suburban homes and designer clothes, fancy jobs and cars.
The Ancients talked a good talk about the return of the Demon but had done nothing to prepare for him.

"She's the only hope we have, Tukufu," she said sincerely.
"I hate that the salvation of her world has to fall on her shoul-

ders, but you and I both know that the Redeemer has to bond with the Omens, and that when she does, she can defeat Sakarabru. She has no choice."

"I do have a choice, Khale."

Neither of them had noticed Eden standing in the living room, barefoot and wearing one of Prophet's shirts. Her dark locks cascaded down her shoulders, and soft, dark, vulnerable eyes darted back and forth between Prophet and Khale.

"You've tried to take it from me my whole life, but I won't let you. I can't."

Khale turned to her. "Then your world as you know it will die, Eden. If you choose to do nothing, that's what will happen."

Khale looked at Prophet. It really was up to her. Khale might not have wanted to admit it before, but now she had no choice. And whatever choice Eden made, he would stand by her and suffer the consequences alongside her.

"It's up to you, Eden," he finally said.

She looked back at Khale. "Where's MyRose?" Her voice cracked. "I need to talk to her."

"Rose is dead," Khale said bluntly.

Eden shook her head. "No," she murmured.

"She died several days ago, Eden."

Rose was an Ancient, a constant who had never failed Eden no matter how many times Eden had disappointed her. She stared at Khale, standing there looking like some geeky gamer chick, waiting for her to say something heartless, like that she was just kidding and Rose was standing outside. Khale didn't even blink.

"She left me?" Eden asked, gradually coming to terms with the fact that this was not a joke.

"No," Khale said, coolly. "You left her."

"Khale!" Prophet snapped at the Shifter.

Eden's whole body shook. He believed that she was going to crumble and break apart into a million pieces, but Eden's expression changed; she walked over to Khale, opened her mouth, and screamed, drew back her arm and swung it at Khale, landing a powerful backhand to the Shifter's face.

The force coming from Eden was so crippling that it lifted Khale off her feet and sent her flying over the railing and out to the sky, sailing over trees that stood at least three hundred feet tall. Khale shifted into an eagle, flew away, and disappeared from sight.

Eden fell to her knees, sobbing. Prophet went to her, picked her up, and carried her up the stairs and back to bed.

"MyRose is gone," Eden murmured pitifully, not willing to let him go. "I should've stayed."

"It might not have made a difference, Eden."

"She was always there for me, Prophet," she sniffed. "I should've been there for her."

She pulled away from him, dried her eyes, and lay back on the bed.

"She was my mother," she said thoughtfully.

"You loved her."

She nodded. "With all my heart."

Eden was starting to cry again, but she forced herself to stop. She'd done too much of that already.

"This is really happening, isn't it?"

He nodded. "Yes."

"I hate Khale," she finally admitted.

"Yeah," he agreed. "Join the club."

PAUL CHAPMAN

In the past I was guilty of underestimating my enemy, Kifo."

Sakarabru was growing stronger with each passing day. He had transitioned from his phantom form and had become blood and tissue again, muscle and bone. He had not yet reached the fullness of his former self, but he knew now that that day would come, and it would come soon.

He slowly circled the creature Kifo had brought to stand before him, examining it and assuring himself that this one had no weaknesses.

"He looks stronger than the others," he said, introspectively.

Naturally this man was not as tall in stature as the Demon, but he was large compared to the others Kifo had brought before Sakarabru.

"He was a fighter in his previous life," Kifo explained.

Sakarabru looked surprised. "A warrior?"

Kifo chuckled. "As much of one as this world has to offer. He's trained in several fighting forms, martial arts, boxing, wrestling."

"And those are the traits of a good warrior in this place?"

Kifo nodded. "Yes, Lord Sakarabru. He has fought and won many battles against his opponents."

Sakarabru bent slightly at the waist to examine the markings on the creature's face—scars, wounds.

"What is your weapon of choice, Brood?" he asked this thing that Kifo called Paul Chapman.

The apprehension of Paul's circumstances filled his eyes. He did not know how he'd changed. He simply understood that he was different and that Sakarabru was his god.

He raised his hands, palms facing up, to Sakarabru.

"M-my hands, Lord Sakarabru," he said, almost as if he were responding against his will. He was a slave to Sakarabru's will now, so his own thoughts were of little consequence.

Sakarabru closely examined his large rough and calloused hands and nodded approvingly. "Are you obedient, Paul Chapman?" he asked, staring the creature in his eyes.

Paul Chapman nodded. His eyes glazed over with tears. "Yes, Lord Sakarabru," he said passionately. "Oh yes. I am the most obedient."

Sakarabru was pleased. He had taken the tale of the Redeemer too lightly. Sakarabru had thought of her as nothing more than a character fit for a child's bedtime story, and because of that, she had defeated him and nearly destroyed him.

"Khale has a great deal of faith in her reborn," he said introspectively.

Paul Chapman stood head and shoulders taller than Kifo. Muscles bulged from every part of him. Kifo had forged him personally and made him the most fearsome creature the human race had to offer. It would be a formidable foe against Khale's new Redeemer.

"She is only human, Sakarabru," Kifo offered. "And without the bond with the Omens, that's all she'll ever be."

"You will find her, Paul Chapman," he said, admiring this new kind of warrior. "You will find her for me and you will kill her before she bonds with the Omens. Do you understand?"

"I understand," he said convincingly. "On my life, I will find her for you and I will kill her."

Paul had memories. He had had another life once, and he'd been someone else. Paul's memories of the man he'd once been were mostly vague, like dreams he'd had and forgotten as soon as he'd opened his eyes and woken up. But there was one he couldn't forget, one he couldn't shake no matter how much he wished he could. It replayed itself over and over in his head, beginning with the man he'd been and ending with the man he'd become.

"Uuuugh!"

Paul Chapman dropped to his hands and knees on the floor of his bathroom in agony and grunted—short, shallow breaths—praying that the searing pain in his gut would mercifully subside.

It stabbed him again and then wrapped around him, raking down his spine like the prongs of a pitchfork. He shuddered. Sweat beaded on his face and dropped in pools on the floor. Paul couldn't help himself, and he vomited, then stared miserably and helplessly at the bloody mess he'd spit up.

Angry hot tears filled his eyes. Fuck! He'd always been such a mean motherfucker, tough as nails and fuckin' fearless! And now look at him. Arms the size of pythons had shrunk down to toothpicks, and he could barely keep himself from dropping face-first into the crap he'd just barfed up. The National Mixed Martial Arts Heavyweight Champion of the World was a goddamned pathetic lump of flesh, too weak to stand up and walk a few feet across the room, a shadow of his former mountainous-sized self.

Paul "Stone Mountain" Chapman, he'd dubbed himself. Paul nearly laughed at that tag now, but his body was too tortured to work up the strength to laugh. Paul was dying. It didn't take a genius to figure that out. He was dropping dead right here and right now in his goddamned bathroom, and there was nothing he could do about it.

Paul lay across the floor, wheezing, his head pounding like someone was stomping on it.

He'd painfully managed to pull himself up using the vanity for leverage. Paul shakily balanced himself and stared at his horrific reflection in the mirror. Once upon a time, he'd been a good-looking guy. Half Italian, the other half German, he was swooned over by women when he walked into a room, and when they did, he'd half smile, run his fingers through his dark wavy hair, dart a green-eyed, hypnotic glance in their direction, and leave them panting after him like the thirsty animals that they were. Every now and then, he'd grab one of them by the hand and welcome her into the fold, at least for the night.

He stared, looking disappointed at himself, or at the remnants of what was left of him. He used to stand six feet four and weighed a solid and muscular 270 pounds. He could bench-press more than 600 pounds. And in the last two years leading up to this moment, Stone Mountain Chapman had been one of the most feared fuckers on the planet.

An invisible vise suddenly gripped his chest and squeezed. Paul's eyes bulged until they were almost ready to pop out of his head. His lips turned a violent shade of purple, and in that moment, he knew it was over.

It was dark all around him, and the darkness pressed down heavily on top of him. Paul struggled to open his eyes but couldn't. He struggled to catch his breath but couldn't do that either. He was trapped, unable to move or to do anything except suffocate. Panic struck like lightning, and he forced his mind to will some part of him to move, to get up, to . . . scream.

A low hummmmmm . . . a whisper . . . a song . . . chanting. In the darkness, he saw something darker . . . hovering over him . . . floating . . . humming. He was terrified, and Paul opened his mouth to scream, but there was no air and he had no voice. He raised his arm on the air and swiped at it—the ghost—with his hand. *What nightmare is this? He kept thinking. Wake up! Wake up, god-damnit! It chanted some kind of prayer or song over him. It waved its hands above him, and it was suffocating like . . . the stench . . . something rotting, molding.*

The whole thing seemed to have lasted an eternity, until the words converged on each other and became one long continuous

sound except for one word: "Sak . . . Sakarabru." The more he heard
that word, the more it eased his pain and his fear. It soothed him
like a cool wind rushing past him on a hot day. It quenched his
thirst and washed over him like cleansing rain. "Sakarabru" was
a word that filled him with hope and purpose, and he began to
miss it when he didn't hear it. He looked helplessly at the dark
figure, chanting, begging him with his eyes to just say the word he
most needed to hear: "Sakarabru."

"You will heed Sakarabru," this being said, his voice haunting
and deep, echoing through the chambers of Paul's mind. "You will
need only him, your master, your savior, your teacher. He will
remove your pain, Paul Chapman. He will be your healer."

Paul didn't resist, he couldn't, because what the ghost said had
been everything Paul had wanted to hear. And as he accepted it,
he felt relief set in and erase all of his doubts, his pain. His lungs
seemed to fill with air, cool and fresh air that couldn't exist in that
place. Yes! He wanted to say. Sakarabru! It was all he needed.

He sat up with a jolt, gasping for breath. Paul clutched at the
stained material of his shirt and coughed uncontrollably, gulping
in buckets of precious oxygen until he finally realized that he was
on his bathroom floor. What the hell happened? he wondered,
sliding on his backside across the floor to the wall. He sat there for
several minutes and realized that the pain was gone. At least he
hoped it was gone, but Paul wasn't convinced, and so he waited
for that shit to grab hold of him again.

He took his time getting up, ready to give in to the fact that
maybe his ass was actually dead and that his bathroom was his
version of heaven, or hell, depending. He looked down at the dark
and crusted stain on the floor that looked like it had been there

for weeks. Paul stood there, feeling pretty good, actually, like he'd really managed to kick this thing, and was even feeling better than he had before he'd gotten sick. His reflection looked like him but it didn't. Shit. He looked even bigger than he'd been before he'd gotten sick; taller, thicker. Paul's shirt felt two sizes too small and the waist of his pants dug into his skin. And then it hit him. He was fuckin' famished. When was the last time he'd had a meal?

Paul rummaged through the refrigerator, grabbed a handful of sliced turkey from the package, stuffed it between two moldy pieces of bread with some mustard, and bit into it heartily. He gagged and spit the food in his mouth into the sink. That shit tasted like dirt. He tried the leftover baked chicken, cheese, even an apple damn near rotted to the core, and it all tasted like crap. He couldn't even bring himself to swallow any of that shit.

The burn in his stomach and the need to eat made him crazy. He'd never felt like this before, but Paul couldn't remember the last time he'd been able to keep anything down, either. Of course he was hungry. The shit in the fridge was spoiled, he concluded. Paul grabbed his keys and decided to go out to get something. He swung open his front door and stared into the frantic face of his manager, Ed Taylor.

"Where've you been, man?" Ed said irritably, pushing past him. "I've been blowing up your damn phone for weeks and banging on your fuckin' door until my knuckles bled! You missed the fuckin' title match! How'd you miss the goddamned title match, Paul?"

Paul stared at him like he had no idea what the man was talking about.

"I'm not speaking Japanese, man." Ed was pissed. "You just blew the title. Do you get that? You forfeited the damn title, and

now some knucklehead kid from Nebraska is walking around somewhere in the world with your shit around his waist."

Paul inhaled deeply and smelled the savory scent of Ed's per-
spiration, and his mouth watered. His stomach growled again.
Crazy thoughts, crazy images flooded his mind. In them, he felt
satisfied, relieved.

"You can stop looking at me like I've lost it and start talking
anytime now, Paul. What the hell happened? Or should I say Who?
You look like shit, by the way. You smell like shit. When was the
last time you took a bath?"

Paul was mesmerized by him, and by the rich, purple-black
color surging just beneath the skin in the vein on the side of his
neck. "This world's gone to fuckin' hell in a fuckin' handbasket,"
Ed paced back and forth. "People are dropping like flies and coming back." He raked his hand across his head. "I know. Right? Who
gives a damn about a prize fight? Who the hell cares?" Paul's heart
raced, and he found himself stepping closer to him, as if being pulled
by an invisible cord drawing the two of them together.

"Fuck!" Ed yelled. "What the fuck's your problem? Is it drugs?
Are you on something, man?"

The hole of Paul's belly burned, his bones and muscles tensed,
and adrenaline surged through his body, filling it with anticipation and an anxious excitement that made him want to jump or
run or fly. Drool began pooling in the corners of his mouth.

Ed Taylor fought for his life, but he lost and he never screamed.
Paul expected him to, but the look on the man's face, the terror in
his eyes, the realization that Paul had sliced him down the middle
with a kitchen knife and then torn open his torso with his bare
hands was too overwhelming an experience to warrant a scream.

Paul saw what he was doing from some distant place in his mind that made sense of it. Paul relished the savory flavors of the other man's blood and skin, and something deep inside of him that he never even knew existed could not understand or accept how wrong it was for him to do what he'd just done.

Paul stood up and stepped over Ed's body on his way to the bathroom, in desperate need of a shower. Days later, Paul had ended up here, summoned.

Sakarabru was pleased with this one. Yes, there was apprehension and uncertainty in his eyes, but there was something else there, too. There was loyalty and dependence so blind that it would never question and never waiver.

"When you hear my voice, you will know it. When I call to you, you will come. You will not hesitate. You will not question. I am all that is all. I am everything to you, and only I can heal you and take away your pain."

He stepped back and examined his Brood once more.

"Go, Paul Chapman," he commanded. "Find her, this new Redeemer, and end her."

REELIN' IN THE YEARS

The scent of bacon woke her up. Eden followed it to the kitchen, where the Guardian Prophet was standing over the stove, cooking. He had his shirt off; his jeans hung low on his waist. Looking at him, Eden guessed that he stood at least six feet five, maybe even six seven or eight, and he was covered in tattoos, a tangled mass of faces, trees, and wild animals. But even under all that ink she could see his huge shoulder blades and two very dark lines, almost black, folds of skin that separated slightly, depending on how he moved.

Prophet's long locks hung slightly below his hips and were blunt at the ends, like they'd been cut. He was the most unusual looking and breathtakingly beautiful thing she'd ever laid eyes on, like a piece of artwork that somebody made up, that couldn't possibly be real. If he looked like this, and he loved Mkombozi at first sight, then she could only imagine how beautiful Mkombozi must've been. The Mkombozi in her dreams, her nightmares, was a hollow shell of the real Redeemer. Eden came to that conclusion just by looking at him.

"Afternoon," he said, turning to her and taking a sip of coffee.

Prophet had prepared two plates and sat them both on the counter.

"Afternoon?" she said, confused, taking in his presentation. "But that's breakfast."

He'd prepared what looked to be a couple of packages of bacon and at least a dozen eggs.

"Yeah, it's uh . . . really all I know how to make," he shrugged. "And coffee. I make a mean cup of coffee." He smiled and raised his cup in a toast.

She made her way over to the counter and sat down. "How long have I been asleep?"

"Long enough to eat all that, I'm sure," he said, motioning toward the food.

Okay, so she was hungry. Eden took a bite of the bacon and moaned audibly. She was starving.

He smiled his appreciation. "Coffee?"

She nodded and shoved some eggs into her mouth. "Yes, please."

Damn! Either this was the best-tasting bacon and eggs she'd ever had in her life or she'd been asleep for weeks and was famished!

After passing her a cup of coffee, he stood there looking mighty pleased with himself.

"Aren't you going to eat?" she asked with her mouth full.

"I ate already."

"Whose plate is this?" Eden pointed to the plate next to her.

He smiled.

She was on her second cup of coffee by the time they went out onto the deck. The view was so beautiful. The house sat in a clearing surrounded by trees as far as you could see in every direction.

"Where are we exactly?" she finally had the presence of mind to ask.

"Vermont."

Vermont. If she'd known that Vermont was as peaceful and surreal as this, she'd have left Brooklyn a long time ago. This place, Prophet's home, was in a bubble, protected and separated from the rest of the world. There was no traffic, no people, no noise, nothing. She hadn't even noticed a television in the house.

"I could stay here forever," she said, more to herself than to him.

"It's tempting," he eventually responded. "But you could go a little stir-crazy in a place like this for too long."

"Not me," she responded. "I've dreamed of living in a place like this my whole life. Someplace quiet and secluded. Someplace safe. It's beautiful here."

Prophet was working hard to be patient. He didn't have to say it for her to know it. He knew that she was afraid, and he knew that Eden was content to deny that the real world ever existed. She appreciated him for not rushing her. No wonder Mkombozi loved him.

"Was she hot?" She looked at him.

"Who?"

Eden rolled her eyes. "Mkombozi. Was she sexy?"

Of course she was. *He* was hot, so it only stood to reason that *she* had to have been sexy.

He was too much of a gentlemen to actually come out and say it, but Eden could see the answer in that sparkle in his eyes and in that half smile he worked hard to hide.

"I knew it." She laughed.

She had a ton of questions. Rose and Khale had told her so many things as she was growing up, but even still, there were things she wanted to know, things that had nothing to do with Omens or destinies or demons.

"Are you a Shifter?"

"Me? Nah." He frowned. "I'm a Guardian."

"Guardian's aren't Shifters?"

He shook his head. "Guardians are Guardians."

She waited for him to elaborate.

Eventually he realized that she was waiting. "We are our own race," he continued.

"But you all have wings?"

"Yes. We all do."

"Do you all guard?" It sounded dumb, but how else was she supposed to say it?

"From a very young age a Guardian is tasked to choose the one he will swear his oath to."

"Does it have to be a woman?" she asked.

"For me, yes. Women are my preference."

Oh, thank heaven for that. "And so you swear this oath to protect this one that you choose?"

"Yes," he nodded. "The oath is eternal, and we don't choose lightly. It's a soul thing, something deeper than a simple choice. A Guardian sees the one that is meant for him, and it's almost as if the choice is made for him."

"Was Mkombozi a Shifter?"

"No."

"But Khale is her mother, and *she's* a Shifter. See, that's what I don't understand. If her mother is a Shifter, then why wouldn't she be one?" Eden thought for a moment. "What was her father?"

He shrugged. "No one knows."

Eden was shocked. "Shut the pump Dior!"

Of course she was confused. "The great Khale née Khale had a kid out of wedlock?"

"She wasn't mated to him."

"Well, well, well," she said, smugly. "Does she at least know who her baby daddy is?"

He laughed. "Mkombozi was no Shifter. She was the Redeemer."

"Yeah, but, I mean, what powers did she have? Like, you fly, Khale can shape-shift. What did Mkombozi do?"

"She was strong, fast, a telepath, and a good strategist and general."

"A warrior, Khale said."

"When she needed to be, but not always. Khale saw what she wanted to see in Mkombozi. I saw everything else."

The sly look she gave him nearly made him blush, if that was even possible.

"She wasn't always the warrior, Eden. She didn't necessarily embrace her fate."

That's not the story Eden had heard about Mkombozi. According to Khale and even Rose, Mkombozi wasn't afraid of anything or anyone, and she pretty much chased those Omens down until she found every last one of them.

"She was afraid."

He thought he was being slick. "Don't even try it, Prophet," she said.

"Try what?"

"Try to make me think that she went through what I'm going through about all of this. Mkombozi was a badass. Eden isn't."

He picked up a stone and threw it into the forest. "I don't know. You looked pretty badass the other day when I found you on that bus."

"That was adrenaline and a fierce commitment to not get eaten."

"Still badass."

"Do you miss Theia?" she said, changing the subject.

It was a dumb question, but Rose seldom talked about how she felt about her world. Eden had grown up believing that it was a war-torn mess, with everybody fighting and dying.

"What was it like for you before The Fall?"

He sat quietly for a few minutes before answering her. "The lesser Ancients worshipped us."

"Lesser Ancients?"

"Not all of us are Shifters or Pixies or Weres," he explained. "Most Ancients look like humans."

"Like MyRose," she concluded, realizing that she'd never seen Rose look any other way besides the way she looked.

"We don't age like humans. We age much more slowly."

"But you do get old?"

"Yes."

"And so these lesser Ancients worshipped Guardians?"

"Guardians, Shifters . . . They looked to us as gods. We lived like gods and we bought into our own hype."

"But you don't think that's what you are or were?"

Prophet was thoughtful again. "In this world, Eden, I have been a god, a slave, a soldier. I have had wives, and now once again, because of you, I am a Guardian. We are who we choose to be."

His words cut into her. "But, according to the prophecy, I have no choice."

He surprised her and laughed. "Prophecy. Ancients are so damn dramatic."

"But that's what I was told, Prophet. I was told that I am who I am because of some Theian prophecy."

"Fine, then it's a prophecy," he said irritably.

"Well, what would you call it?"

"A Seer told Khale about the future," he began to explain. "Larcerta is her name, and she is one of six Seers, all trolls. Very unattractive, and I'm not the only one who thinks that, but she's influential."

"I know of the Seers."

"Larcerta told Khale of a possible future, not a definitive one."

"But you heard Khale. My future, according to her, is set. It will happen the way I was taught and I have no choice in it."

"Khale is driving the train," he said sarcastically. "This so-called prophecy or destiny will go where she wants it to go. Until someone else takes over."

"So none of this has to happen? That the damn Demon didn't have to come to my world and fuck it all up? And that I don't have to bond with any Omens or die saving the planet?"

"No."

She couldn't help it. She punched him. Prophet grabbed his arm and spun around, grimacing as if he were in some real pain.

"Oh God!" She stepped back. "Did I hurt you?"

"What I'm saying is that, yes, Larcerta saw all of these things and that they are happening the way she said that they would."

"Then Khale was right! I don't have a choice."

"Larcerta can't see your choice, Eden," he told her. "You could stay here in this house for the rest of your life, however long that may be, and never face the destiny that has been told belongs to you. You could do that."

Eden stood up and began pacing back and forth. "I could do that?" She looked at him.

"You could. If you want to stay here, then stay here. But if you do—if that's the choice you make—understand that it is your choice but that it will come with consequences."

She stopped and just stared back into those silver eyes churning like a storm was raging in them.

"You can choose not to do this, and the world will take care of itself, Eden."

That happy and contented feeling she'd briefly basked in quickly faded. Even without a television or the Internet, Eden could almost feel the change in this world taking place in the air. This house in Vermont may very well have been heaven on earth, but hell was surging all around it, and it would only be a matter of time before it actually showed up here.

"You do have a choice," he said again.

She smiled at the sincerity with which he said it, but if she had any kind of conscience whatsoever, then no. No, she didn't.

SMOKESTACK LIGHTNIN'

Jarrod Runyon and his kind were never on Khale's side. Not on Theia and not here and now in this world. Her side chose him, when the Demon's Brood Army killed his pack in the Valley of Halo before The Fall of Theia.

In the Were Nation, Jarrod Runyon was Alpha, but no outsider would know that by looking at him. He had always preferred to live simply. Jarrod had founded this small town in rural Kentucky hundreds of years ago, but to humans, he was the great-great-great—maybe even one more great—grandson of the original founder of Halo, Kentucky. It was a lie that perpetuated with time, and one that he'd grown quite fond of.

The Great Shifter, Mother General of the Ancient forces, Khale née Khale, looked about as out of place as she felt on his ranch. She'd flown into this place like some sort of hawk, only to land and shift into the form of a young human woman with glasses bigger than her head, standing two feet away from a mound of bull dung.

"Watch your step, Khale," he said, snidely.

She looked down at the mess around her in disgust.

"You sure you don't wanna change into a cow or something?" He laughed. "You'll fit right in."

"We need to talk, Were."

Were. Humans called them werewolves, and had filled in the missing blanks of what they actually were to create their own version of the legend. Some of his favorites included: *"Werewolves can only change into their wolf form when the moon is full."* Another one: *"You can only kill a werewolf with a silver bullet."* And his all-time favorite: *"Any human bitten by a werewolf will change into a wolf at the next full moon."*

His kind had no interest in taking a bite out of any nasty-ass humans. But whatever. Their stories made for pretty decent entertainment if nothing else.

If Khale expected him to climb down from his horse, she was going to be disappointed. He had no love for Khale or any other Ancient that fathomed themselves gods. The truth was that when Theia fell, so did the Ancients, along with their fancy titles and stations in life.

"So talk," he said, in the southern accent he'd adopted as his own. It was an earthy drawl, one that the common man embraced, and it came from the heart.

"The Demon is back," she said, visibly flustered as she swatted at a fly.

Jarrod had seen the news. He knew what was happening in cities all around the world, and he felt sorry for the humans, he truly did. All in all, most of them were decent people and none of them deserved what was happening to them.

"Yeah, I know," he said, shaking his head.

"We have to come together, Jarrod. Sakarabru will destroy this world rebuilding his army and then he will come for all of us. No Ancient will be safe. No one spared."

Jarrod looked out across the vast acreage of his ranch and remembered the first time he'd come face-to-face with Sakarabru's army. He'd had a family on Theia. He'd had a wife and children. That damn Brood Army took them from him. What choice did he have after that, except to fight on the side of the Shifter?

From the look on her face, Jarrod and the boys could tell that she was not nearly as happy about the rewards of their hunt as they all thought she'd be.

Alaine looked at each one of them, and then back to the half dozen dead creatures laying on her kitchen table.

"Did you just put those dead, vile things on my clean table?"

"The boys caught them on their own," Jarrod said proudly, thinking somewhere in the back of his mind that somehow she'd be less inclined to get upset if she knew that.

Alaine stared back at him like he'd just told her that he was a Guardian.

He nudged Cobi, the oldest.

"Yes. Loe and I caught them all by ourselves." He swallowed.

Alaine's angry gaze drifted from one boy to the other. A bitter smile curled the corner of her lips. "Then you and Loe can take them out back where they belong."

"*I'll carry them!*" Loe grabbed the end of the rope that the animals were tied to, dragged them off the table, ran straight for the door, and bumped into Jarrod's brother, Natholu.

"*What is this?*"

The boy held up the animals. "*Cobi and I hunted them and caught them on our own,*" he announced proudly.

"*And you and Cobi can skin them, too,*" Alaine shouted. "*With your father's help,*" she said, glaring at Jarrod.

"*We can eat them tonight for dinner,*" Natholu said, licking his lips.

"*You weren't invited to dinner, brother,*" Jarrod said.

"*Since when has that ever stopped him from showing up?*" Alaine quipped.

"*It never has before, Natholu.*" He smiled.

Alaine laughed, shook her head, and turned back around to finish peeling the vegetables she had on the counter. Jarrod nudged his brother in the side with an elbow.

"*What?*" Natholu asked, sounding as dumb as he looked.

Jarrod nodded his head in the direction of the door, signaling that he needed his brother to leave.

"*Oh,*" Natholu said, finally figuring out what his brother meant. "*Yes, so . . . uh . . . I'll see you tonight at dinner, Alaine.*"

Jarrod came over to his mate, placed a hand on the counter on either side of her, and sniffed a trail down the side of her neck. He loved the way she smelled. It had been sealed into his mind, his heart. It had traveled the winds to him, and he'd followed it until he'd found her. She was made for him.

"*Those boys will be busy for a couple of hours,*" he muttered, and then kissed her neck.

She laughed. "They'll know. They always know."

"Then let's take a walk." Jarrod took the knife from his mate's hand and entwined his fingers with hers. "It's better outside, anyway."

She moaned and turned her face to press against his. "You know I'd love that."

He wrapped his other arm around her waist and pulled her closer to him.

"I know." He kissed her neck again.

"Mother!" The voice of their son Loe warned them that he would be coming through the door at any moment.

"I told you, they always know," she said, and smiled.

Moments later, the boy burst through the door. "Cobi's got the only knife, and he won't let me skin my catch."

Jarrod stared at the boy. "So what are you saying, son?" He struggled to hide his frustration.

The boy shrugged. "I need my own knife."

Alaine found a nice sharp one in the drawer and started to follow the boy outside. "And I need salt and flour if you want me to cook these hairy creatures for supper," she said, smiling over her shoulder at Jarrod.

His heart melted when she smiled. His erection, on the other hand . . .

Seconds after she and Loe left, Natholu walked in. "Damn, brother," he laughed. "That was quick."

Jarrod shrugged off his disappointment. "Come on," he said, ushering his brother out the door. "We have to go and get supplies."

"Now?"

"Yes now, if you want to eat."

They hadn't been gone long when Jarrod caught the scent. He and Natholu locked gazes.

"No," Natholu said, shaking his head slowly. "That can't be . . . it can't be . . . real?"

It was different, but both of them knew undeniably exactly what it was. And it was coming from home.

Jarrod's heart pounded like a drum.

"Hurry, brother!" Jarrod started to change as he turned to run. "Hurry!"

"Please let us be wrong," Jarrod muttered. His family.

The sounds of screams pinned back their ears miles before they got to the colony. And in that instant, the brothers knew that they weren't wrong.

"Run!"

It was Alaine's voice.

The brothers' transformation into Were form was effortless. Both large in stature before their change, they doubled in size after they were transformed, and their nature, more animal than not, took over as they charged and attacked Sakarabru's Brood soldiers. Instinctively, they knew which areas on the Brood bodies were vulnerable: throats, eyes, and chests.

Alaine had told the boys to run, while she stayed behind and fought. Jarrod saw her, battling like a warrior, slashing her butcher knife into the throats of Brood attacking her. She was not a Were creature, so she could not change. Jarrod fought to get to her, but the Brood Army seemed to come from every direction at the same time. It had been a long time since he'd fought. Maybe too long. They were strong. They were Brood. And there were so many of them.

Alaine whipped her knife through the air like a skilled swordsman.

"Mother!" he heard his son Cobi cry out.

"Run, Cobi!" she screamed, catching a Brood from behind and raking the knife deep across its throat.

But Cobi couldn't run. He was being stalked by a Brood not much bigger than him but still stronger. Jarrod's boys were hybrids of both parents. They could only turn at will when they had time to concentrate and focus—when they weren't afraid. He crouched low and raced across the field to Cobi. The small Brood turned in time to see Jarrod's thick and razor-sharp claws slice through the air, slicing through it like a hot knife cuts through butter.

"Papa!" The boy jumped up and ran to his father.

"Where's your brother?" Jarrod growled.

The boy couldn't answer.

"Find him!" he commanded, turning to get to his mate.

He could see her, fighting, slashing, and growling, but the Brood were too many, and he wasn't fast enough. She never saw the one come up behind her and twist her head until her neck snapped. Jarrod watched her body fall lifeless to the ground, her beautiful brown eyes fixed on him.

Jarrod's growl pierced the air like thunder. The Brood would fall. He knew it as soon as he saw the gray Were creature lunging at him, teeth bared, claws extended, and crazed. The beast in the Were raged, leaving reason and logic behind. Jarrod killed everyone who crossed his path without hesitation. He killed with abandon, snatching life out of anything that remotely resembled a Brood until his coat was soaked with their blood.

The small colony managed to kill the Brood that had attacked them. But the Brood had killed many of them too.

Jarrod cradled Alaine in his arms like a small child. His sons were at his side, crying.

"They came because he sent them," Jarrod said, through his tears and grief. "Sakarabru sent them." He looked at his brother.

Jarrod looked down from his horse at this small, almost insignificant version of Khale. He had heard the stories about the return of the Demon. And he knew that when the Demon returned, so would the Redeemer. Khale had messed with fate and instinctively he knew that that couldn't have been good.

"So what of your reborn, Khale?" he asked, cautiously. "What of this new Redeemer? Where is she?"

"She is with the Guardian," Khale told him.

"Is she ready? Has she bonded with the Omens?"

"He will make her ready."

Yeah, right. "The last one fucked up everything. And you said she was ready. We all ended up here, our world is gone, and the Demon is back. So why should we believe that this one can do what the last one couldn't?"

His question, his doubt, had offended her, but Jarrod didn't give a damn. Khale had no answers. "The Redeemer is our only hope," she said with resolve. "I expect your cooperation, Were. Or sit back and watch while Sakarabru destroys everything you claim to love about this world. Your choice." She did her shifting thing and changed back into that bird she was when she showed up, and she took off.

HE PLAYED ONE

He'd walked for nearly eighty years, and when the pain became unbearable, he crawled. Dave Jensen stood at the end of a road leading up a hill. At the end of this road was the one he had been searching for all these many years. And finding her would be his end.

"Finally," he said tearfully.

It was a word he'd waited too long to say. And hearing it filled him with such relief that he suddenly felt as light as a feather, and if a good stiff breeze were to blow by in that moment, he was sure that it would carry him away.

He stared at the path of that winding road and drew in a deep breath. Never in a million years would he have guessed he'd end up here. His quest had been too grand, his responsibility and purpose too grave to end in such a quiet and insignificant place. But who was he to question *her* and what *she* wanted. It looked so peaceful compared to what was happening in the rest of the world. He closed his eyes and listened intensely for the sounds of screaming and guns firing, for men calling out orders over megaphones. He heard none of those things. All he heard was peace and he heard quiet. He smiled in a show of grateful and private gratitude to her, for finally giving him what he had needed since he first found her. Dave raised the bloody stump of his foot and took the first step leading him to the end of this long and arduous journey.

It was warm for spring, especially for being so far North. The buds on the trees made this place look like something out of a fairy tale, and she truly could live here for the rest of her life and never miss one second of the outside world.

Eden had been going on and on about not being ready to take on the responsibility that she had supposedly been born for. But there was nothing or no one who could've ever prepared her for this. This was her world falling apart. Forget the Ancients. They had their world and they lost it. This one was hers.

Eden was no hero or warrior. Her only aspiration in life was to eventually get married and maybe have a kid or two. She'd dreamed of being a manicurist, for crying out loud. Who dreams of being a manicurist?

Khale would be back soon, spewing the same old rhetoric to Eden since she was a toddler. Prophet had a different strategy for getting the message across to her, but it was still the same one. Eden had a choice, yes, and she didn't. Deep down, she knew that.

"It's hard at first."

An old man seemed to come out of nowhere and stood in the clearing behind the house with her. He stood there, layered in dirty clothes, his smile revealing gaps where teeth should've been.

"Wh-what?" Eden asked, suddenly afraid. "What?"

He stared back at her with tears streaming down his face.

"You're prettier than I imagined," he said feebly. He took a step toward her and started to sing, "One for three . . . Bring me. . . . Redeem me." He sobbed and came even closer. "You die the lamb."

Eden hadn't even realized that she sang with him.

Touch her.

He stumbled toward her. Eden wanted to run but stood frozen.

"Touching you will end this torture," he yelled. "Take it." He grabbed hold of her arm.

A shock wave of pain jolted her whole body as Eden disappeared into the blackness of her screams.

Eden ran, but the sand beneath her feet gave way to prevent any friction she tried to get. She opened her mouth to call for help, but there was no air in this black place. She couldn't scream because she couldn't breathe, and it was getting closer.

The harder she fought to get away, the deeper she sank into the sand, burning her skin. Help me! Guardian! *She called to him in her thoughts but he wasn't there.* Khale! *Eden was alone. She couldn't do this.* No.

One for three . . . Bring me. . . . Redeem me. One for three . . . Bring me. . . . Redeem me.

Eden's eyes grew wide with fear. Her lungs burned, fighting for breath. Jagged shards of blackness cut into her flesh, digging deep until they scraped against bone and sliced into her like a thousand hot blades all at once. The pain was too much and it was snatching the life out of her, stealing away her soul, until she was too weak to fight. Eden was without hope. The agony of this moment had stolen what determination she had once had to save her own life.

One for three . . . Bring me. . . . Redeem me—I am yours. I am yours. Yessssss.

She closed her eyes. Eden stopped struggling to breathe and submitted to the death that had enveloped her body, mind, and soul. Burning. Burning inside and out. Breaking— snapping to pieces as easily as a twig. She felt herself wither and fade and life left her. This was death. This was . . . nothing.

We are unfulfilled. We are incomplete. Our Redeemer. Our Sister. Bond with us. Make us one.

I'M YOURS

K hale seemed to appear out of nowhere. "No! Eden! Help her," she yelled, looking desperately to the Guardian.

The whites of Eden's eyes turned blood red. The veins in the sides of her neck pulsed and swelled to massive proportions, gorged with blood flooding her body.

The two of them stared at her, knowing that she would not survive this. Eden was no Ancient warrior, just the memory of one. She was nothing more than a weak and scared little girl, being tortured literally to death. Prophet glared at Khale, wondering what in the hell she had been thinking to do this. She'd been wrong for using this human girl. They had all been so very, very wrong.

"I am amazed by your brilliance, Khale," he said venomously, "that you should be so wise as to resurrect your Beloved into something as fragile as this."

She stared back defiantly at him. "Watch your tone with me, Guardian," she threatened.

He laughed. "Or what, Ancient?" He stared at the pitiful young woman lying in his arms, swallowed by unimaginable agony. "She couldn't do it," he said to Khale. "You knew she couldn't."

Khale started to say something, but of course there were no words for what she knew was the truth. Eden may have been the vessel to hold Mkombozi's spirit, but her body was very human and incapable of sustaining itself against the torturous bonding process with the first Omen.

"You need to leave," he said. Her business here was done, and Khale was of no consequence anymore. She was not allowed to bear witness to what happened between Prophet and Eden from this point on, and she knew it. Eden was his responsibility now, and he would be the one to bury her.

"Take care of her, Guardian," she said weakly, before shifting into bird form and flying away.

He looked down into Eden's face, frozen in shock and fear, and his heart broke in half for her. "Better care than you did, Shifter."

The Guardian was prepared to protect Eden at all costs. He was prepared to save her, even from her so-called destiny. Whatever she was suffering was more than she could survive and so much more than her body could bear. He couldn't let her be taken like this. And he prepared himself to do the only thing he could do.

He had just found her. And now to lose her again . . . But he couldn't let her suffer like this.

"Eden." He whispered her name, put his hand at her throat, and wrapped his fingers around her neck.

He knew her pain. He could feel it as if he were there with her! He could sense her terror.

"Eden, I'm so sorry," he said softly.

Prophet turned his face from hers and began to squeeze. Suddenly the sky darkened above him and then wrapped around the two of them together. He couldn't understand it. She'd fallen while there was still daylight. The darkness fell like a blanket covering them. He couldn't see his hand in front of his face. He couldn't even see her, and though he hadn't summoned them, he could feel his wings spread from his back.

The air grew thin and warm, no—hot. And then he felt Eden grab the hand on her neck and squeeze her fingers around his.

"Eden?" he said, stunned by her actions.

Was she . . . fighting? Could she hear him? "Eden! Baby, if you can hear me . . ."

He released his grip on her neck and pulled her tightly to his chest. There was a chance—a small one. . . . "Eden." He said her name over and over again in her ear. "Come back, sweetheart. Come back to me."

All of a sudden she shook, her whole body went rigid, and Eden gasped for air.

She took a breath. Prophet couldn't believe it—she was breathing.

"Eden," he said, sweeping locks from her face.

She looked at him. Tears streamed down the sides of her face. Her lips moved, but the words . . .

"It's all right," he said, happier and more shocked than he ever thought possible. "I'm here. It's all right."

Fuck. How the hell had she survived that?

"I . . . heard . . ." She struggled to speak. Eden swallowed.

"It's okay," he said. "It's all right."

"I . . . heard . . . you," she managed to gather enough strength to say.

She was shaking so hard he worried that she might break something.

"I heard . . . you," she repeated, sobbing and raising her hand to touch his face.

"You heard me." He laughed. She was so beautiful. He stared at her as if he were truly seeing her for the first time. "You heard me?"

She nodded. "I heard . . . you call my name."

This shit had just gotten real. Until this moment, he thought he knew . . . , but now he was certain, more certain than he'd ever been about anything in his long life. This Eden Reid was his Beloved. She was the one he thought he'd lost when their world was destroyed, and she was the one he'd spent the last four thousand years waiting for.

He raised her to him, pressed his lips to hers, and savored the flavor of this beautiful young woman.

———

Eden was exhausted and needed time alone. He'd run a bath for her and left her in the tub with her thoughts. One thing was certain: she had a hell of a lot to process. She had survived the first bond with the first Omen. The damn thing should've killed her, and no one was more surprised than Prophet that it didn't.

He sat in the living room, staring out of the window, watching the sun set. The Omen had somehow solicited the old man who looked to be almost as old as Prophet to find the Redeemer and bring itself to her. Maybe it grew tired of waiting, or maybe it knew that Eden wouldn't go looking for it. But whatever the case, and ready or not, the first bond had taken place and Eden was still alive.

He hadn't heard her come down the stairs.

"I don't think I can sleep alone tonight," she said softly, standing across the room wrapped in a towel.

He held out his hand for her. Eden came to him.

How good it felt to have her here with him. Through the years there had been women, plenty of women, who claimed to love him, need him, and want him. But not one of them had filled the void in him that she'd left behind. That nagging ache of emptiness was gone, and he never wanted to feel it again.

Eden dropped her towel and stood naked before him. He had thought she was too thin, but looking at her now, he couldn't help taking in the delicate curves of her slender figure and appreciate the perfection of it. Eden's waist was so small his fingers nearly touched when he held it in his hands. That lovely waist curved nicely down into soft hips and up into round, firm breasts with dark nipples begging to be tasted.

He pulled her down onto his lap and noticed the marking on her upper arm. It was the brand of the Omen. The bond had been made.

She noticed him looking. "It doesn't hurt," she said softly.

He smiled. "Good."

Had she been with a man before? He didn't want to know. She had never been with him before, and when it was over, she would never want to be with anyone else.

Eden leaned forward and planted hesitant kisses on his lips, staring into his eyes and daring him to even try to close them.

"I had given up," she quietly explained. "It expected me to."

It—meaning the Omen.

"It was dark, Prophet. Darker than the regular dark. Suffocating and heavy."

He'd felt it, too.

He pulled her closer and wrapped his arm around her waist as she pressed against his dick, growing thicker by the second.

Eden leaned closer, held a rope of his hair in her hand, brought it to her nose, and inhaled. She closed her eyes. "I heard wings." And then she opened her eyes. "I heard you flying toward me and then you called my name."

She pressed her lips together as she contemplated how to continue.

"You were looking for me, and I knew that if you didn't find me, that you would die, too."

She had no idea what she had done. Eden had yet to realize that she hadn't heard him from some faraway place on the other side of her nightmare. She'd pulled him into it.

He loosened the buckle on his belt. Eden pushed her body up enough for him to unzip his jeans and free himself. And then she slowly, carefully began to lower her body down onto his, until she stopped at the discovery of his size.

He held her by the back of her neck and pulled her face even closer to his. She could not stop this. Not now.

"Slowly," he whispered, grazing his lips across her. "Take your time."

She gradually eased down onto him until her body melted around his and the connection was made—fully and completely.

Neither of them wanted to move, as breath flowed between them and they shared an energy that was as old as time.

"You are mine, forever, Beloved," he said in his Ancient language.

Eden responded in kind. "I will never leave you, Beloved. I swear."

PRIME TIME NETWORK NEWS
We interrupt this program for breaking news . . .

Russ Bradley had been reporting the news for more than thirty years, but never had a story left him speechless.

Russ, producers, the camera crew all sat there for several minutes watching recorded footage of the horror streaking across skies all around the world, leveling cities, military installations, energy and fuel plants, and corporations.

"The truth is," he swallowed, and all color had washed from his face, "we don't know what it is," he said gravely, forcing himself to look into the camera.

He hadn't slept in days. None of them had. Russ rubbed his burning eyes and worked hard to try to compose himself.

"It uh . . . appears to glide through the air like a . . . um . . . a speeding storm cloud. Lightning or . . . fire." He shook his head, confused. "It's big." He nervously cleared his throat. "And fast. Reports have been coming in that it is faster than even military jets can keep up with."

More distracting images flashed on the screen behind him, but he could see them on one of the viewers behind one of the cameramen. Images of people running and screaming, bodies littering the ground.

"Christian leaders are calling him—it—the Antichrist. The . . . Angel of Death," he stroked his hand across disheveled hair. "Thousands have been killed," he continued. "And thousands more, maybe even tens of thousands have been gathering . . . coming together in cities and towns around the world, worshipping this . . . 'Worshipping'?" He looked confused. The word had actually appeared on his prompter. "Really?"

He had never seen anything like this before in his life. No one had. And he didn't know—he just . . . if he could've described what the end of the world would look like, it would look a lot like this.

DEMON SEED

Fear was universal. No matter the world, the species, or the time. Living things feared that which they did not understand, and Sakarabru was one of a kind. The Demon had not been born. He had no origin, as far as he knew. Sakarabru just . . . was. For as long as he could form a thought, his nature had been to rule, to conquer, to reign over those he knew to be beneath him. This Earth was no different than Theia.

Not all Ancients who fell to this world the day Theia was destroyed were loyalists to Khale. In addition to his Brood Army, Sakarabru had those, like Kifo, who were steadfast to him. When they found out that the Djinn had lived up to his word and brought the Demon back from the brink of destruction, they came crawling out of the recesses of their lives back to him.

Their numbers had dwindled, but still they were key to establishing a precedence in this new world, which was necessary if these people were to understand that Sakarabru was unlike any other foe they'd ever encountered. These Ancients had blended in with these humans. They lived and worked alongside them and even mated with them and reproduced. Being the strategist that he was, he quickly took advantage of their positions to disrupt the flow of energy in this world by planting that seed of fear until he was strong enough to show them who and what he was—and what he was capable of.

They looked human, these men and women standing before him wearing their military uniforms that labeled them generals, admirals, and soldiers of the human military forces. Others were doctors, businessmen and -women, mothers, fathers, pilots, and even a dog walker. Underneath their facades were Shifters, Djinn mystics, and Vampyres. They came to him now as the Ancient beings that they were, prepared to follow him into whatever battle awaited him.

The other Ancients standing in that room watched on the large visual monitors as images of the Demon speeding through skies like lightning carved out paths of destruction from continent to continent.

"Even in my weakened condition," he said wearily, leaning back in his chair, "they have never before encountered the likes of me."

This world was smaller than Theia, but its resources were similar and plentiful. These lands would serve him well.

"They don't know what to do," one of the Ancients

volunteered. This one was what was referred to as a policeman. "They don't know how to fight against you, Lord Sakarabru."

"The humans are gathering together at summits to discuss defenses and retaliation," another one volunteered. "They are even talking about the use of nuclear bombs. It's the most powerful weapon that they have."

"Those nukes would destroy them and this world too," an admiral stepped up and said. "Weapons like that are always a last resort."

Sakarabru watched them debate among themselves as to what actions the humans could and would take against him. Sakarabru was not concerned, because he knew that there was nothing they could do to defend themselves against him and his army.

"They have already began building their sanctuaries in all the major cities," he heard one of them say.

"Sanctuaries?" the Demon asked.

"Compounds to keep people who haven't been infected by the plagues safe from those who have been," she explained.

"My Brood suffer from no plague, Ancient," he said, gathering his strength to stand.

"No, Lord Sakarabru, but the humans believe that they do. And they want to isolate themselves from them and kill those that they think have the sickness."

The Demon pondered this, imagining these people erecting walls and believing that they could keep themselves safe from Sakarabru's army. This would be impossible. "There is no sanctuary that can protect them."

He had finally become strong enough to call to them, to gather them to him. He had come across a method that would help him to reach out to those who were too far away to make the journey to him. Sakarabru nodded to the one behind the camera, and suddenly his image was flashed on every flat-screen monitor hanging on the walls in this massive auditorium. He was assured that his face would be broadcast across screens like this all at once so that his Brood could finally see him and hear his voice. They needed to know that he was real and that he was here. They needed the kind of order that only Sakarabru could provide them.

"You are not mindless beasts," he said, turning slowly in the center of the room, relishing the sight of himself on those screens.

The transition back to the living had been long and difficult, and signs of the journey had taken their toll. Sakarabru had been young and handsome before The Fall. He had been strong, with a broad chest and shoulders. Kifo assured him that he would come to be that way again, in time. For now, he looked old, his hair white, his skin weathered. He had managed to gather enough strength to terrify humans, but it had taken his energy to do so, and recovery was slow.

"I am your Lord," he spoke with authority to no one in particular, and yet he knew that all of those who were meant to hear him hung on his every word. "I am Sakarabru. Come," he said simply. He knew that they would. They had been conditioned to heed his call and to obey his commands. "Come."

The Demon crossed the room. The Ancients and the one with the camera followed as he slowly made his way down the winding staircase, across the foyer, and finally out of the main door.

Of course they were waiting. Many fell to their knees at the sight of him. The sounds of crying filled the air; hands reached out to touch him.

"Lord Sakarabru," he heard them say over and over again.

Not all of them had made this journey to New Orleans, but he knew that wherever they were, they would see him and they would hear him and feel him reaching out to them, commanding them, leading them.

"You are my Brood Army," he said proudly, nodding his appreciation that the pieces of his life were falling back into place. "And together we will survive. Together we will thrive."

The humans were nothing to him, less than nothing. Let them bring their weapons and build their fortresses. They would not be able to stop Sakarabru from achieving his goal of domination.

"We love you, Lord Sakarabru!" the Brood cried out to him.

Thoughts of Khale's reborn Redeemer were never far enough away from him. And she was all that was standing between him and his victory.

Khale watched, in horror, the broadcast from her Manhattan apartment. She could hear his name being called outside her window.

"Sakarabru! Lord Sakarabru!"

Martial law had been established in most US cities. In

some places, those suspected of having contracted this plague were shot on sight. In other places, Sakarabru's new Brood were more organized and hunted in packs. Barricades were going up in cities, around neighborhoods; schools had been shut down, and air travel had been stopped. Military troops were tasked with trying to keep peace and order where chaos reigned. And all the while, the Demon was growing stronger.

Khale's once-mighty Ancient forces had dwindled down to nearly nothing before The Fall. Those Ancients who were left now, who weren't loyalists to Sakarabru, were few and far between. She had managed to convince the Were Nation to stand with her, and the Mer Nation, but they could fight only if Sakarabru brought his war to their shores. And she'd managed to gather some of the other Shifter Nations together, but most of the Ancients that were here now, were never warriors.

Khale's cell phone buzzed, and she received a cryptic text message from a number she didn't recognize.

"She survived," was all it said.

She immediately called the number, and her heart jumped when Tukufu answered. The last thing she needed to do was to get her hopes up, but . . . "What?" she asked shakily.

A long pause passed between them before he finally responded. "She survived the bond, Khale. Eden is alive."

MAGIC MOMENT

Even Kifo couldn't help being overwhelmed by the sight of Sakarabru walking through those doors to salute his army. This moment had been four thousand years in the making. Kifo had devoted his time, energy, his concentration into bringing Sakarabru back. Yes, the Redeemer had defeated him, but not all of him. Khale destroyed her before she could, and all that was left behind of Sakarabru was a molecule, two or more atoms joined together. But through Kifo's magic, he had found it, kept it, and willed it to come together again until it was him, Sakarabru.

Mysticism was not magic, and it offended him anytime someone referred to it as such. It was a science of life, of spirit, and of will. With these things, the Djinn had worked the most horrific miracle this world had ever seen.

"He's beautiful," she said from behind him.

Kifo never knew when she would come to him, but it was never often enough.

He closed his eyes when she leaned close to him and whispered. "Look at what you did, Kifo."

Lilith was her name and she was his lover. She came around and sat down next to him on the sofa. This time her hair was gold, the color of the sun, and her eyes were a deep blue. Her full lips were painted red. Lilith's skirt was so tight, it was a wonder that she could sit down at all. Mounds of beautiful breasts spilled from the top of her blouse. She had been his for longer than he could remember, and she had promised that she always would be.

"He is proud of you," she said softly. Lilith's hand trailed from his shoulder to his chest and finally rested in his lap. "He favors you above all, Kifo."

Sakarabru had been the most powerful being on Theia, and he would be here as well. Soon the humans would have no choice but to bend their prideful knees and succumb to his rule. It was inevitable and it had all been made possible by Kifo.

She leaned in close to him and grazed her lips against his earlobe, his cheek, and the side of his neck. Lilith was intoxicating. She squeezed his cock until it nearly exploded.

"Not . . . yet," she whispered.

She stood up, slid her skirt up just far enough to reach underneath it and pull off her panties. Lilith sank to her knees on the floor at his feet, laid on her back, and spread her thick, delicious thighs, exposing her moist and sweet pink pussy.

His mouth watered as he watched her slide her finger in and around the folds of her sex.

"Taste me," she commanded him. Lilith spread her legs wider. "Stick out your tongue," she coaxed, "and taste me."

Kifo stretched out on the floor, flat on his belly, and lapped her up like a thirsty dog drinks water. Her juices flowed down his chin and spilled onto the rug underneath her as she writhed and moaned underneath him.

"I want you," she eventually told him, grabbing hold of his collar and pulling on him until he hovered over her, wrestled to free himself from his pants, and drove into her with such force that both of them cried out.

Kifo was drunk on her sex! He could never fuck her hard enough, fast enough, or deep enough, and he could never have her enough! He looked down at Lilith, kneading her own breasts until her nipples were hard little pebbles that demanded his attention. Kifo took one in his mouth, and then the other, licking and nibbling on each of them until they looked as if they might burst. But he was the one who burst! Kifo came so hard that he nearly lost consciousness, but even still, it wasn't enough.

He made love to her on the floor, in the shower, and eventually in his bed. Kifo was exhausted, but he couldn't bring himself to sleep when she was there. Lilith lay next to him, sound asleep with the corners of her lovely mouth curled into a slight smile. She disappeared when he closed his eyes, so he'd learned long ago to keep them open for as long as possible to keep her with him for as long as he could.

His thoughts drifted to Sakarabru and how quickly the Demon had changed this world in so short a period of time. Kifo shouldn't have been surprised. It wasn't in Sakarabru's nature to be subtle about anything or to be patient long enough to let his body come back fully to itself.

"He tortured you, Kifo."

Khale's words had been haunting him since she'd spoken them, stirring uneasy and gnawing feelings in him that he couldn't shake. There were all types of spells, most of which were spun with words that took root and festered in a person's mind, feeding on insecurities and fears.

Khale had been known to spin a few spells, and he suspected that she'd cast one on him, counting on him to fall for her lies and turn him against Sakarabru. The Demon had saved his life from the desolation she'd left behind when she killed the mystics and left Kifo to die.

Lilith moaned seductively in her sleep and rested her hand on his chest. Kifo brought it to his lips and kissed it. He had more pleasurable things to focus on than Khale's twisted versions of the truth.

Despite Kifo's best efforts, sleep was starting to get the best of him, and he started to doze off to the rhythm of Lilith's soft breathing. Kifo began to feel warm, too warm. In that state between being asleep and being fully awake was where his darkest thoughts lingered.

"Run, boy! The dragon! It's Khale! Run!"

He tortured you.

"Little one. Little Magician. That's it, boy. Bite your tongue."

Shhhhh . . . Listen to me and I'll make it stop. Listen to me and I'll make it go away. Listen to me, little Djinn.

His eyes opened to the sight of Lilith smiling down on him. "Ready for round two, baby?"

His cock rallied to attention as if he hadn't just come half a dozen times already. She slid down the length of him, grabbed hold of his rigid instrument in her hand, opened her mouth, and wrapped full, supple lips around it.

He tortured you, Kifo.

Khale is a liar.

He tortured . . . Khale is a liar. Khale is a liar. Khale is a . . .

"Yessssss," he said, silencing the thoughts punishing him and focusing instead on what she was doing.

Kifo was drunk on Lilith and he could have her. He could have all of her as long as . . . he was obedient.

COME TO MY WINDOW

Passageways. Ever since Eden and the first Omen had bonded, all she kept seeing in her mind's eye was herself wandering through a maze of passageways. She felt as if she were living outside herself, looking in at her life, disconnected and far away. Eden had to constantly remind herself to be in the moment, to be aware of where she was at any given time of the day or night. Prophet would say something to her and she'd have to ask him to repeat himself, or she'd pretend that she had heard every word.

From the balcony of the house, she stared down at the burnt imprint on the grass of the old man who had brought the Omen to her. Prophet had gotten rid of the mound of dirty clothes left behind where his body had been, but the rest of him had turned to ash. They'd found his wallet with his driver's license still in it from the 1930s. His name had been David Jensen. The Omen had forced him to find Eden. It had made him search for her until he found her—until it found her and forced the bond, which it must've known Eden was reluctant to make.

Eden heard Khale's voice. She turned slightly, glancing over her shoulder to confirm that the Shifter was here, standing in the living room talking to Prophet. Eden had no idea how long the two of them had been there.

" . . . a miracle, Guardian. Making the bond was difficult for Mkombozi, but she was an Ancient. Her strength and fortitude were unmatched, so imagine my surprise when I found out that Eden survived this."

"She's pretty strong too, Khale, and damn if she isn't going around here constantly flashing that damn fortitude of hers like a badge," he said sarcastically.

Eden smiled.

"You know that's not how I meant it," she retorted.

Of course that was how she meant it. Khale talked a good talk and even tried convincing Eden that she believed the hype of this reborn Redeemer, but the truth was, she didn't. She never did. Eden realized that a long time ago. Khale didn't have the faith in Eden that Khale had had in Mkombozi, and Eden couldn't fault her for her doubts. Maybe Eden was her reincarnated daughter, but then again, she was Eden too. Just Eden.

"But now is not the time for celebration or to bask in this one victory," she said, coming out onto the balcony. "I know that you feel safe here, Eden," Khale said carefully. "I know that this place must feel like heaven on earth to you now, but hell has fallen on the rest of the world, sweetheart."

"Khale, it's too soon," Prophet chimed in.

"It's been a week," she snapped at him. "And in that week, the Demon has made his presence known to the people in this world. He's stronger. Images of Sakarabru—what they can capture of him—are all over the news and the Internet now! He's destroyed entire cities and military installations, Eden. He's turned people against each other and has called his Brood Army to order! It's not going to go away, and it's only going to get worse the longer we wait!"

Khale was afraid. Eden could hear it in her voice. The Great Shifter was terrified, and she had every right to be.

"We don't even know where to find the second Omen, Khale," Prophet argued. "But even if we did, she's not ready. The first one nearly took her life, and I won't put her at risk again until and unless she tells me that she wants to do this."

"Can't you see, Guardian," Khale said, frustrated. "It's not up to you. It's not even up to Eden. It never has been. The Omen found its way to her. They will all find their way to her whether she wants to be found or not."

"She's right," Eden finally said, looking over her shoulder.

Again, Eden saw herself winding through dark corridor after dark corridor in her mind. She took a deep breath, and squeezed her eyes shut to shake the visions.

"One is incomplete without the others," Eden murmured to herself, realizing that she had not come by that knowledge on her own. The Omen had given it to her.

"Eden . . ." Khale started.

Without thinking, Eden jumped over the railing of the balcony and landed on her feet, fifteen feet below on the ground. In an afterthought, she stood there for a moment, wondering why or even how she'd even known it was possible for her to do that without hurting herself. Eden needed to be alone.

"No, Khale," Eden heard the Guardian tell the Shifter as Eden started to walk away.

There was no more running from this. Eden knew that now. She walked until she reached the edge of the clearing and entered the forest. Eden was following a passageway. What was this that she was seeing over and over again in her mind? What was this place? And where would she ultimately end up if she just . . . followed . . . ?

Eden saw a door and she stopped. In her mind she stopped and stared at it. In reality, there was nothing but trees before her. A wave of anticipation rushed over her. Fear of the unknown held her back. But she had to know what was behind that door. She had been coming to this same place in her visions over and over again, only to stop and turn away and try to pretend that it wasn't real—but it was. It was time to stop running.

Eden stretched out her arm and pressed her palm flat against the door in front of her and slowly pushed it open. There was a small fire burning in the middle of the room, and sitting next to it was a hooded man. All of a sudden Eden stood inside the room and the door closed behind her.

The hooded figure turned his head slightly toward her, but the dark shadows casting across his face made him impossible to identify. It was a mistake coming here. She knew it. Eden began to back away to where the door had been, but when she turned to find it, it was gone.

"You dare come into this place." The sound of him was not like any sound she'd heard before. His voice came from him and all around him and through her.

She pressed her back against the wall. She conceived a scream that rose up from her stomach and wedged in her throat.

He stood up, and when he did, she could no longer see the top of him. He came toward her. Calves as round as tree trunks, wrapped in sinewy muscle the color of blood, flexed as he walked. The air closed in around her as he pressed closer. It was him. She knew instinctively that this was Sakarabru.

"You dare come to this place," he repeated.

"I'm sorry," she screamed, crying. "Oh God." Eden turned and began scratching at the wall behind her until the tips of her fingers bled.

It was him. It was the Demon. She'd made a mistake.

"Eden. Eden. It's me."

"Prophet," she exclaimed, realizing that she was actually in the forest surrounding his house and that it was broad daylight. She wrapped both arms around him and held on to him with all of her strength.

He'd come for her. Just like before, he'd come for her.

"They didn't tell me," she said breathlessly. Khale, and even Rose hadn't told her the whole truth about the Omens. "They didn't tell me everything, Prophet."

"What are you talking about?" he asked, stroking her back.

The revelation of this truth was so big, so much bigger than she could embrace fully.

"Eden," he said softly. "What is it?"

Why hadn't they told her everything? Eden pushed away from him and stumbled backward. Twigs and dried dead leaves crunched beneath her feet. She looked at him and then wondered if he had known, too? Mkombozi had to have known, and she would've told him.

"The Omens," she started to explain, her chest heaving. "The Omens are a part of him." Saying it out loud made it sound even more unbelievable. "The first Omen is connected to Sakarabru," she continued, panicking. "It's his mind or his thoughts. It's him, Prophet, and now it's a part of me. I'm a part of him," she yelled. Looking at him, she immediately understood that he did know.

Eden backed away from him, shaking her head.

"Eden," he reached out to her.

"You fuckin' knew?"

Khale came up from behind her. "Eden we . . ."

Eden's heart broke in half. "MyRose knew, too," she sobbed. "You all knew?"

"It would've been difficult to explain!" Khale shouted. "You wouldn't have understood, Eden. Mkombozi didn't understand until she also bonded with the first Omen."

Eden looked past Khale to Prophet. Khale was Khale. She and Eden had never been close; they'd never seen eye to eye on anything, and Eden wouldn't trust the Shifter as far as she could throw her, but Prophet—he knew, too, and never said anything.

"It wasn't my place to tell you, Eden," he said gravely, knowing instinctively what she was thinking.

Her knight in shining armor wasn't shining so brightly anymore, and Eden realized that all of them had been in on this betrayal filled with half-truths or no truths at all.

"I had no idea how much you remembered, and I didn't want to tell you something that you weren't prepared to hear," he tried explaining.

Eden shook her head in disbelief. "I don't expect anything from her." She motioned to Khale. "But I . . . Mkombozi trusted you, Guardian. She trusted that the truth, all of it, should come from you."

Eden felt more alone than she'd ever been before.

"No one knows what this is like," she said sadly. "None of you can understand what this is doing to me inside." She pressed her hand to her heart. "You don't know what it's like to have to depend on finding out the truth about yourself from people who hardly know you. I don't know if my thoughts are my own or if they belong to her. I am stuck in a place between Eden and Mkombozi. It sucks. It shouldn't be like this. I shouldn't have to pay the price; none of us here should have to pay for the mess you left behind on Theia."

The first Omen saw to it that the bond had taken place, and it would no doubt lead her to the second Omen. There was no turning back now, and if Eden was going to be forced to fight in this war, then she had better get off her ass and figure out what the hell was going on. The only thing she knew for certain was that in the end, one of them was going to die—Eden or Sakarabru. She didn't know about him, but at this point, at least for her, death would be a relief.

FIGHT THE POWER

We don't have time for this," Khale snapped at Prophet after Eden stormed away. "I'm sick and tired of coddling that girl. The hope of this civilization is pinned to her, and all she can do is whine and throw tantrums about it." She folded her arms across her chest. "If it weren't for the fact that she'd survived that first bond, I would question if she truly was Mkombozi. She never acted like this."

"Yes she did, Khale."

The Shifter had selective memories of Mkombozi. He needed to remind her of that.

"She acted just like this."

She looked at him as if he'd just told her that Mkombozi had had three heads. "She was afraid, Tukufu," she said, forcing herself to calm down. "But she knew what she had to do, and she did it."

"Mkombozi knew her role, she played it, but she was as afraid as Eden is now," he explained. "The only difference was that Mkombozi loved you." He decided to leave it at that.

"This should not be my fate, Tukufu, my responsibility. It is too much," Mkombozi said, *crying after she had bonded with the first Omen.*

It was late, and he woke up to find her sitting on the side of the bed, unable to sleep. Prophet reached out to her, but she shrugged away.

"I am my mother's general, and I am proud of that. I will lay down my life for her without hesitation."

He sat up in bed. "She knows that, Mkombozi. You are a great warrior."

She shook her head. "I am a coward." She argued. "I am afraid of this thing inside me, and I am afraid that I could be consumed by it."

"No. No, that's not going to happen," he said, reassuring her. "You're too strong for that. You'll use the Omen, all of the Omen, to defeat the Demon and then . . ."

She turned to him. "And then? The bond is eternal, Tukufu. Once a bond has been made, it cannot be broken." Tears streamed down her face. "I do not want this. I do not want to lose myself to this but I fear that I will. What will happen then?"

"She was as afraid as Eden after that first bond, Khale."

"You need to show Eden the truth of what's happening in her world, Guardian," Khale challenged. "Turn on the news and make her watch. Power up the Internet and let her see the destruction that's already begun here. Hiding her away from it won't make it go away, because eventually that devastation will bring itself to your doors."

If Khale wanted to believe that he was keeping Eden secluded here for her benefit, then let her believe it. The truth was, he had been keeping her here, away from the distraction of everything going on around them, for his own selfish reasons. It was a fantasy he had had and lost when he first made his oath to Mkombozi, a fantasy that included just the two of them, alone.

Khale turned to face him and stretched out her T-shirt for him to read.

DENIAL IS A RIVER IN EGYPT

"I wore this one especially for the two of you today," she said with a weak smile. "Sakarabru underestimated the power of the Redeemer before, but I guarantee you, he won't make that mistake again." She swallowed. "No one, not even the other Ancients loyal to me, believe that Eden can do this. Until she survived this bond, I didn't either," she admitted. "She needs to make the next bond, Guardian, and she needs to do it quickly. The time is here, Tukufu. It's now."

Khale didn't wait for him to respond before she transformed into a butterfly and fluttered away.

An hour after Eden had left him and Khale, Prophet finally went inside the house. Eden was just coming out of the shower. He pulled a remote control out of the nightstand drawer near the bed and pressed a button. A large flat-screen television ascended from a hidden compartment at the foot of the bed, and he turned it on.

Together they watched in horror as he flipped through

channel after channel of news coverage reporting chaos and deaths happening in cities around the world.

"Linköping, a small town in Sweden, has been overrun with these . . . cannibals, for lack of a better word."

"Military forces in Washington, DC, are in the process of setting up a fortified perimeter around the city, creating a sanctuary for those who are uninfected with the virus. However, orders have been given to shoot to kill on sight and if anyone tries to penetrate barrier walls without proper authorization."

"Experts say that he stands at least nine feet tall, but what he is . . . He appears to have some sort of influence, if you will, or control over those infected with the virus. They flock to him like rats to the Pied Piper."

Major corporations had fallen. Bodies littered the streets; homes and businesses burned, all while Prophet and Eden had been here at his place, like birds in a nest. Neither of them said anything for several minutes after he turned off the television. There was no hiding from this. There was to be no running away from it. And they no longer had the luxury of time.

"Mkombozi never told me what it was like." Prophet finally spoke, breaking the heavy weight of silence in the air. "I just watched her change."

He tossed the remote onto the bed between them.

"She said that she could feel what he felt. The Omen forced her to know his mind intimately. In the beginning it scared her, but eventually she understood it," he said solemnly. "And she started to shut me out, Eden."

She looked so small and so vulnerable, still wet and shivering in that towel wrapped around her. But the fate of the world rested on this young woman's shoulders, and no one or nothing could stop it. What scared him most of all, though, was the thought of what would happen to her, even if she succeeded in defeating the Demon.

"The bond is eternal, Tukufu. Once a bond has been made, it cannot be broken."

He had made an oath to this woman thousands of Earth's years ago, and it was a oath that had surpassed death, destruction, time, and space. She didn't look like his Beloved from Theia, but he knew better than anyone that she was her. The oath wouldn't let him make the mistake of committing to another.

"I've waited four thousand years for you," he said, humbly.

Finally, Eden looked at him, and he melted under the weight of those beautiful brown eyes of hers, as if he were falling prey to them for the first time, all over again.

"I failed her, Eden," he confessed. "It was my job, my sole purpose in life to protect her, even from herself, and I failed to do that."

She started to come to him, but he held up his hand to stop her.

"It's said that a Guardian will follow the one he's sworn himself to, to her death." Prophet shrugged. "I could have done that, and I would have, except that I knew that I didn't deserve that honor. I deserved to have to live without her. It's been an empty life. I've lived it half full, but it's no less than I deserve."

She looked at him as if she felt sorry for him, and it pissed him off.

"Don't you dare." He shook his head in frustration. "Don't pity me."

"I'm not. I . . . I just . . ."

"I will not make the same mistakes with you that I made with her." Prophet locked gazes with Eden. "And I won't let you make the same mistakes she made. You will not shut me out, Eden. You will not turn away from me, and you will not leave me behind again." He was nearly shouting. "I want to know everything. You tell me every damn thing that's going on in you, with you, to you. Details. I want fuckin' details so that I can know how to be here."

She nodded, but he wasn't convinced. He studied her, this human, twenty-four-year-old woman, filled with her insecurities, her stubbornness, and her awkwardness. She was not as graceful as Mkombozi had been, not as tall or as confident in who she truly was at the core of herself. This world, and perhaps Rose and Khale, had been guilty of trespassing on her life when they had no right to do it, but she had a role to play, and the first Omen had seen to it to pull her into this game. If she'd had a choice before, that choice had been removed from her.

"I can't help you with the Omens, Eden. They are your burden, but know this"—Prophet took a deep breath—"you are mine."

He needed some air, fresh air, as far away from the ground as he could get beneath him. He needed to fly.

SPITTIN' GAME

In the normal course of things, changing a flat tire would be of little consequence to a man. Forty-two-year-old Joe Huey worked feverishly to get that old pickup truck back on the road and into Morgantown, Pennsylvania, where he belonged. He'd have been the first to admit that he'd been an idiot, and that it had been his own stupidity that landed him in this mess, stuck out here in the middle of nowhere on this lonely dirt road. All he wanted to do was to hurry up and get home. Joe had been gone for nearly a week on a fishing trip and hadn't caught a damn thing worth cooking and eating.

As he struggled to get that last lug nut loose on the wheel, he heard a noise coming from the open field on the other side of his truck. He stood up and stared hard into the brush across from him but didn't see anything. It was probably just a rabbit or maybe a fox. Or it could've just been the wind. He decided that he was just being paranoid and went back to changing his tire.

He finally got that last lug off, removed the flat tire, quickly mounted the spare, and hurried to tighten the lugs. Joe was nearly finished, and relief started to set in, knowing he'd be back on the road again in no time. As he stood up, he heard a noise again coming from the field. But this time, he did see something. A tall dark figure of a man stood maybe a hundred yards or so away from him. Whoever he was just stood there, staring back at Joe and standing still like a statue.

"Hello?" Joe called out apprehensively. Maybe the man was lost or needed help. Joe swallowed, hoping that's all it was. "You need help out there?" Joe asked, and waited for the man to respond, but he didn't say a word. Suddenly, he began to move, slowly, toward Joe's truck. Joe resisted the instinct to panic. "What do you want?" No answer.

Joe moved over to the driver's side door and tried to pull it open and then realized it was locked. He frantically searched his pockets for the keys, but then he looked inside and saw them dangling from the ignition. The man in the field had started to run. Joe grabbed his tire iron and ran in the opposite direction, disappearing into the thick wooded area on the other side of the road. Branches slapped him across the face, and he tripped several times and stumbled forward at full speed, refusing to let himself fall. He didn't have to see the man to know that he wasn't far behind. Joe could feel him, and he felt the ground echo with the heavy pounding of the man's footsteps, taking one for every two of Joe's.

The space between them pushed hard against Joe's back

as the man drew closer. Joe's lungs burned from running faster and longer than he had in years. His heart banged hard in his chest, and a merciless cramp coursed his side. But in his hand, he held on tight to that tire iron. Joe gripped it, knowing that this was the only weapon he had and that he was going to have to hit that fucker upside the head with it.

Joe's legs began to give out on him, and the man was closing in fast. In desperation, Joe Huey stopped, reared back that tire iron, and, as he turned, swung it hard at the man's head, half a step behind him. His eyes widened with astonishment and his arm froze in midair as the beast, at least two feet taller than he was, towered over him, caught him by the wrist, and with a twist of his own, snapped the bones in Joe's arm. His fingers loosened their grip on the tire iron from the agonizing pain surging through his arm, and it fell to the ground at his feet with a thud. Joe yelled and was forced to his knees on the ground by the giant, who reached down and grabbed hold of Joe's bottom jaw and pulled.

One man's glassy-eyed gaze fixed unblinking up at the black sky. The other stood there amazed by the fact that life in the Pennsylvania woods went on like it always did, without so much as a hiccup or a cough. A man's soul was gone from this world, and the world didn't seem to give it much thought. Toads croaked and crickets chirped uninterrupted. A light breeze passed by calm and soothing, and he couldn't help inhaling deeply to take in as much of it as he could.

Chapman rose up from the ground like a spirit and then

closed his eyes and let his head fall back. He spread his massive shoulders and moaned, satisfied at the fullness in his belly. Blood soaked into his hair and skin and filled his nostrils. His jaw ached from tearing flesh from tendons and bones, but he felt more energized and renewed than he'd felt in a long time, ready to pursue his mission with an invigorated purpose. He had promised his master that he would find the reborn, and he would.

The best he could figure, Sakarabru was some sort of demon or fallen angel, or someone who talked in riddles about things that didn't make any sense, but Paul listened and he watched, and soon he came to understand that nothing in this world was as it appeared.

Most people didn't like the looks of him, and when he walked down the streets, they ran from him. He was a big man. Bigger than he was before he was remade. Paul now stood close to seven feet tall, and weighed maybe 350 pounds of solid muscle. Paul's heavy shoulders were as big and round as bowling balls, damn near, with a massive head and neck that reminded him of a big tree stump. It was all in there together, packed tight. His chest was broad, his back strong, but all that narrowed down into the kind of torso most men would envy. He looked odd, even to himself, but it suited him.

Paul was a bloodhound. He was a general and now he was a hunter. There was nothing or no one he couldn't find when he went looking for them. Well, Sakarabru wanted him to find the Redeemer, and Paul had set out to do just that.

"I want her dead."

Paul had to find her to kill her. The Djinn led him. Djinn were sort of like Genies, but they didn't live in a bottle and they didn't wear cute pink harem-girl outfits. Most of them looked like shadows, whispering directions to him that would lead him to her.

"*Go South,*" one of them had whispered to him moments before he'd come across the guy with the flat tire.

Others had warned him: "*Beware the Guardian.*"

Paul had no idea who or what a Guardian was, but he pushed on without hesitation because the Demon had commanded him. Paul no longer had a will of his own. He lived for Sakarabru and blindly obeyed his every word. Pleasing him was the only thing that mattered to Paul. Proclaiming Sakarabru as the sovereign had taken away his pain. Swearing loyalty to him had given Paul unimaginable pleasure, which he looked forward to every time he laid down his head to rest.

Lilith was her name. And to have her, all Paul had to do was make a wish.

DREAM WEAVER

Andromeda was like a thread weaving her way through time and space, connecting aspects of each to the other. It was said that no one could be in two places at once, but that was false and a lie. At any given moment, she could be in five: the past, present, future, and someone's idea of heaven and of hell. Her sense of being transversed in confusion and chaos, and it played out where her screams should have been.

"We shall overcome. Like my page and Khale hid her good. Too—save us God of hosts! Aye! He who is and was and all and all!"

Sakarabru was beautiful to look at. His shocking green eyes shone like gemstones; ink-black tresses of hair fell in waves past his shoulders broad and strong. Even in her agony she couldn't help admiring his regal stature and being entranced by the deep, seductive rumblings of his voice. Even in his threats, he was intoxicating.

"It is said that you hold the secrets to the ages, Seer," he said, stalking circles around her.

His naked chest and torso ripped with sinewy muscles that carved him into the magnificent creature he was and had always been. Sakarabru stopped behind Andromeda, hanging by her wrists from chains suspended from the ceiling. Some things were out of her control. Some things were just her fate and she couldn't stop them no matter how much she wanted to.

The glamour of the Troll Seer Sisters was legendary, and with a single thought, they could transform into the most beautiful female creatures alive, irresistible to any male who saw them. Andromeda's beauty morphed constantly as her thoughts and maybe even her form transcended all times and places at once.

Blue eyes changed to green and then to brown. Red hair turned ink-black, to brown, to blond. Her clothes changed from fitted jeans and tank tops to elegant ball gowns, and then every once in awhile the troll in her revealed itself, too, and those beautiful brown eyes would widen farther apart on her face, spread by a thick, mush-roomlike nose, and turn a putrid yellow color that Sakarabru obviously didn't find appealing. Slim, delicate hands would momentarily turn into clubs with thick, fat fingers covered in warts and thickened gray fingernails.

"It is said that you have discovered the secret to defeating me," he said in her ear, his hot breath washing over her naked, ever-changing form.

The heat of skin being peeled from her bones far exceeded the tortuous sounds of it being ripped away. He held up part of her flesh between two fingers in front of her face and then let it fall to the ground like spoiled meat.

"You will tell me your secrets, Andromeda," he murmured again. "Tell me, and I will take away your pain," he promised. "I will stop your suffering and I will comfort you, Seer. I will save you."

In one moment, she was in two places. Or maybe she was several moments in all places. Andromeda was never sure, but while the Demon tortured her there, Andromeda also sat here, in the electronics section of an abandoned department store, watching Sakarabru on television, as fascinated by him as every other creature was who had ever laid eyes on him. The looters hadn't made it to this Sears store yet, probably because people didn't shop at Sears like they used to anymore and they'd all but forgotten about it.

She'd found an abandoned sandwich shop too, made herself a couple of sandwiches, one for now, and one for later, grabbed a few cans of pop, and crouched low in the electronics section of the store, watching the news of this Sakarabru and his crimes against the people of this world.

It was hard not to think of what he was doing to her now in another time, another space. Andromeda believed that it was happening behind her, in the past. That's what most folks called the behind. They called it the past. She couldn't be sure, but if she let her mind stay there, then her body would stay there, too, and the pain would come back again, and the fear would come back again.

"Do you think Khale will save you? Are you waiting for her to come to your rescue, Seer?" He laughed at her.

Andromeda lay crumpled on the floor, raw and bleeding. He stood over her, staring down at the open wound that he had made on her, and he laughed.

"They call me the monster, but the Shifter is her own special brand of monster." He knelt before her. "She lies to you all, Seer. You know what I am saying is true, Andromeda. You know that Khale is an imposter and a liar. You know that she is false."

He placed his hand underneath her chin, and Andromeda cried out unintelligibly at the agony of having exposed muscle touched by another.

"You have seen all, Andromeda, and you know how this all ends."

"Our love has come along," she said. "Marc Anthony does not love. . . . Li'l Wayne is the best rapper. . . . Sssssssss, said the beast! Reborn! Heed our call!"

He stared curiously at her. "Marc Anthony? Li'l Wayne?" he laughed again and shook his head. "You are such a fascinating creature, Seer. Redeemer? Who is the Redeemer, Andromeda?"

All of a sudden, her surroundings changed again. Andromeda was no longer with the Demon or even at the Sears store. She was where she was happiest. She was home.

The sun shone warmly on her face through her kitchen window. Andromeda was happy here. If she could stop the momentum of her life and make it stop at any one place, it would be here in this small cottage, where she would spend her days sipping tea, eating chocolates, and petting the cat purring in her lap.

The Redeemer should be awake now. She stood up so abruptly that the cat fell out of her lap, landing on all fours on the linoleum floor and hissing angrily at her. Eden was awake, but she would need some tea. Andromeda hurried to fill her cup and carried it steaming to the small bedroom on the other side of the living room.

The young Eden was so lovely, but tormented. The bond was complete. Eden and the Omens were one, and it was only a matter of time before . . .

"*I grow weary of your impudence, Andromeda!*" Sakarabru shouted.

He had lifted her off the floor again by her shackled wrists. Andromeda's body hovered over the open flame burning below her, its heat rising and torturing the fragile and delicate tissue he'd left exposed. Andromeda wished for death, she willed it, but it seemed to stand off in the far reaches of her mind somewhere, mocking her.

"*Or is everything I've heard about you a lie?*" *he asked, stopping to glare at her.* "*Perhaps you are not the visionary you claim to be.*"

She had never claimed any such thing.

"*Perhaps Khale and her kind have a false god in you.*"

Andromeda was no god.

"*It is only time that is on the side of Khale and her army now, Seer. This legend of their Redeemer is nothing more than that. A legend. A myth. They have no savior who is powerful enough to stand against me.*"

He was such a fool. The savior, the Redeemer, had been born. Her name was Mkombozi, and she was the daughter of the Great Shifter, Khale née Khale, and of the Demon, Sakarabru, conceived before the two of them decided to become enemies.

"*All of a sudden,*" *he said, wearily,* "*you are of no use to me, Seer.*"

Sakarabru waved his hand in the air and turned to walk away as Andromeda's body fell into the flames. She may have been of no use to him, but he had been of use to her and Andromeda now had the last element she needed to complete the final Omen. In his quest for answers to the question of his end, Andromeda had suffered greatly, but her suffering had not been in vain. As she managed to roll off of the fire, screaming, and fall onto the floor, she found it—a bead of sweat from the beautiful Demon's brow. She collected it and saved it on her tongue.

Andromeda rummaged through bags scattered on the floor in that Sears store, tossing aside napkins and condiments. Pickles. Damn! She'd forgotten to put pickles on her sandwich.

THIS LOVE

Hours had passed since they'd spoken to each other. Eden found him, sitting alone in the dark in the room he called his library, filled with books, old maps, even a record player and a collection of LPs gathering dust in one corner of the room. That old leather chair had seen better days, but he looked comfortable in it. After he'd turned off the television in the bedroom, Eden had turned it back on and watched channel after channel of news covering stories from all around the world of the drastic turn of events that had unfolded in the last week. It was painful to watch but even more painful not to.

He was sleeping but stirred awake when she stopped and stood in front of him.

"What is it?" he asked, confused and running his hand down his face. "You all right?"

She couldn't help smiling. "I'm all right, Prophet."

Eden had spent the last few hours coming to an emotional place of resolve. Maybe it was that Omen inside her, or maybe it was watching her world fall apart right in front of her eyes. Whatever it was, she felt a sense of purpose.

"Are you still mad at me?" she asked softly.

He leaned back and looked at her. "I was never mad at you."

Prophet's silver eyes glowed softly in the dark. He held out his hand to her. Eden took it and he pulled her onto his lap. Prophet held the power of touch over her. Whatever savage, immature, sobbing, self-pitying beast that decided to rear its ugly head in her at any given moment, he could calm it just by touching her. She wondered if he had had the same effect on Mkombozi. She wondered if he knew how much power he really held over her.

"So you told me to tell you everything," she began.

He waited.

"I had never been so scared then when that bond happened, Prophet. I felt like I'd been pulled into a vacuum of darkness and fear that was suffocating, and all I wanted to do was die. I think that for a moment, I did die."

Prophet stroked her bare thigh with his thumb, but still, he sat quietly and waited for her to continue.

"My world's gone to shit," she said, tearfully. "And I mean that in more ways than one. I'm sitting there watching it all fall apart on television; watching people being killed and losing everything, every aspect of their lives changed forever, and then the question came to me: If I had the power to stop this madness, would I?"

For as long as she could remember, Eden had been enveloped in a blanket of self-absorption.

"It's not about me anymore," she finally admitted. "And I need to stop acting like it is. As much as I hate to think about it, we have to leave this place. I have to make the second bond."

Saying it out loud sounded even more terrifying than thinking about it. The first one nearly killed her, and Eden could only imagine what the second Omen would do to her. No. She didn't even want to imagine what it would do. Her first step was getting out of this house and back out into the world. That was going to be a big enough challenge by itself.

He thought for a few minutes before finally responding. "We'll leave in the morning."

Prophet put his arm under her knees and braced her back with his other arm, placed her on the floor, and nestled between her thighs as he lay on top of her, balancing on his elbows so as not to crush her.

"Tonight," he said, kissing her softly, "you can bond with me."

Eden locked onto the silver reflective pools of his eyes as he kissed her, praying that he wouldn't close them. She lost herself in those eyes of his and rode the wave of his kisses as they carried her away, far away from the burdens of this life with him, just the two of them, alone.

Prophet was a patient lover. Maybe the fact that he was more than four thousand years old had something to do with that, but he took his time, making love to every inch of her. He inhaled her as he kissed her neck, between her breasts, her stomach. She moaned when he dipped his tongue into her. Eden arched her back and pressed her palms down flat on the floor on either side of her, succumbing to the delicious pleasure he gave her with his mouth. Eden gasped and held her breath, building to the inevitable climax she knew would come if he kept going.

"I want you," he whispered, raising his body over her and then slowly easing his thick, throbbing cock into her, pulsing gently until he'd worked himself into her as far as he could.

Eden cried out and locked her legs at the ankles around his waist, then rolled her hips and squeezed her body around his. He thrust into her, forgetting that she was still not fully acclimated to his size yet. Prophet looked lost. He'd been so careful with her, so in control of himself with her, but now he was hurting her.

Make him stop. No. She wanted this. She wanted him and she needed him. Eden reached up and grabbed him around the neck, raised her knees higher, and pulled his face to hers. The pain was excruciating and lovely because it was all of him and all of her, meeting together in the middle of this explosion that was inevitable. Their mouths met, locked, and stifled her cries.

Waves of pain and pleasure washed over her body. Tears slid down the sides of her face as the two of them branded each other's bodies with their own.

He's mine. He's everything.

Eden broke the seal of their kiss, let her head fall back, and screamed as she came and her juices flooded onto the floor underneath her. Prophet growled as he drove inside her and released an orgasm so intense that his whole body went rigid and then finally collapsed fully on top of hers. Eden let her eyes close. Her body went limp underneath his, and for the first time in her life, she felt a part of something, of herself and of him.

Prophet eventually caught his breath. "I hurt you, Beloved," he whispered in her ear. "I'm sorry. I didn't mean to. . . ."

Eden wrapped her arms around him and kissed the side of his face. "You loved me, Tukufu, as you needed to," she said in the language of the Ancients.

He raised his head and looked into her eyes. Eden smiled. He was so freaking gorgeous!

The next morning Eden came out of the house. Prophet leaned against a black SUV, with his arms folded across his chest, smiling.

"You have a car?" she asked, perplexed.

He had wings. Why the hell would he drive, why would anyone drive, if they had wings?

In gallant fashion, he opened the passenger door for her.

"I've got lots of cars," he announced proudly. "This one's great for road trips." He smiled and motioned for her to get in.

"But we can fly," she reminded him.

"First of all, it gets pretty cold at ten thousand feet. Second, they're shooting down anything—or anyone—without a clearance to fly, and though I'm not quite as big as a jumbo jet, I'm pretty damn big enough to shoot down with a missile. And third"—he smiled broadly—"I love driving."

She shook her head, smiled, and climbed into the passenger seat. He climbed in next to her, started the engine, and then just sat there.

"Do we know where we're going?" she asked.

"Well, we'll start by getting down off this hill." He looked at her.

Eden swallowed and nodded. "Baby steps."

"Baby steps," he repeated, pulling away from the house.

CASUALTIES OF WAR

H e who is the author of a war lets loose the whole contagion of hell and opens a vein that bleeds a nation to death." It was a quote from the English-born American writer Thomas Paine that Kifo recalled as he surveyed the results of his work on the humans. He'd chosen not to be seen by Sakarabru's Brood Army, so that he could study each of them more closely. The lines had been firmly drawn in the sand, and the groups divided into those who had been changed by Kifo and his Djinn mystics, and those who had been spared. Spared. Had they been spared? No. They'd just been cast into another kind of hell.

The unaffected humans rummaged through what was left of their societies like scavengers, hoarding what they could and hiding where they could, arming themselves like militia from a *Mad Max* movie. Sanctuaries sprouted up like weeds, surrounded by barbed-wire fences and snipers. Lines to get into them stretched for miles, and people waited for days, hoping to be let inside.

Despite the plight of the humans, it was the Brood who truly captured and held Kifo's attention. These transformed humans, these slaves to Sakarabru's will, stirred an unexpected curiosity in him. Kifo watched them as they organized into platoons, strategized attacks on military installations, government headquarters, even cell phone and cable companies.

"Entry points are here, here, and here," one of the Brood generals told the others gathered around him hovering over a blueprint laid out on the table. "I can guarantee you that they'll be snipers here and here. You can see everything from up there."

"So we come in behind them," another responded, shrugging.

"We send a decoy," the general offered. "An expendable."

Expendables were captured humans or lesser Brood, those who weren't soldiers.

Kifo wafted through them like a spirit, listening to their conversations, some of them whispered in huddled groups.

"I told her, when this is over, we're getting married." The young man's eyes lit up like beacons as he spoke of his fiancée. "I never thought it was possible to love a woman as much as I love her, but damn! She's my life."

"Yeah, well, I met somebody, too," his friend said, blushing.

"Where'd you meet her?" the first young man asked.

The second man thought for a moment and then smiled. "In my dreams."

They all laughed.

"I'm serious, man! I don't know. One minute it was dark. And then I opened my eyes and there she was, standing over me in the hospital, smiling at me and staring at me with the biggest, bluest eyes I'd ever seen before in my life."

The other young men glanced nervously at each other, but they stopped short of saying her name.

"When she made love to me," his eyes glazed over, "I knew that I'd never want anybody else. Being with her erased every bad thing that ever happened to me."

Kifo knew that feeling, having experienced that same kind of love himself.

Kifo had grown tired of listening to the news reports. Music annoyed him. He sat alone in the darkness in his penthouse apartment, staring out the floor-to-ceiling window across from him. The city used to be lit up like a Christmas tree, but now it was nothing but darkness and the sound of gunfire.

Memories as old as his were buried so deep that he almost couldn't reach them, but Kifo concentrated long and hard. Searching for a history almost as old as he was. He'd remembered the images of the Dragon soaring over them in the sky spewing fire down on this village. Kifo remembered wandering the desert lost and alone and being rescued by the Demon. He remembered the making of Sakarabru's first Brood soldier. But there was a blank space in his soul, hollow and empty, that eluded him, like an itch that couldn't be scratched. Kifo felt things he couldn't explain, a sense of panic and apprehension cowering in the recesses of his thoughts. Thinking about it now, it had always been there, but he'd always turned away from it just before it came into view. This time was different. This time, Kifo didn't turn away. He concentrated, took a deep breath and stared into the darkest void of his life until he finally found them, and he wished with all of his heart that he never had.

"*Never go looking for what you do not wish to find, Kifo,*" one of his mystic brothers had told him once. "*Some things are better left hidden.*"

"*There are no screams left, little Djinn, because there is nothing left of what you once were.*"

Kifo lay on that table, staring up at the ceiling, wondering why death had forsaken him and left him here to suffer.

Sakarabru stalked slowly around Kifo's naked, raw, and bloody body, but Kifo was not afraid anymore. The Demon had done too much to him, so much that nothing else could add to the agonizing pain that enveloped him now.

"*You have no family, Kifo. The mystics are all gone. The Dragon killed them because she knew that I would come for them. And yet she made the mistake of leaving you behind and alive.*"

Khale had killed his teachers, his family, and all of those he had loved. She should've killed Kifo too. She had made the mistake of overlooking the boy.

Sakarabru stopped where Kifo's head lay, leaned down, and whispered to him. "I am all that you have left, little mystic." His warm breath singed Kifo's exposed muscles and burned his lidless eyes.

He had no strength left to fight for what small glimmer of life was left in him. He had no desire to resist. Kifo just wanted the pain to stop; he wanted the quiet to linger and a cool glass of water to coat the back of his throat.

The Demon seemed to read his mind. A flask appeared suspended in the air close to Kifo's face. Sakarabru held it over his mouth and allowed a few drops of cool water to coat his lips. Kifo traced a trembling tongue around them to take in as much of the liquid as he could. He was so grateful.

"You need me, little Djinn," the Demon whispered softly, letting a few more drops of water drip onto Kifo's tongue. "You are so young. You are alone in this world now."

Yes. Kifo was all alone. He had lost so much and there was no one—nothing—left.

"You need someone to care for you, Kifo," he continued, gently. "To protect you and to heal you."

The sadness Kifo felt was overwhelming, even more overwhelming than the open wound that was his body. Who would want him? Kifo had been abandoned by his own mother and left to the mystics to raise. She hadn't wanted him. The mystics were dead. Who would want him now? Who would take care of him? Teach him? Feed and clothe him? Who would be there for him when he was afraid? Who would love him?

"There are times," Sakarabru said, crossing the room, "when one must break the body to free the mind, Kifo."

The sounds of chants—healing chants—began to fill the room. The melody from them rose up like a cool mist, soothing the parts of him that felt as if they were on fire.

"Forgive me, little Djinn," Sakarabru told him. "It was the only way."

He didn't have to see it to know that his skin was being regenerated, starting at the tips of his toes and fingers.

"I am all you have, Kifo. I can and will be here for you. I can keep you safe. I can heal your wounds."

The sound of Sakarabru was in harmony with the melody of the chants. And as he spoke, Kifo's body began to heal. His mind began to rest, and he focused on the beautiful sound of the chanting mystics around him and on the hypnotic voice of Sakarabru.

"I will swear myself to you, little Djinn, if you swear yourself to me."

How long had Kifo been here? How many times had Sakarabru said these very words to him before? He'd been here too long, and he had said these same words to Kifo too many times.

"I can take the pain away, Kifo."

Kifo let his eyes close. He hadn't been able to close them before, but now . . . Tears slid down the sides of his face at the joy he felt to finally be able to release them. He sobbed quietly, grateful for the relief enveloping him.

"I will swear myself to you, Kifo," Sakarabru said again, "if you swear yourself to me."

A beautiful and fragrant scent filled the room, and soft hands moved the wisps of hair from his face.

"Drink, Kifo," she said, the sound of her voice compelling him to open his eyes. "Drink."

She held up his head, put the flask of water to his lips, and waited patiently as he greedily gulped it down until it should have been gone, but the water in the small flask continued to flow as if there was no end to it.

Her beautiful blue eyes locked onto his, and a timid smile spread her full crimson lips. "I am Lilith," she said. Her long dark hair brushed across his cheeks.

"Swear yourself to me, Kifo," Sakarabru said again. "I need to know that you are obedient."

Kifo had no one. He had nothing. Sakarabru had taken away the pain.

"Say it," she whispered to him. "I promise you will not regret it."

Kifo managed to sit up. Lilith's fingertips grazed a trail down his spine as she came around the table soaked with his blood, pressed her mouth to his, and kissed him.

"Do I have your loyalty, Kifo?" Sakarabru asked. "Do I have your obedience?"

The boy nodded. "Yes, Lord Sakarabru." He looked at the Demon. "Yes."

"Kifo?" the sound of Lilith's voice broke through the silence of his apartment. "You should come to bed." Her hand rested on his shoulder.

She conveniently came to him when his thoughts were darkest. It was as if she knew when it was time to cast her spell on him to keep him true to his word. He was loyal to Sakarabru. The Demon had saved him, and above all else, Kifo was obedient.

GOODWILL HUNTING

Paul Chapman studied that video footage every chance he got. The damn thing had gone viral. Too bad that the person who'd shot it didn't live to see it. Paul stared at the small screen of his own phone, watching the video feed and studying every single nuance of it.

"Oh God! Oh God!" the person shooting the scene whispered over and over again to himself.

He was hidden underneath something. Paul assumed that it was a seat or something, since it looked like the video was being shot from a train or maybe even a bus. Bodies lay everywhere, and moans came from all around, and then screams, as the ones inside the train or bus were attacked by others. He could make out blurred images of people being pummeled and pounded on by others. The shaky hand of the person holding the camera made it nearly impossible to see the details, but Paul knew instinctively that the attackers had been

Brood. And he knew that the Brood were feeding on those people.

All of a sudden, another image streaked across the screen, a person wearing a gray hoodie, jeans, and sneakers. At first he thought it was a boy, but when the hood came off, he could tell that it was a girl, and she was kicking Brood ass in a big way, breaking jaws, arms, and legs. She was strong and fast. She jumped out through the main window, and Paul lost sight of her for a while, but then a huge dark figure appeared on-screen, overshadowed her, and—*poof!*—she was gone.

The polarizing effects of Sakarabru had divided the world dramatically into three very distinct kinds of individuals. There were the humans, who had pretty much stayed the same, except for the fact that they were now afraid for their lives. And then there were the nonhumans. Most of them seemed to be littered in among humans, but they were different. Paul had never noticed them before when he was . . . well, who he used to be. But he saw them now, and they were everywhere. Some looked as human as Paul, but ever since he'd been changed, he could tell the difference. It was as if this transformation had given him a superpower like X-ray vision or something. Paul could see a hundred humans standing together lined up next to one another, and he could pick out every single one of those pretenders as if it were nothing. They weren't of this world but had become a part of it. Aliens.

Finally, there was another type of being in this world now, brand new, and precariously straddling the fence between life and death, human and nonhuman. Monsters were real. He knew this because he had become one.

Sakarabru had commanded him to find the Redeemer. At first, Paul had no idea what the hell that meant or how he was supposed to find her. But the master had sent him out into the world with this one mission, and Paul was driven to see it through to the end.

It made sense to him that the humans would know nothing of this woman. So Paul sought out the nonhumans. Most were ordinary enough, but others were changelings and witches and even some vampires. Some helped him when he showed them the video of the girl being swept away.

"If she is the Redeemer," a skinny, sun-deprived dude, who called himself a vampire, told him, "then she'll have a Guardian."

"What's a Guardian?" Paul asked.

The scrawny, frail little dude smiled. "A big mean motherfucker with wings. Guardians guard, man. The legend goes that the reborn is the reincarnation of the first Redeemer. And the Redeemer had a Guardian. So this reborn must have one, too."

"Where do I find this Guardian?"

Skinny man shrugged his bony shoulders. "I don't run in those circles, dude. They don't give me the 411, but you might wanna check with some other Ancients."

Ancients. That's what they called themselves as a whole.

"Shifters would know. Some of the Mer creatures would know, if you don't mind getting wet." He grinned. But Paul minded getting wet.

"There's a colony not too far from here of Weres."

Paul looked confused.

"Werewolves," he clarified. "They tend to be selective about loyalty and shit. They might be feeling generous and tell you what you need to know."

They weren't.

This shit wasn't like in the movies. As soon as Paul stepped out of his car, they began to surround him and transform, almost as if they knew what he was. There was no full moon, and they didn't change into dogs or even wolves like he'd seen in movies. These were some big-ass men, who turned into even bigger-assed mutants, that stood upright and taller than him with arms that damn near dragged the ground, six-inch-long fangs, elongated faces that sort of looked like snouts, and fucking muscles bulging out of places where no living thing should have muscles.

Paul never saw the one come up behind him and sink his teeth into Paul's deltoid. He did see the one barreling toward him, lowering his massive shoulder and driving it into Paul's solar plexus with such force that Paul fell backward and on top of the one behind him, crushing the damn thing's chest. It yelped like a dog.

Paul rolled off the one underneath him, grabbed the one on top of him underneath his arms, planted his feet, and raised himself up on the tips of his toes, using all of his strength to flip that sonofabitch overhead. He turned right into another one, who met Paul's chin with what looked like a hand with long thick talons at the end of it. Paul's head jerked back so hard when he fell backward that he thought his neck had been broken.

The Weres were powerful. They were fast, but they attacked like pack animals. Half a dozen of them stalked around him while he lay there, waiting for him to make an aggressive move. In his previous life, Paul had been a fighter. He'd been a champion, all six feet four, 270 pounds of him. Since this change, he stood closer to six eight, six nine, and weighed more than 300 pounds. He was outnumbered, but the damn things weren't the tacticians that Paul was.

He looked for the biggest one and found him. Paul would start with that fucker right there. As the big Were passed by Paul's outstretched arm, Paul grabbed him by the heel and pulled it out from under him. In the blink of an eye, he was sitting on the bastard's chest, holding his bottom jaw in one hand and his upper jaw in another. It clawed and swiped at Paul. They were all over his back, biting into his thighs and arms, but the sound of jawbone breaking startled every last one of them long enough for him to drive his elbow hard into the skull of another. Paul reached behind him to the one driving those fangs through the muscles in his shoulder, and dug his fingers viciously into the eyes, until it let him go and fell over yelping and howling. Paul forced himself to his feet, walked over to the blind Were, and drove the heel of his boot into its throat to shut it up.

Out of the corner of his eye, he saw one run off and disappear into the woods. One remained, limping away from Paul as he stalked toward it, and gradually shifting back into a human-looking form. He was young, no more than twenty, twenty-five. Paul could've snapped his little ass like a twig, but he needed him.

Paul hurt all over, but he wasn't even out of breath. The

scent of his own blood was sour, foul, like something spoiled. The boy put up his hands in surrender.

"Where is the Guardian?" Paul blurted out, still coming at the boy.

He looked up at Paul and shook his head. "What?"

The little bitch had taken a bite out of Paul at some point. He was sure of it, and looking at him now, it took everything inside him not to break his scrawny little neck. "The Guardian!" he yelled. "Where's the fuckin' Guardian!"

"I don't know," the boy cried, and fell helplessly to his knees. "I don't _ ."

Paul stopped and stood over him and then reached down, grabbed a handful of dark curly hair, and pulled the kid up until he dangled a foot off the ground.

"The reborn has a Guardian," he spat in the boy's face. "Where do I find this Guardian?"

The boy couldn't tell him anything except where he could go to find someone else who could. The Were boy had pointed Paul in the direction of "that way" before Paul punched his fist through his chest. *That way* ended up being north, less than ten miles from where he'd found these dudes on a back road that led him to a clearing where an old trailer sat on cinder blocks. Paul didn't bother to knock. Vincent Larimer had pretended to be a teacher throughout the centuries. A learned man, he shined a whole new light on the term "Ancient History," even filling Paul in on the legend of this reborn. Unlike the Vamp or the Were boy, it was obvious to Paul that this Vincent was an elitist, trembling behind his desk, wearing a tailored button-down shirt, cuff links, designer jeans, and old, weathered Air Jordans.

"I'm looking for the Guardian," Paul said without the courtesy of a formal introduction.

"W-what?"

Paul decided that there was no need to repeat himself. Eventually, Larimer figured that stalling was wasted on Chapman.

"H-he lives in Vermont," he finally volunteered.

Again, Paul waited for this pissant to finally realize that he needed to narrow the scope a little.

Vincent swallowed. "I'd have to show you."

Paul took one step toward the Ancient, and the fool wet his pants.

The next night, Chapman pulled up into the circular driveway of the house Larimer had led him to. Paul kicked in the front door and dragged Vincent Larimer in behind him by the collar and dropped his pathetic body on the hardwood floors. The place was dark. He cautiously searched each room, finding signs that the place had been recently inhabited. There were dishes in the sink and food still fresh in the refrigerator. He stepped over Vincent, still lying there and moaning on the floor, and went upstairs. The bed in the master bedroom was unmade, and on it lay a small tank top. Paul picked it up, raised it to his nose, and inhaled. He didn't need anyone to tell him that she had worn this. And now he had her scent committed to memory and finding her would be a piece of cake.

SERPENTINE FIRE

Prophet stuck to the back roads as he drove, but even the smaller towns hadn't been spared the devastation caused by the Demon. Most of them were abandoned, or at least they looked that way on the surface. They'd been shot at twice, and on several occasions, people would scurry from their hiding places like roaches, rushing toward the car, begging for them to stop and help them.

"Prophet," Eden whispered, staring at a family carrying children chasing behind them on foot.

"We can't stop, Eden," he told her. "It's not safe."

It was one thing to see it on the news, but to actually be a part of a world that had changed so much in so short a time, like this, was overwhelming. Prophet drove like he knew exactly where they needed to go. The weight of despair and of the part Eden was supposed to play in all of this was draining, and all she wanted to do was to close her eyes, and each time she did, her thoughts drifted back to the same dark place.

The fire was still burning. Eden sat on the cold floor with her knees drawn to her chest, fixated on that flame, as it seemed to dance at the sound of his voice. The Demon could hardly take his eyes off of it long enough to even notice that she was still there. She couldn't get out. If Eden could have left this place, she would have, but the door she'd come in through was nowhere to be found.

Eden didn't want to move. She didn't want to draw attention to herself out of fear that it would provoke him. Her eyes were becoming adjusted to the darkness. She studied him and his fire, watching everything from the way he moved to the way it responded to him. It was lonely here and quiet except for the sound of his occasional sigh.

"You watch me too closely," he said, slowly turning his head toward her. "Too intently."

The sound of his voice caused her to tremble, but Eden pulled herself into an even tighter ball and tried to make herself as small as possible.

"What are you looking for?" he asked, standing up slowly. The hood still fell over half of his face and kept it hidden from her. "What do you hope to see?"

Eden buried her face in her knees and shook her head. Stay away! she wanted to scream but didn't dare to say a word. Eden could hear his footsteps crossing the room and coming closer and closer to her, and in her panic, she pushed herself up off the floor and stood trembling.

He walked slow circles around her, staring down on top of her, the weight of his gaze trying to push her to her knees, but Eden refused to give in to the pressure. If she sat or knelt, then she would be nothing more than a bug to him. He would squash her under his foot. Eden squeezed her eyes shut and willed herself awake from this nightmare.

"What is your name?" The heat of his breath rained down on her.

She pressed her lips together to keep her words from escaping. She couldn't tell him! He couldn't know who she was, because if he did . . .

He stopped in front of her. Eden felt his hand under her chin, and her whole body tightened. She clenched her fists, and curled her toes. The sensation of his touch sent shockwaves through her body. He raised her chin.

"Look at me," he commanded.

She didn't want to look. She didn't want to open her eyes.

"Look—at—me."

It was like he had power over her eyelids, and all of a sudden Eden couldn't help herself. She opened her eyes and looked up at his shadowed face and piercing emerald-green eyes burning into her.

"What is your name?"

The word swelled on her tongue until she had no choice but to answer him. Eden opened her mouth to tell him her name, but something else came out of it instead. It was her voice, but it wasn't.

"I see you, Demon. Peeeeee-cuuuu-leeeeee-aaaaaarrrrr!"

Eden opened her eyes. Prophet was driving along just as he had been before she'd drifted off to sleep.

They were in Jersey, or maybe Delaware now. She couldn't tell, but it was late when he pulled his SUV up in a lot filled with other cars parked on the sand surrounding a beach house on stilts and facing the water.

He came over to her side and held the door open for her. "You all right?" he asked, closing the door and kissing the top of her head.

She nodded. Anxiety churned like butter in her stomach, but she worked hard not to let him see her sweat. Wherever they were, whatever they were doing here, it was another step in this journey of hers to wherever the hell she was going. Eden wasn't ready to know, so she made up her mind not to ask any questions. He held her hand and led her to the entrance.

"None of us can deny him any longer. Sakarabru is back, and he has pulled us into a war, just as he did before our world fell."

Khale stood in the center of the room, surrounded by Ancients of every different species that Theia had to offer, more than Eden had ever seen at any one time in any one place.

She still insisted on keeping that small-girl-bug-eyed-glasses-nerd thing going, though. Khale stopped when she saw Eden step out from behind Prophet. Every eye in the room shifted to Eden.

Khale looked at Eden and sighed. Her features softened, and she looked genuinely glad to see her. "Please . . ." She motioned for the two of them to sit down.

"Take a seat, love," Prophet whispered. "I'll stand here."

Eden found her way to a place on the sofa. Other Ancients made room for her, but it was pretty obvious that they weren't as happy to see her as Khale was.

"He is as determined to rule here as he was to rule Theia," Khale continued. "The humans have no idea how to combat a foe like Sakarabru."

"And we don't have the numbers anymore, Khale," someone shouted. "He is pulling resources for his army from the seven billion humans of this world. We can't compete with that."

"We can fight a different kind of war, Aelia," Khale argued. "What we lack in numbers we can make up for in our strategy and cunning. We have fate on our side."

"You mean her?"

A tall shapely raven-haired woman stood up. She was so beautiful that Eden's chin dropped just looking at her.

"Isis, please," Khale protested

Isis? *The* Isis?

"You know how we feel about this, Khale. Prophecy or no prophecy, we're not all willing to put our fate in her hands again. She nearly destroyed all of us."

"I didn't destroy you," Eden murmured under her breath, shocked that this gorgeous woman would accuse her of being responsible for what happened to their world. No one heard her.

"It's not for any of us to decide, Isis," Khale argued. "It's fate and that means it's done."

"What is? The Demon? Us? This world? Or all of the above?" Isis shot back.

Suddenly there was a commotion in the back of the room.

"Hold up," Prophet said, stopping a man from bursting in. "Who are you?"

Breathless, the man said, "I need to see Khale. It's about the reborn."

"Let him in, Guardian."

Eden sat frozen on the sofa, her hands clasped tightly in her lap. Her heart was racing as the man stumbled into the room and dropped to his knees at Khale's feet.

"Who are you, Were?" Khale asked.

Another man weeded his way through the crowd to get to the one who had just crashed the party.

"Argos?" he said, kneeling next to him. "What's wrong? What's happened?"

Blood dripped down the side of the man's face. "He's coming for her," he said, finally managing to catch his breath.

"Who? What are you talking about?" Khale asked.

The other man put his hand up to quiet the Shifter.

"A big-ass Brood, man! He came into the colony." He swallowed. "We tried to fight him off—six of us. I'm the only one who got away, Jarrod." He said, panicked. "He killed the rest. . . . But I heard him ask Donovan . . . I heard him ask about the Guardian. The reborn's Guardian."

Eden didn't know when Prophet had showed up next to her. She didn't even remember getting up from that couch, and she knew for a fact that no one in that room had told Argos who she was. He looked right at her.

"He's coming for you. He's coming for her."

WHO YOU ARE

Six of us went at him," Argos explained, sipping on a beer that Jarrod had given him. "Six male Weres in full regalia"—he shook his head in disbelief—"and he handled us like we were rodents."

"How'd you get away, Argos?" Jarrod asked.

"I ran, man," he shrugged. "I saw what he was doing to the others, and I knew . . . that at least one of us needed to escape so that we could tell you about it." The shame he felt was evident in his eyes. The Were were proud and loyal creatures, albeit stubborn and defiant. They looked after their own with the kind of conviction that was envied among other Ancients. Leaving his brother behind had not been an easy decision.

"Human Brood aren't like Theian Brood," he said anxiously. "I get that. But this dude"—he glanced up at Jarrod, standing over him—"he was, Jarrod. He was as fierce a fighter as any Theian Brood I'd ever come up against, and you know that I know what I'm talking about. His strength and his skills were the shit that legends are made of." He shrugged. "He made it look so fuckin' easy."

While Argos spoke, Khale studied Eden for a reaction. A few weeks ago the girl would've gone running and screaming from the room, but now she just stood there, stone-faced and rigid. She had changed more than even she probably realized in a very short period of time.

"Why don't you go get some rest, Argos?" Jarrod said, patting him on the back and escorting him out of the room.

Prophet closed the door behind the Were as he left. "So what the fuck does this mean, Khale?" He glared at her as if she'd been the one to send the Brood into the Were colony.

"It means that the Demon is determined not to let history repeat itself," Khale said, not taking her eyes off of Eden, who was staring back at her. "Would you two gentlemen leave us alone, please?"

Jarrod left without hesitating, but Prophet lingered until Eden smiled at him and nodded.

"Ever the Guardian, I see," Khale chuckled as he closed the door behind him. "Even where I'm concerned."

"Or especially?" Eden murmured.

She liked this new Eden, this one so filled with confidence and certainty, who hadn't burst out in tears once since she'd first walked through that door.

"I can see in your eyes that you now understand the gravity of these times."

Eden dropped her gaze and nodded.

"This is bigger than you, Eden. It's bigger than me. The damage that Sakarabru has done can never be undone. Even if he is defeated, the people of this world will suffer from this deep and terrible scar he's inflicted upon them for generation after generation, and the word 'normal' will evolve to mean something totally different than what it once meant."

"So he's trying to kill me before I bond with the other Omens?" Eden asked apprehensively.

"He had heard of the legends of the Redeemer just like we all had. He had heard the stories of how she was to be our savior and his demise, but the legends were nothing more than stories to him. Fairytales. He ignored them, and it wasn't until after she'd made the last bond that Sakarabru had no choice but to come face-to-face with the only creature alive who could put an end to him."

Tears flooded Eden's eyes, but she impressively blinked them away.

"My guess is that he's not going to make that mistake again. And yes, Eden, it seems that he is trying to get to you before you can make the final bond."

Khale was careful not to say the word "kill," but that didn't stop it from being the elephant in the room.

They had never had the kind of relationship that Khale had imagined they'd have when Eden was first born—or reborn. Rose had quickly stepped in as her mother, and Khale sort of hovered around the perimeter, waiting for the day to come when she could step in and be the mother to Eden that she had been to Mkombozi, but that day never really came. Looking at her now, it was impossible not to see Mkombozi in Eden.

Most of the similarities were subtle, and they always had been, but Eden had come to possess a regalness about her, a stature that had never been there before. Khale wondered how much of this change had come about because of the bond with the first Omen, how much had come from her relationship with the Guardian, and how much of it had come from seeing her world fall apart around her and knowing that she alone could save it.

Khale wanted so badly to reach out to her and to hold her and whisper to her that everything was going to be all right and that Eden could do this. She was the one who had been chosen to do it because she was the only one who could. But she knew that Eden would shun any such show of affection from the Shifter.

"Does anyone know where the second Omen is?" Eden eventually asked, glancing back at Khale.

"I had hoped that somehow you would know. I had hoped that the first Omen would lead you to the others."

"The first Omen shows me the Demon's mind," she explained, reluctantly. "I'm worried that it might show him mine," she admitted. "He doesn't know who I am, but he's curious," she said introspectively.

"Are you curious?" Khale asked.

Eden thought long and hard before answering her. "Yes." Did she really just admit that out loud? And more importantly, did she mean it? "But I don't want him to know me, Khale. I don't want him to pull me in."

That's the part that frightened her the most. It was the feeling she had that he could somehow trap her and make her want to stay in that place with him, almost as if he had the power to change her or make her like him.

Khale walked over to her. "But *in* is where you must go, Eden," she said, gently.

Instead of arguing, Eden nodded. "I know, Khale. It's just . . ." Eden shrugged. "How much of me will be lost when I do?"

She said *when*—not *if*—but *when*. Khale couldn't help herself, and she reached out and took hold of Eden's hands. If history was not to repeat itself, then Khale had to do her part to see that it wouldn't. She had to be open with Eden and tell her the truth.

"The mind of Sakarabru is a trap," she admitted. This time, it was the Shifter who was struggling not to cry. "Mkombozi fell victim to it in the end, Eden, and that's why I . . ." She swallowed. "That's what destroyed her."

"Then it's going to destroy me too," Eden added quickly.

"It doesn't have to." Khale raised her hand to Eden's cheek. Of course, that was a lie, the one that Khale had to keep until the end. "The Redeemer is born for this because she is the one who has the ability to resist the trap of what the Omens hold. The Demon's mind, his power, his destruction—Mkombozi held those things back for a time, but eventually they took her."

"Mkombozi was an Ancient warrior, Khale. She was born to fight. She was born strong and she was one of your generals. So, if she fell victim to the power of these things, what's to stop it from happening to me?"

Khale stared into the warm brown pools of Eden's eyes and saw this young woman struggling to be brave, still struggling to grasp this huge responsibility that had been put on her, and her heart ached for her.

"You, Eden," she said, softly. "You can stop it."

"How, Khale? If she couldn't then . . ."

"I can't tell you how, anymore than I could tell her. There is something in you, inside you, that is more powerful than you can know, Eden. When you survived that first bond, I knew it. Yes, Mkombozi was an Ancient. She was a warrior and a general, but it was never a question of whether or not she'd survive the bonds. I questioned yours."

"Thanks, Khale," she said sarcastically.

"It wasn't meant as an insult. You're human. Your body can only take so much, Eden, but you fought through it, you lived, and I have never been more proud than when I heard that my human girl from Brooklyn"—Khale smiled—"had survived the impossible. Do you understand what that means?"

Eden shook her head.

"It means that maybe, just maybe, you are even more powerful and more of a warrior than Mkombozi. And she was fierce." She laughed, warmly.

There it was. Khale saw it, even if only for a moment, but Eden couldn't hide it no matter how much she'd wanted to—that glimmer of pride, of hope. It was just a spark, and a small one, but it was there. And for now, it would do.

AND SHE WAS

She was cute, the little Redeemer—savior or destroyer of the galaxy, or whatever. Jarrod didn't expect to see anybody out here this time of night, least of all her. He surveyed the area, looking for the Guardian, but he was nowhere to be found.

"Some Guardian," he muttered under his breath.

Eden sat at the end of the pier dangling her feet off the edge. For a moment, Jarrod had the wicked thought of some Mer creature suddenly coming up and grabbing hold of her ankles, scaring the shit out of her. But they knew better, just like Jarrod knew better. If this Eden was who Khale said she was, then far be it from him to try to sneak up on her.

He coughed just to let her know that he was coming up from behind her. Jarrod had not chosen a side in the Theian wars, but a side had been chosen for him when Sakarabru wiped out his colony and killed his mate, Alaine. He'd joined forces with Khale for a chance to make the fucker pay, but the Redeemer, Mkombozi, had gotten to him first.

He sat down on the pier on the other side of Eden's cowboy boots.

"Shouldn't you be asleep?" he asked, staring into the black inkwell of water at her feet.

"Shouldn't you?" Eden responded apprehensively.

He was like the other Ancients, leery of Eden and what she was becoming. And she was leery of all of them. There was a determination in her expression, a bold but subtle challenge in her eyes that almost dared him to make just one wrong move. Jarrod was a Were and he knew this look well. What he didn't know was if her courage was because of the bond she'd made with the Omen or if it was just a good old healthy dose of human self-preservation.

"So, is it commonplace for that Guardian of yours to just let you go wandering around in the middle of the night without him?"

She shook her head. "No. Fortunately, he's a sound sleeper." She actually smiled. "I needed time to myself."

"You want me to leave?"

She paused and then shook her head. "No. You don't have to."

Eden wasn't too tall, but the shapely legs that dangled off the edge of that pier were rather attractive, as legs go. She wore cutoff jean shorts, a black tank top, and an overcoat that looked a lot like the one the Guardian wore. Dradlocks were pulled up into some kind of knot and twisted on top of her head. In theory, it should've looked stupid, but on her, it worked. He couldn't believe that he even knew this word, but it came to mind and shocked the shit out of him: "delicate." And she had some beautiful tits. He could tell that even hidden inside that jacket, because he was a man obsessed with boobs.

"It's only a matter of time before he senses you're gone and comes looking for you."

Small talk wasn't his thing, but hell, it was the effort that counted in his book. She wasn't one of them, but thanks to Khale and her bag of tricks, she'd been dragged into some shit that had to have been mind-blowing. Jarrod couldn't help it. He felt sorry for her.

"Eventually, I'm sure he will," she said, not bothering to even look at him.

This was Khale's reborn Redeemer. She was young, and she sat there looking exactly as she should, like a young woman who had the weight of the world on her shoulders. Shit! He could curse the Shifter out for this one. Khale could've found somebody else, like a sumo wrestler or a linebacker. Why in the world did she pick this one?

"How old are you?" he asked without thinking.

This time she did look at him. "Twenty-four."

And she looked all of twenty-four. She was a fuckin' kid! Damn! If he thought he could get away with kicking Khale's ass for this, he would.

Jarrod could feel her staring at him now. "What?"

"So, you're a werewolf?"

"I'm a Were. Humans came up with this notion of a werewolf."

"Based on your kind?" she probed.

He nodded. "They put their own spin on it, of course," he said casually.

"Like?"

"Like that whole myth about us taking chunks out of people," he explained, frowning. "That's pretty damn disgusting."

She laughed. "Have you ever tried eating people?"

"Nah. Took a bite out of a chick back in the seventies. Just 'cause I was curious, you understand. Took weeks for me to get that taste out of my mouth."

She surprised him and smiled. "What about silver bullets?"

He shrugged. "They hurt."

This time she laughed. "But they don't kill you?"

He looked at her like she'd just asked him to pull a snake out of his ass.

"I'm just asking," she said, raising her hands in surrender. "I mean, I only know what I see on television. I just figured that since you're here, I might as well get it from the source."

"Humans were afraid of us," he started to explain. "They hunted us, and a lot of Weres died early on." Those memories were painful and surprisingly vivid to Jarrod. "We learned to be more discreet, and they learned to empower themselves by making up the rules to their legends and myths. They made it up in their minds that we could only change during the full moon; it gave them a sense of peace and superiority, I guess. Same thing with the bullets. It made them feel more in control."

She mulled over what he had said before asking the question: "But why'd you let them? You were, or are, obviously capable of overpowering the humans. And I'm sure you scared the hell out of them. You could've killed them in retaliation for them attacking you. Why didn't you?"

Jarrod smiled. "It's not our nature, Eden. The Were are a proud and close-knit nation. Just because we're capable of being monsters doesn't mean we are. This was their world. We were strangers and lucky to be alive. Our role, the role of all Ancients, has always been to respect the people here and to live quietly among them, if we can. We found ways to do that and, until recently, we were happy."

He sounded like a fuckin' Hallmark card. Jarrod swallowed the bile that had come up from his stomach, because spitting would've been rude.

"It's peaceful out here," she eventually said. "Almost as if the rest of the world hasn't gone to shit at all."

But that's exactly what was happening to it. Jarrod looked at her.

"It's going to suck to have to leave. . . ." Her voice trailed off.

Jarrod was on the outside looking in with these other Ancients. Khale only needed him to fight, and the Guardian just glared at him. He had sort of accidentally found out that Eden was the reborn, and he had some idea that maybe she had bonded with the first Omen, but he couldn't be sure. So he figured it couldn't hurt to ask.

"Did you find the first Omen?"

She looked at him. "It found me."

Okay, so he was an Ancient and that sounded crazy even to him. He could only imagine what it must've done to her. "Uh . . . damn."

Eden nodded. "Damn is right."

"So the bond was made?"

"Yep," she said, swinging her feet back and forth.

"How do you feel about that?" On the surface, it was a dumb question, but Jarrod had his reasons for asking.

Eden gave it some thought before answering. "I wanted to be a manicurist," she said suddenly. "I wanted to get my license, set up shop somewhere, and maybe even open up my own nail salon." She looked at him. "But now I'm bonded with an Omen, and my mind is stuck in a room with a Demon's. I'm scared to death that too much is being expected of me, and even more afraid that I'll actually live up to this shit, or worse, be an overachiever and kill every-damn-body. But other than that"—she shrugged—"I feel pretty good."

Jarrod, like most Ancients, didn't look forward to the return of the Redeemer because that would mean that the Demon was back. But also, like most Ancients, one was just as bad and just as dangerous as the other. Khale and the Guardian were the only two beings in the universe who romanticized the Redeemer. The rest of them were terrified of her, and of what she had done and could do. She was powerful enough to destroy Sakarabru, yes. But Mkombozi had done so much more than that, and having her reborn again as their savior was scary as hell.

The Ancients had put up a good fight on Theia. They had come together, sworn their loyalty to Khale, and fought against

Sakarabru, wiping out as many of his Brood solders as he had of theirs. But the Demon had proved to be too much for all of them, even Khale. And it wasn't until the Redeemer came into the fullness of the power of the Omens that any of them had ever even seen Sakarabru vulnerable.

Eden could very well kill the Demon the same as Mkombozi. And she could just as well kill everybody on the planet in the process, but the way Jarrod saw it, it was pretty much on its way to being dead anyway.

That moment was on him now to say what needed to be said. Damn! He'd hoped he could get by without ever telling anybody, but she had just made that impossible.

"Do you know where to find the next Omen?" he asked, irritated with himself more than he'd been in a long time.

She shook her head. "Khale thinks that the first one will eventually lead me to it."

Well, hell! The first one had led her to him, so maybe there was something to this prophecy shit after all.

"I think I know how to find it," he said, regretting every painful word of that statement.

She looked at him.

"But," he quickly added, "I want you to think on it, sleep on it first," he warned her. She had been pulled into this mess, but prophecy or no prophecy, she did have a choice as far as he was concerned. And he wasn't about to take that away from her. "You think about this, Eden. How far are you willing to go? How far do you want to go?"

"Eden."

The Guardian appeared out of nowhere behind the two of them.

"It's up to you," Jarrod added.

"Eden!" Prophet said more urgently.

Jarrod quickly stood up and held out his hand to help her up. He pulled her close to him. "If you want to find it, let me know. If not, then we'll forget I ever said anything. It's up to you." He let go of her hand.

Prophet held out his hand to her. "Let's go."

She looked back at Jarrod with uncertainty in her eyes.

"Your choice," he said to her. "Not anyone else's."

Of course the big dude glared at him with those creepy in glow-in-the-dark eyes of his. But Jarrod stood by his word. Ultimately, it was up to her how this thing played out.

She deserved at least that.

BROWN-EYED GIRL

Prophet didn't know how many Ancients were staying here in Khale's beach house, but he knew that he didn't trust any of them alone with Eden. Khale hadn't said it, and she never had to. The Redeemer didn't have the fan club in other Ancients that she had in Prophet and the Shifter. The other Ancients were afraid of her, and they resented everything she represented. Mkombozi had not only destroyed their world, but she had, in essence, destroyed their lives. The threat of her coming back, in any form, was terrifying enough to make all of the Ancients dangerous, and her vulnerable.

She'd dozed off after Prophet had brought her back to the room, but it was a restless sleep. She didn't talk about it, but he knew that the nightmares were getting worse. He also knew that whatever she and that Were had spoken about needed to be discussed. Prophet sat out on the balcony overlooking the inlet waiting for her to wake up. He'd pressed her last night about what she and the Were had talked about, but Eden insisted on being tired and needing to sleep. It was the secrets that came between him and Mkombozi. Prophet was not going to allow them to come between him and Eden.

Eden moaned, sat up in bed, and locked onto him sitting on the balcony. "What time is it?"

"Nearly noon," he said.

She stretched. "I didn't mean to sleep that long." Eden tossed back the sheets. "I've gotta pee."

He watched her stumble toward the bathroom. "Pee, and then come out here, please."

Eden stalled with taking an exorbitant amount of time to wash her hands and then of course brush her teeth. But Prophet had waited four thousand years for this woman. Another five or ten minutes wouldn't hurt.

"It's so quiet out here," she said, coming out onto the balcony.

He took hold of her hand and pulled her down onto his lap. Eden kissed the side of his face.

"Are you okay?" he asked.

"All things considered." She shrugged. "I don't know. Are you okay?"

"Well, since you asked . . . not really." He looked into her eyes. "Why don't you tell me what you and the Were talked about last night?"

Eden smiled mischievously. "Are you jealous?"

"Yes."

She looked at him like she expected for him to say more,

but as far as he was concerned, there was nothing more
to say.

"Just about . . . what Argos had told us," she lied.

"Are you really going to do this, Eden?"

"What?"

"I'm not the enemy."

"I know. I never said that. . . ."

"Then why treat me like I am?"

"That's not what I'm doing."

"We talked about you being open with me."

"I am," she argued.

Prophet leaned back, stared up at the sky, and sighed his
frustration. How could he do what he needed to do if she
refused to do her part, which was to keep him aware of any
and everything going on with her?

"He knows where to find the next Omen," she finally confessed. "He told me that I had to make a choice as to whether
or not I wanted him to tell me where it is."

He sat up. Of course Prophet wouldn't trust that fool as
far as he could throw him. "You believe him?"

She thought about it. "Why would he lie?"

Hell. He'd like to set her up. To lead her into a trap of
some kind. Shit. "How would he know something like that,
Eden?"

"I don't know," she said, frustrated. "He just said he knew.
How am I supposed to know how he knows?"

The shit didn't make sense. No one knew where the
Omens were, so how was it that this Jarrod Runyon had come
by that information, and why hadn't he said anything last

night with everyone present? Why had he waited to tell her when the two of them were alone? There were just too many questions that led nowhere.

"You don't believe him?"

He shook his head. "No. I don't."

"He has no reason to lie about something like that, Prophet."

"None that we know of," Prophet countered. If the Were was telling the truth, then he should have no problem telling it to Prophet. "Wait here."

Prophet followed the sounds of voices coming from the kitchen on the lower level. Runyon was sitting at the table, finishing breakfast.

"Outside," Prophet commanded him.

The Were took his sweet-ass time, but eventually he showed up and held out a cup of coffee to Prophet.

"It's good," he offered.

Prophet knocked it out of his hand. "What the fuck did you tell her last night?"

Jarrod wasn't as tall as Prophet. He had the typical thick Were build, especially across the shoulders and in the legs. The wolf shone through, even in his non-Were form.

"Oh, we talked about a lot of things, Guardian," he said flippantly. "Did you know that she had planned to open up a nail salon before all this mess happened?"

Prophet was not going to be baited by this fool. "You told her that you knew where to find the next Omen," he said calmly.

All humor left the Were's face. "Is that what she told you?"

"I want you to tell me."

"What's going on out here?" Khale interjected, coming out of the house.

Prophet waited for the Were to volunteer the information, but Runyon all of a sudden became mute.

"Your Were friend here told Eden that he knew where to find the next Omen."

Khale looked stunned. "Is that true, Jarrod?"

Jarrod raked his hand through his hair. "I don't know for certain, Khale."

"Then what do you know?" Prophet challenged.

Runyon glared back at him. "Does this look like fuckin' Theia to you, Guardian? You talk to me like you got some goddamned sense, with respect and not like some fake-ass deity sitting up on a throne like you used to back in the good old days." The Were took a threatening step closer to Prophet. "I don't give a damn about you." He looked at Khale. "About any of you." Runyon turned his attention back to Prophet. "But Eden on the other hand is stuck having to clean up the mess we started, and I got an issue with that."

"Do you know where the second Omen is or don't you?" Khale demanded to know.

The Were ignored her and kept his gaze fixed on Prophet. "Who the hell are you to deserve a second chance?" he asked, angrily. "You lost your mate in one world only to turn around and find her reborn here in this one? You couldn't fuckin' protect her on Theia, Guardian." His resentment was powerful. "What the hell makes you think you can protect her now?"

Prophet wasn't going to cave to this beast's war with words. No one knew better than he did how he'd let Mkombozi down, and no one knew better than he knew now how determined he was not to let the same thing happen to Eden.

"Do you really think it's that easy to provoke me?" Prophet drew back his shoulders. "Then you're way more fuckin' pathetic than I gave you credit for."

Runyon slowly eased into beast mode, literally. Prophet watched the male grow a foot taller. His shirt ripped at the shoulders and across the chest, and his arms swelled with muscles the size of bowling balls.

"If you have to transform to have any chance of winning this fight," Prophet said, coming toward him, "then bring it."

Khale stepped in between the two. "Idiots," she blurted out irritably. She spun around and soon stood as tall as the Were. "Stop wasting my fuckin' time, Jarrod. Do you know where the Omen is or not?"

Runyon shifted back to his unimpressive self and forced back his rage, turning his attention to Khale. "Ever since The Fall, we've looked after the twins," he explained.

The twins were the youngest of the Troll Seer Sisters, Ursa Major and Ursa Minor, the Seers of Heaven and Hell, but no one really knew which one saw heaven and which one saw hell. The two had always been inseparable.

"No one has been able to find them since The Fall," Prophet interjected.

"We didn't want anyone to find them. They didn't want to be found."

"And you think that they know how to find the Omen?" Khale asked suspiciously.

"The sisters talk in riddles. They share sentences, so you never fully know if it's heaven they're talking about or hell or both. They sing this song." He thought about it before repeating it: "Uh . . . Two for three. Redeem . . . something, and/or die the lamb," he recited.

"Two for three. Bring me. Redeem me. Or die the lamb." Eden recited it correctly as she came out of the house and stared at Jarrod.

"I thought it was just gibberish until they said the word together: 'Omen.' And they only said it once." He looked hard into her eyes. "It's up to *you* if you want me to take you to them, Eden. Not *them,* and not *me.*"

Prophet saw the hesitation darken her eyes and then he saw something else. He saw resolve.

Eden slowly nodded. "Take me there, Jarrod," she finally said. All of them were speechless. Eden glanced back at Khale and Prophet once more before going back inside. Jarrod looked as if the world had come crashing down on top of him. Prophet knew that it had come crashing down on all of them.

"Be ready in an hour," Prophet said, pushing between Khale and Runyon and following Eden inside.

STATE OF THE
UNION ADDRESS

Good evening,

"This is Vice President Ronald Crawford, addressing you now as acting President of the United States of America. We've received reports earlier this afternoon that the President of the United States, President Lawson Reynolds, has been . . . lost.

"The President took ill three days ago, as did forty percent of our Senate, and forty-seven percent of our House of Representatives. Although the White House is still under government control, it has since been reinforced with extreme security measures, and trespassers will be shot on sight.

"In addition to our losses suffered here at the federal level, we are no longer in communication with the leadership from the following states:

Alabama
New York
North Carolina
South Carolina . . ."

LIFE IN TECHNICOLOR

E den didn't know whether she should feel like the queen of England being transported by the royal guard or a prisoner being taken to Rikers. She rode in the Hummer with Jarrod, while Prophet and other winged Shifters flew ahead of them and others trailed behind. They drove down every back road they could find for two hours from the beach house, traveling to Bennottsville, South Carolina.

Creedence Clearwater Revival's "Proud Mary" blared from the speakers. Eden had memorized the very limited rotation on Jarrod's MP3 player. Next would come "Born to Run" by Springsteen, and "Old Time Rock and Roll" by Bob Segar and the Silver Bullet Band. She'd have killed right now for a cheeseburger, fries, and a new playlist that wasn't the personal theme music for Jarrod Runyon.

"Khale didn't know that you knew where to find the Omen?" she asked.

She barely knew him, but the silence coming from him during this ride seemed so out of character. He had barely said two words to her since they'd begun this journey. Jarrod's mood had turned 180 degrees since she'd spoken to him last night.

"Nah," was all he said, staring straight ahead out at the road.

He was handsome. Jarrod looked every bit the disheveled, cowboy rocker that personified the kind of music he loved. He'd pulled his long, golden brown waves of hair back away from his face into a ponytail, and since last night the scruff on his face was noticeably thicker. He had the most beautiful brown eyes she'd ever seen, though, sort of a translucent honey brown.

"So, what made you tell me?" she probed.

They drove at least another mile before he finally responded.

"Sakarabru was a mean motherfucker," he said. "Evil mean. He's the kind that would peel his own mother like a grape and think nothing of it."

It didn't take a genius to realize that Jarrod had suffered his own losses at the hands of the Demon. Eden could hear it in his voice, and see the pain in his expression.

"Mkombozi came through like a champ," he continued. "She took it to him in a way that none of the rest of us ever could. Put her foot in his evil ass and saved us. We all believed that she done it and we were right. She had killed the Demon only she didn't stop—killing." He glanced at Eden and then turned his attention back to the road. "You know the story. Right? I don't have to explain it."

No. He didn't have to explain it. Eden knew it. She'd been told that story for as long as she could remember.

Khale and Prophet were always so careful with the things they'd told her about Mkombozi. They were careful to tell Eden everything that had been good about the Ancient. Jarrod seemed willing to offer up another perspective.

"There was no other way to defeat Sakarabru, though," Eden offered. "She was Theia's last hope."

"Was she?" he asked quickly. "I mean, I don't know. Maybe she was." Jarrod shook his head and shrugged. "Mkombozi, Khale, the Guardian—they were in a different class than my kind, Eden. They were your generals in the war, but the rest of us were just soldiers. We followed orders and did what we were told. I wasn't a part of that inner circle. I had heard rumors of a Redeemer who was born with the ability to defeat the Demon. And I saw her do that. I watched her do what none of the rest of us had even come close to doing, which was to not only destroy his army but Lord Sakarabru himself." He looked into her eyes. "It was poetic. It was beautiful. But then we all saw that as she destroyed him, she started to become him. The ground shook, the sky seemed like it had cracked wide open. Khale was screaming, 'Stop it, Mkombozi!' " He quietly reflected on those moments, reliving them again in his mind.

She started to become him. The words made her sick to her stomach.

"It was a matter of time before I knew that I'd have to tell somebody about the other Omen," he finally admitted. "I never bought into all that prophecy/destiny/fate shit, until Sakarabru came back. I didn't want to believe that he would." Jarrod swallowed. "I don't know how or why she did it, but for some reason, Khale decided to dump all this shit on your shoulders. Ultimately, you're caught in the middle of cleaning up the fallout from a world you don't even know. You're a scapegoat for the bullshit we created. And you shouldn't have to be. I said that it's up to you how you want to do this, or *if* you want to do it. Not Khale, not the Guardian—but you. That's why I told you. So that you could decide what to do next."

"No," she protested, "it's not up to me, Jarrod, because it's not just about the Ancients or Sakarabru. If I don't do this, my world is dead. He's destroyed everything I know and love, and it's never going to be the same. We won't recover from this."

Families had been left devastated. Governments all over the world had fallen. This wasn't just a New York thing or an America thing. Sakarabru's destruction touched every corner of the globe. And if she was the only thing standing between him and what was left of it, then Eden didn't have the luxury of walking away.

"It's said that Andromeda created the Omens," she continued quietly. "Do you know what the Omens are?"

He shook his head. "Not really. Spells. Trinkets. Hell, I don't know."

Eden pulled her sweater down off of her shoulder and

showed him the brand that had formed there after the first bond. It had long since healed: a starburst with a small circle in the center.

"I think that they are all a part of Sakarabru," she explained.

Jarrod stared at the symbol.

"The first one connects mind or soul or whatever to his."

Jarrod raked his hand down his face. "Like now?"

She shrugged. Eden didn't know if this was a figurative thing or if it was literal. If she was aware of him, was he as aware of her? She had no way of knowing.

"So what does the second Omen do?" he asked.

"I was hoping you could tell me."

"Shit, Eden. I don't know. I mean, the twins sing that song, and every now and then the word 'Omen,' but I have no idea what it does."

"The longer I'm in that room with Sakarabru, Jarrod," she offered for the first time to anyone, "the less afraid I am of becoming him."

The Were was speechless and maybe even a bit afraid too now. The Sakarabru in her mind was becoming less of a threat to her. In her thoughts, Eden saw herself coming out of that dark corner of that dark room and sitting across from him on the floor in front of his fire. It was warm.

She started to become familiar with him and even drawn to him.

"I've never wanted to believe that I was Mkombozi," Eden confessed. "I'd never wanted to be extraordinary or powerful. But from a very young age, I think I've always known that being Eden was never more than a fantasy. Being plain old boring, underachieving Eden was my dream come true. But she was never real. She was never meant to live forever."

Eden stared out of the window, letting the background noise of Springsteen's voice fade away like a whisper. Rows of timber flashed past her sight, hypnotizing her and taking her back to a place she had never seen with Eden's eyes. Eden saw Mkombozi, young, athletic, and beautiful, running parallel to the Hummer. She carried something in her hand, but Eden couldn't make out what it was. She ran barefoot through the shrubbery, moving as quickly as that truck moved. Long hair whipped across her face as she turned and looked at Eden. Mkombozi leapt into the air like a gazelle, stretching out long toned legs and pointing her toes and then faded away.

Eden remembered that day, the way the air smelled, the way the ground felt under her feet. Eden remembered her lungs filling to capacity as she'd run for miles and miles— running away . . . running to . . . That part was a mystery.

The fire is warm.

The Demon nodded. I keep it warm. It comforts me.

It comforts me too.

It should. It is a part of you now.

She should've been afraid. She should've wanted to run away. But she didn't.

TIGHTROPE

H ey, Dad."

"Hay is for horses."

"What?"

Paul laughed. "That's a joke from the old days."

The boy laughed. "Hay is for horses. That's dumb, Dad."

"Yeah, but it made you laugh." *If it made the boy laugh . . . The boy. His son . . . What was his name?*

"You promised to pick me up early this weekend. So, don't forget."

The boy had been an unplanned event in Paul's busy life, but he'd never regretted him. Not for a second.

"Mom and Todd are leaving for Hawaii tomorrow and I don't want to stay here with boring old Consuelo."

Consuelo. The housekeeper. Paul remembered her, but how come he couldn't remember the name of his own son?

"I'll be there bright and early on Saturday morning," Paul
promised. "You just be ready."

"I'm already packed," the boy—his son—said noncha-
lantly.

Paul laughed. He was as excited to see the boy as the boy . . .
was to see . . . him?

"Aaaaaaaagh!"

This . . . thing. This dark and terrible . . . thing pressed
in around Paul from every corner of the room like a vise. It
had a face, cloaked, but he could see its mouth move, utter-
ing a continuous whisper of words that cursed the blood
surging through Paul's veins.

Paul lay naked, curled into the fetal position on the concrete floor of the abandoned warehouse he'd found to rest
for the night. He'd fallen asleep and started to dream of another man's life—of his life before . . . before he'd . . .

Where was his son? And how come Paul couldn't recall
the boy's name? He had loved him more than his own life,
and yet for some unexplainable reason, he couldn't remember his name or his face.

"My boy!" he called out, his voice echoing in the hollow
and wide-open spaces of the warehouses.

They had taken things from him. They had violated Paul
in the worst ways, stripping him of his life, of the people most
precious to him. And in his dreams, Paul fought to get back
to his son—his life. He fought to get back to the man he had
once been, the fighter—the champion.

If only he could drown out the deafening sounds of the phantom's whispers. The words were silent to his ears but clanged together like metal inside him. Blood began to seep from his pores, and Paul knew that he had soiled himself more than once. He had been a man. He had been . . . human. He had been a father. And now this damn thing was trying to turn him into something else.

"*Sakarabru. Sakarabru. Sakarabru.*" The word, his name, burned like a brand into Paul's memory, replacing . . . replacing . . . his son's name, his son's face. Paul rolled off of his side and onto his knees. His muscles thickened under the pressure of the pain building from within. The phantom came close to him and put his face close to Paul's. Paul fixed his gaze on its lips, moving faster, speaking faster in a language that Paul didn't understand except for the one word— "Sakarabru."

"You have forgotten your first commandment, Paul." It was her voice.

He would know it anywhere. Paul took a deep breath and inhaled the scent of her perfume. It was the phantom that he saw, but it was Lilith that now had his undivided attention. The unyielding burning of pain pulsed inside him, but it was her touch that lighted on his skin and raised goose bumps on his back and arms.

"Sakarabru," she said in unison with the phantom, who continued chanting in his own language, "has commanded you to find the reborn, and yet you stray, Brood," she said seductively.

He closed his eyes and shuddered as she swept her

fingertips through the strands of his hair touching his shoulders.

"You're dwelling on the wrong things, baby," she whispered in his ear, leaning close.

The sweet warmth of her breath against his skin was like nectar to him. The anticipation of Lilith was a drug, a narcotic that mixed beautifully with the agony still boiling inside him.

"Find her, Brood," she told him.

Paul opened his eyes and watched as the phantom drifted away from him, leaving just her. Beautiful waves of red hair cascaded down her shoulders and created windows for erect pink nipples peaking through them. The delicious nakedness of Lilith instantly made him hard. The phantom still chanted, but the sight of her and Paul's desire for her had overcome the sound of the words that had been so deeply embedded in him.

Lilith got down on all fours and slowly crawled toward him seductively, like a lioness stalking her prey.

"Promise me that you will find her, sugar." Lilith rolled over on her back and spread her soft thighs, exposing the sweet treasure hidden between them.

Paul growled low and deep in the back of his throat, rolled over on top of her, and slowly eased himself inside her. Lilith was the drug he needed to ease his pain and to bring clarity to his mind.

"Promise me!" she demanded, thrusting her hips against his.

Paul stared into her ocean-blue eyes. She had taken away his pain. She had bought him back to his purpose. She had given him more pleasure than he had ever had in his life. "I promise."

"We know where they're taking her."

The next morning, Paul emerged from the warehouse and saw three men standing outside. They were Brood. He studied each of them and finally reached the conclusion that he had allies. Either Lilith had sent them or maybe even Sakarabru. But in any event, if they had come with a lead on how to find the reborn, he'd take what he could get.

"Where?" he asked, focusing on the one who appeared to be the leader.

"South," he told him. "They're staying close to the coast but not getting on any of the major roads—sticking to backcountry mostly." He looked back at the other two men. "We can get you onto their trail easy enough."

"She's traveling with the Guardian?" he asked.

They looked at each other. "She's traveling with a convoy: the Guardian, a few Weres, and a few Shifters. They've got her pretty well protected," the one leaning against the car added.

Paul pulled his keys from his pocket, headed to his car, climbed in, and started the engine, following them on this trail leading to the reborn.

The funk of their all-night fuck session permeated the entire warehouse. Lilith and the Brood were long gone, but Kifo knew exactly what had gone on here and why. Lilith was a master dream weaver, a spell caster of sex. She had tricked men and women into believing that they loved her, needed her, and couldn't live without her. And she had made them believe that *she* actually loved them, too.

She and Sakarabru had played Kifo like an instrument. The Demon had broken him, torn him down, and nearly destroyed him, only to send her in like the cavalry, to pick up those broken pieces and put him back together again using the lovely spell of pussy and promises. All in the name of Sakarabru. It had worked on Kifo, and it worked on Sakarabru's most incredible and formidable monster here on Earth, this Brood. It had happened so long ago, and Kifo had been so young and so caught up in the love of Lilith that he never thought to ever question how someone like her could come to want to be with someone like him. But now he understood. Kifo understood everything with such clarity that it sickened him.

BURNIN' DOWN
THE HOUSE

You could cut through the despair with a knife. Jacksonville Sanctuary. In the last week Khale had traveled from one US coast to the other surveying the devastation caused by Sakarabru. She had finally come to Florida and found this place as dismal as any other. She snaked her way slowly through the masses littering the playing field inside what used to be the professional football stadium. Thousands upon thousands had been living inside this place for weeks, and thousands more waited outside the perimeter, hoping to get in. Armed military men perched high in the stands with their guns loaded and ready to shoot those on the outside who tried to break in and those on the inside who may have wanted to leave.

The conditions inside were horrible. The stench of urine, feces, and cigarettes smothered the air. Frightened women and children huddled together in groups. These people were like animals, fighting over any little morsel of food available. Trucks hauled in large boxes filled with food and supplies, but order had given way to chaos, and it truly was the survival of the fittest.

Khale had always loved this world. She'd watched humanity take root and blossom over time, siphoning their notion of culture, religion, languages from what they'd learned from Ancients, some of whom, for a short time, were worshipped like gods. But as mankind developed and thrived, the influence of the Ancients diminished, and they were eventually, and mercifully, forgotten. Khale and her kind assimilated and blended in to avoid persecution by a race that fell in love with logic and out of love with legends.

She had, in essence, become one of them, and she had never regretted it. As Khale née Khale, the Forever and Ever, and the Great Shifter, she could adopt whatever form she chose and had experienced this world from a thousand different perspectives. Khale loved her life here, and her heart went out to these people.

So as not to frighten them anymore than they already were, she ducked behind a shed, transformed into a small bird, and flew outside the walls of this new kind of prison. She had a very important meeting to attend on the other side of these walls, and Khale did not want to be late for it.

Saint Simon's Island, off the coast of Georgia, was barren now. The humans had all escaped inland and to the larger cities, hoping to get into sanctuaries. Without humans to feed on, the Brood found no use for places like this.

Khale stood staring out at the ocean rummaging through all of the regrets she had had since even before her world had fallen. Of all of them, Sakarabru had been her first mistake, and the one with the most lasting consequences.

"Am I the last to make love to you, Khale?" he asked, appearing behind her.

Her knees grew weak at the sound of his voice, and Khale silently cursed herself for the effect that he still had on her. She closed her eyes, and without thinking, shifted into a height more compatible with his. Khale slowly turned to Sakarabru and gazed into the depths of his emerald-colored eyes.

Sakarabru's charm for Khale began with his beauty. On Theia, when they were much, much younger, his hair had been a dark contrast to the rich color of his eyes. Time had changed it to white, which made him even more breathtaking.

He reached down and carefully took her hand in his. In the mind of that young and naive and careless Shifter, this was the Sakarabru that she loved, then and now. Her heart fluttered at his touch.

He raised her hand and studied it intently and then he laughed.

Khale noticeably tensed.

"Forgive me, Beloved," he said, stroking the back of her hand. "It's just that, I can't help but to find it amusing that you would lessen your own beauty to suit what is accept-able to the humans." He raised her hand to his lips and kissed it. "Such a waste," he said, gazing into her eyes.

Khale had taken a huge risk coming here. She was liter-ally taking her own life into her hands by agreeing to meet with him. Sakarabru was not back to the fullness of his strength, but the influence of who and what he was was as strong as it had ever been.

"Know thy enemy," she murmured, removing her hand from his. "You are still my enemy, Sakarabru."

The flirtatious spark in his eyes faded quickly. "I am most definitely your enemy, Shifter."

"Why'd you ask to see me?" she asked coolly.

"Why did you agree to come?" he challenged.

This time, it was her turn to be coy. "Because my ego is just as big as yours, Demon," she said, stepping away from him. "But let's just say that I was curious to see what I am really up against after four thousand years."

"Look around you, Ancient," he said casually. "I am well rested and I am ready to rule again. It is in my—"

"I know," she said irritably. "It's in your nature. You al-ways say that as if it's all the excuse you need to inflict death and destruction on nations."

"Well, if those nations would just cooperate, maybe the transition to being under my rule wouldn't have to be so destructive."

"These people were not your enemy, Sakarabru. You didn't have to do this to them!"

"I needed an army, Ancient, by any means necessary."

"An army against—us?"

"If by the word 'us' you mean Ancients, then yes."

Did he believe that there were more Ancients than there actually were? Had Sakarabru set out to build this massive Brood Army to combat an army he believed Khale led?

"You mean to destroy us all," she said somberly.

His expression changed, softened, and for a moment he looked sincere. "You've always forced my hand, Shifter," he explained. "Your destruction was never what I wanted, but it's always been what you've insisted on, pitting that army of yours between you and me." He shook his head disapprovingly. "But I still believe that I could love you like no other, Shifter."

Sakarabru had sprung up on Theia like a lush tree in the desert. He had just appeared one day, radiant and intoxicating. Khale was young and curious and mesmerized by him. She'd given herself to him completely. She'd loved him and would've done anything to spend eternity with him.

"I remember Kahah," she said introspectively. She didn't have to raise her voice for him to hear her. "They believed that they could be safe in the valley hidden in their caves." She watched his expression harden as she recalled this story. "I can still hear their screams. Their cries still echo in my head."

"Khale! Help us, Khale! Save us!"

But she and her army arrived too late. Sakarabru's Brood swept through that valley like a cyclone, wiping out an entire race.

"They were farmers, Sakarabru," she said bitterly. "They

were helpless, and you killed them, squashed them like insects. There is no love in you, Sakarabru. There never was and there never will be."

"You wound me, Khale." He pressed one hand to his chest. "I left evidence of my love in your womb."

She stiffened.

"And you made her my enemy," he said callously. "Did Mkombozi ever know the truth?" He laughed. "I will admit all day long that I am a monster, Khale. But when will you admit that you are one as well?"

Angry tears fell from her eyes. "You don't know what you're talking about," she shot back.

"The depths of your deceptions are legendary, Ancient. At least to me. Play the victim if you must, Khale, but know this:" He stepped toward her. "You will not get away with using my own flesh and blood against me again. Your reborn—our daughter—will not see the second bond."

"I already know that you've sent soldiers out to kill her, Sakarabru. They won't get close enough to lay a finger on her!"

"Your forces are small, Khale. Your reborn is a human. If she survives all three bonds, she'll still have me to contend with, and I promise you, Daddy will be prepared this time."

The Demon walked out into the water, pressed both arms close to his body, and began to churn, creating a giant waterspout that spun out across the ocean until Khale could no longer see it.

Mkombozi had not known that Sakarabru was her father, and Eden would never know, either. But Khale knew.

And he knew. It was the reason that Mkombozi and now Eden had been designated the Redeemer. Only the offspring of the Demon could bond with the Omens because they were made from the most powerful and dangerous elements of him and were already a part of her.

WAKE-UP CALL

Seer twins Ursa Minor and Ursa Major looked more like eight- or nine-year-old children than Ancient Seers. They squealed and jumped up and down with delight when they saw Runyon dumping out bags of chocolate and red licorice and unloading bottles of rum all over the kitchen table. He laughed at their enthusiasm as they both grabbed handfuls of candy and alcohol, ran circles around him, and collapsed on the floor at his feet.

This place looked like something out of a storybook. A warm, inviting fire burned in the fireplace. Pretty wallpaper with yellow flowers and pristine white-painted wainscoting decorated the walls, along with framed photographs of two girls, both with curly red hair tied with pink ribbons, bright blue eyes, and rose-colored cheeks, together, always smiling and indistinguishable.

Eden soon realized that those images were glamour images of the Troll Sisters, but in reality, they looked like trolls wearing blue ribbons in the thin and oily strands of dirty-blond hair.

"How are my girls doing?" Runyon asked enthusiastically, kneeling down next to them.

"What took you so long?" the one on the left asked.

"You said you were coming weeks ago. We've been waiting."

"Forgive me," he said, apologetically. "I lost track of time, but I promise I'll make it up to you."

The one on the left looked over his shoulder. "Who is he?" she asked, referring to Prophet standing in front of the door. Eden stood right next to him, but they only asked about him, which she found odd.

"He's my best friend," Jarrod responded sarcastically. "And she's Eden."

The two girls leaned in close and whispered, "We already know who she is."

Prophet started to take a step toward the sisters before Runyon raised his hand to stop him. "How do you know her?" Prophet asked cautiously.

"She won't tell you," Runyon explained, standing up and walking over to him. "Neither of them will. Nobody knows which of them is the Heaven Seer and which is the Hell Seer, not even the other Seer sisters. And until now, nobody knew where they were but me."

"Why you?" Prophet asked suspiciously.

"Because he brings us licorice and chocolate," one of them said.

"And rum," the other one added, grinning.

"The sisters are inseparable. They have to be. It's all about balance with these two."

"What do you mean?" Eden asked.

Runyon turned his attention to her. "Imagine knowing the secrets of the universe. Imagine knowing all the good all the time, and all the bad all the time. Too much of anything is a problem, and too much of anything extreme can be crippling. All they need is each other—and me showing up once a month with sweets and booze. They don't leave the house, and no one else until now has ever come inside."

"How do they know me, Jarrod?" Eden asked quietly. Part of her didn't really want to know, but she couldn't help being curious.

Jarrod just looked at her. Without saying a word, he'd spoken volumes.

Eden turned quickly and pushed open the screen door. "I need some air." She was going to be sick.

Prophet followed her outside but stood on the porch and waited while she threw up in the bushes. A few minutes later, Eden came up for air and sat down on the bottom step to steady herself. It felt like the rest of the world was sitting still and she was the one spinning. He came and sat down next to her.

"This is insane," Eden finally said, holding her head in her hands. "How can they know me? They see into heaven and hell, but whose heaven and whose hell? And correct me if I'm wrong, but wouldn't you have to be dead to be in either one of those places?"

He shrugged. "Depends on who you ask."

She looked at him. "What the hell does that even mean?"

"It means that you don't know what it means. Are heaven and hell literal or figurative? Are they actual places or just someone's idea of what either one of those places is? I don't know," he said irritably, responding to the look she was giving him. "I'm just speculating, Eden."

He was trying to help, and Eden appreciated his efforts to try to minimize the gravity of this situation, but deep down she knew that this was one of those things he couldn't protect her from. Prophet couldn't follow her to wherever it was she'd probably have to go to get the second Omen. But it didn't matter. She wasn't so anxious or prepared to go after it anymore, either.

"Sakarabru has destroyed everything," she said to Prophet. "It's never going to be the same."

"No it's not, Eden. So, what are you really trying to say?"

She was about to ask him to take her far, far away from this place, when Khale appeared out of nowhere.

"She has to be dead," Khale said gravely.

Neither of them saw the knife that she drove into Eden's chest.

"Forgive me! Please! Forgive me, Eden!"

Eden heard the roar of the Guardian. She felt the warmth of her own blood soaking into the front of her clothes. She felt the blade of the knife driven into her chest, and she looked up at the stars and took her last breath.

———

Khale couldn't transform fast enough. The Guardian barreled into her and drove her petite form hard into the ground on her back.

"It needed to be done!" Khale yelled, transforming into a silverback gorilla.

Prophet pounded her hard in the face several times before she growled and rolled him over onto his back. She locked her fingers together, raised her powerful arms over her head, and brought them down hard into his chest, knocking the wind out of him. Blood sprayed from the Guardian's mouth.

"It needed to be done!" she yelled again.

"What the hell?" Jarrod slammed open the door.

"The second Omen is in the afterlife! She needed to die!" Khale shouted.

Prophet slammed a solid uppercut under her chin, forcing Khale to roll off of him.

Jarrod rushed down to Eden, lying on the steps with a knife sticking out of her chest.

"Guardian!" he yelled.

Prophet stopped and looked at Eden's lifeless body in Jarrod's arms.

"It needed to be done, Prophet," Khale said desperately, as she began to shift back to Katie Smith. "It is the only way that it can happen."

"This isn't up to you," he said, stumbling over to Eden and gathered her in his arms. "You have no fuckin' right."

"I have every right! Eden was born for this. Nobody else can do it, Tukufu. No one else can save this world."

He didn't want to hear it. Khale had caused all of this. She'd forced this so-called destiny on Mkombozi, and when Mkombozi was lost to it, she killed her, paving the way for Sakarabru to come back. She'd put this bullshit on Eden, leaving it up to her to clean up the shit Khale had created.

"Let's get her inside," Jarrod said solemnly.

Prophet picked her up and carefully carried her up the stairs and inside.

"You're not welcome here, Khale," Jarrod said as he turned to her.

"You can't keep me out of this, Were," she said defiantly.

"Between me and the Guardian, we can give you a run for your money, Khale. If you walk through this door, we'll kill you."

Khale stood frozen, shocked by what she'd just done. But she knew—she knew the moment Jarrod revealed his secret about the twin seers that Eden had to die to make the bond. There was no other way.

"She has to bond," she murmured anxiously. "She has to bond and she has to live."

But what if Khale had sealed their fate? What if Eden couldn't recover from this?

NOW I'M ON MY KNEES

Eden's body gave in to its natural instinct to inhale, but there was no air in this place. Panic set it.

Khale. Khale had . . . Eden reached for her chest—the knife. It was gone, but . . . She staggered to her feet and stretched her eyes open wide to see. . . . She opened her mouth and desperately tried to breathe.

Nothing. Eden turned slowly, looking all around her to try to figure out where she was, but there was nothing. Flat, muted, airless, and soundless. She couldn't even hear herself gasping for air or starting to cry. Eden wrapped her arms tightly around herself and realized that she was naked, but what difference did it make? It was a revelation that meant nothing.

Walk.

The word came out of nowhere but was everywhere, pressing down on top of her and all around her. She began to turn in circles again, looking for the source, looking for who had said that, but she saw no one. There was no one else here but her. Who could've said that if she was the only one here?

Walk.

She took a step and stopped.

Another.

Eden had been confused. She had woken up here afraid that she was completely and utterly alone, but she wasn't. Someone else was here. She opened her mouth and called out to them. But Eden's words were lost in this vacuum of nothingness.

She took another reluctant step and then another and another. Time meant nothing here. Eden had tried to count in her head the number of steps she had taken, measuring the distance that it took for her to move from one place to another.

She walked and walked, but how far? How long? Where was she walking to? She had no idea if the person who'd told her to walk was still here. Eden stopped and waited, listening for the sound of the voice again. Despair set in when she didn't hear it. Hopelessness washed over her. She was alone. Eden stood there, trembling and searching all around her for signs of something, anything.

His name was gone from her memory. The one she had . . . No. She would call him and he would come, but . . . she couldn't remember his name, his face. She slowly sank to her knees and desperately searched her memories for him. He would help her. If she could remember him, then she could call him and he'd come. He'd take her from this place and she'd be all right. She'd be fine because the two of them would be together, but she needed to call out his name, which escaped her.

Eden was suddenly off the ground. Her body was being pulled through the air with a terrifying force.

I said walk.

She landed facedown and at someone's feet. A woman's feet. Eden raised her head to see who was standing in front of her, but a blow came out of nowhere, her head jerked back, and Eden sailed again through the air, landing on her back.

How dare you defy me?

Before she could even recover from the last blow, another one jolted her midsection, another followed to her chin, and another cracked the middle of her spine.

How dare you make me wait?

Who are you? Eden wanted to ask. What do you want with me? Her own words were her enemy. They betrayed her and left her helpless against this . . . thing.

How dare you leave me here?

Another crippling blow landed on Eden's side and forced her over on her back. She looked up to see the face of this . . . this . . . She had no face.

She squatted down next to Eden, grabbed a handful of Eden's hair, and jerked back her head. She pressed the sharp tip of a weapon against Eden's jugular.

She had no face. She was naked like Eden but stronger, bigger, more powerful.

Now you come for me?

She had no face, no mouth, so how was it able to speak?

Now you choose me?

She released her hold on Eden's hair and viciously slammed her head back down onto the ground, then slowly stalked circles around her, whispering a song in Ancient tongue. That song—familiar! Eden had heard it before, but where? How could she know this language? How could she know this song?

Two for three
Bring me
Redeem me
Or die the lamb.

Eden struggled to sit up and mouthed the words to the song, sung by the female circling her. Two for three. Two. She had said two and not one. This was her, the second Omen. Dear God! Eden wasn't ready! Pain ripped through her broken body, but this song held a place in her memory, an Ancient memory born long before Eden had come into her own life.

Eden continued singing without noticing that her voice had finally come to her and blended with that of the other female. She continued singing long after the other female had stopped and towered over her.

This was the song of the Omens. It was the song of her destiny.

You can have me, the female told her, *but you will have to fight for me.*

Fight for her? This bitch wanted Eden in a battle? She

couldn't take her eyes off the weapon the female gripped as she circled Eden. The handle was wrapped in what looked to be gold threading or rope. Three long blades that looked like spearheads extended from it, two in the front, curving downward, and one straight blade extended from the back. A shorter extension came from the center of the unit, which splayed out on either side with smaller curved blades, looking almost like a boat.

She kicked Eden in the face again, grabbed her by the throat, and hooked one of the larger blades around the back of Eden's neck. She forced Eden up off of her knees and held her up in the air until the tips of her toes barely scraped the ground underneath.

Fight me, Redeemer. Win me. Or stay here with me—for eternity.

She let Eden's body fall and crumple to the ground. Eden closed her eyes. Was this her death? Her hell? Certainly it wasn't heaven. The image of the fire came into focus in her mind's eye. Eden saw herself sitting near that flame, warmed by it, mesmerized by it and entranced by it.

"*She will keep you there,*" *the Demon said, sitting across from her.* "*She will torture you*"—*he laughed*—"*while you beg your God to intervene, but no intervention will come.*"

Claim me, Redeemer. If you can.

Eden looked at him, his face still cloaked by the hood of his robe. "*She's too strong.*"

He leaned back and sighed. "*Then it ends here, Eden.*" *The Demon knew her name. He waved his hand and put out the flame.*

Darkness closed in around her, smothering her, filling her with un-
natural fear, Isolation, and something else.

"Bring it back!" *she shouted to him. Eden's voice echoed all*
around her. Rage ran hot through her veins. "Bring it back to me,"
she demanded again, wringing her hands together.

She had feared that fire. She had loved it. She had recoiled
from it, but eventually she had been drawn dangerously close to it
and had found comfort in it. He had no right to take it from her.
Eden had been brave. She had been careful with it, and she had
honored it.

"Bring it back, Demon," *she demanded.*

But it was gone. It wasn't coming back. He had taken it from
her, and she had nothing.

Eden opened her eyes again in time to see the bottom of
the female's foot less than an inch from her face. Eden caught
and held it.

I am the warrior, Redeemer. I will not be claimed so easily as
my sister.

Eden had wished for death time and time again, and now
that she had it, she realized that the peace she'd hoped it
would bring didn't exist here. She pushed the female hard
enough to knock her off balance, stumbling backward. There
was no peace in death for her.

Fight me!

All of a sudden, Eden noticed that the symbol on her arm
began to glow and grow warm.

Coward! The female shouted, steadying herself. She ran
toward Eden.

The sound of the Demon's laughter came to her. *"She is your enemy, Redeemer. She is your prize."*

Eden planted her feet, drew back her arm, and landed a fist that sent her opponent sailing through the air. This female was the warrior in him, his rage. But she lacked reason. She lacked control and intuition. She lacked the strength of Sakarabru's mind.

The female landed on her feet and came running back to Eden again. Eden stood there, watching the chaos that was the second Omen. The first Omen could control her. Maybe.

Eden lowered her head, drew back her arm, and curled her hand into a fist, planting it hard into the jaw of the female, caving it in and forcing her to drop to her knees at Eden's feet.

The first Omen was the mind, the very soul of the Demon, and this one needed the mind to control it. It was time, finally, to claim what was hers.

Eden spun around, raised her leg, and landed with a kick to the side of the Omen's head. As her body disintegrated, Eden stepped back, raised her arms, inhaled, and waited.

SAVE THE NIGHT

Prophet had long since drowned out the incessant giggling of the two Seers in the living room, getting high on sugar and drunk on rum. Runyon's attempts to somehow calm or comfort Prophet had fallen on deaf ears as the Guardian gradually shut out the rest of the world and cleared his head to hear only the sound of her voice. Eden lay on a bed in a small back room of the house, and for all intents and purposes, she was dead.

Prophet knelt on the floor beside her with his head bowed, his eyes closed, and waited. If even a hint of her was still there then he would go to her, he would get her and bring her back from whatever hell she was in, even if it took him another four thousand years to find her again.

Khale would pay for this. He raised his head and stared into Eden's beautiful face. Had he ever told her that he thought she was beautiful? No. He couldn't remember ever saying it, but he believed it. She was her own kind of beauty, effortless and timeless. There was vulnerability in her eyes, but also a determination that showed just how strong she could be when she put her mind to it.

She had a subtle, quiet attraction about her that was stunning when you stopped and paid attention, and over time Eden would mature into a breathtaking and regal older woman. He'd hoped he'd have a chance to watch it happen. Prophet had waited four thousand years to find her, and she had been worth every single one of them.

He needed to stretch his legs and stood up and walked over to the window. The sky was clear tonight and gave no indication of the madness taking place in this world. What if she didn't wake up? If she didn't, then this life would have no more use for him, and he doubted that Khale had put another plan in place to rebirth another Redeemer. And even if she did, what difference would it make? He had waited for this one. And this one was the only one who mattered.

"We've got company," Jarrod said, bursting into the room.

Prophet glanced down into the overgrown brush behind the house and saw movement.

"I think they're Brood," Jarrod added.

Prophet stood there, rigid and unreactive.

"You coming?"

Why should he? This battle would be one of many that they would all ultimately lose. The Demon had taken this world. Fighting for it now seemed fuckin' pointless.

"Guess I'm on my own then," the Were said, frustrated, before leaving.

There had to be dozens of them down there, judging from the activity Prophet could see from the upstairs window. He turned to look at Eden. The growl of the Were invited him to a fight. They'd come looking for her. And they'd found her but too late. He wouldn't let them desecrate her remains. No. Even in death, the Demon still could not have her.

Prophet crashed through the glass, leaping from the window, and landed on his feet as he hit the ground.

Paul wasn't interested in the Were or even the Guardian. She was inside. She was the reason that he was here. He waited in the darkness, watching from a distance as the Brood went at the Ancients, but these two were behemoths compared to the smaller and inexperienced Brood. The Were was much larger than those he'd fought a few days ago. Even without asking the question, Paul could see that he was an Alpha.

The Guardian came from behind the house, cracking heads and breaking backs as he circled to where the Brood attacked the Were. If nothing else, the Brood at least had numbers on their side. But none of them were as big or as strong as Paul. They had their purpose though, as he had his, but he needed them to create the distraction. While the Guardian and Were were occupied, he snaked his way through the trees to get to the back of the house.

Paul forced open the door that had been dead-bolted and went inside. The first room was a kitchen, small and outdated. He walked through to a dining room and then into the living room. Two strange-looking creatures sat crossed-legged on the floor, looking up at him. They were fuckin' ugly as all get out, with what looked like chocolate smeared around their mouths. One of them turned up a bottle of what looked to be whiskey, like a seasoned alcoholic, and then swiped the back of her hand across her mouth.

"She's dead upstairs," the one on the left said.

"But you already know that," the other one finished.

He expected them to scream or to come at him with maybe some weird ninja skills, but they just wallowed in the debris of empty wrappers surrounding them and continued eating as if he didn't even matter. Paul stepped over them, glanced out of the window to see that the two Ancients were still occupied, and then ascended the stairs.

Paul pushed open three doors before he found her. He walked over to the bed and looked down at this woman—small, brown, her shirt covered in what looked like blood, and then he looked around the room as if maybe there would be someone else in there. She couldn't have been what had Lord Sakarabru all up in arms. He leaned down close to her and put his ear to her mouth to see if she was even breathing. She wasn't.

"He's upstairs with her," he heard one of those girls—or whatever—say to someone.

Then he heard the pounding of somebody running up those stairs. Paul had a choice to make. Get the girl and go, or kick some ass, then get the girl and go? He grabbed the reborn's lifeless body, tossed her over his shoulder, and burst through the shattered glass window of the bedroom. As soon as he landed, he heard her take a breath and twisted her small body from his grasp.

He hadn't seen the weapon when he'd grabbed her. She was fast. Too damn fast. The reborn stayed low to the ground, using her size to her advantage. She spun like a top, turning from right to left, swinging that damned thing into his calves and thighs, stabbing him over and over again until his legs began to feel like tenderized meat.

Chapman was suddenly grabbed from behind, around his neck. A knee pushed into his spine, forcing his belly outward. She sliced him across the middle. Chapman reached over his head, grabbed a handful of dreadlocks, and twisted the head of the Guardian until his body had no choice but to follow and flip over his shoulder, nearly landing on top of and crushing the girl. But she slid between Chapman's legs before she was crushed, and from behind, drove one of the blades of that damn weapon deep into his side.

The Guardian was up too quickly. Fuckin' giant black wings came out of nowhere! He grabbed Chapman by the collar of his coat, and the next thing the Brood knew, he was airborne. He fought, pounding on the fists of the Guardian as hard as he could, but the motherfucker was determined. Paul had no idea how high they had flown or how far they'd gone, but the last thing he remembered thinking before the Guardian let go was *It's gonna fucking hurt when I hit the ground!*

Prophet didn't hang around to see him land. Eden called to him.

"Guardiaaaaaaannn!" she screamed over and over again hysterically.

He flew faster than he'd ever flown in his life, landed, and stared at her as if he were looking at a ghost.

The Were looked scared shitless. Eden, covered in blood, stood in the middle of the yard trembling and holding what looked like a *kpinga*, an Ancient blade once used for ceremonies on Theia. She seemed to notice it for the first time and then she looked for him.

"It was hers," she said, wide-eyed and breathless. "I fought her. She made me fight her—the Omen—the second Omen!"

"You bonded?" Prophet asked apprehensively.

Eden nodded. "It's mine now," she said, referring to the weapon and then she thought for a moment. "She's mine, Prophet. The second Omen is mine now." Confusion filled her eyes as she ran to him and jumped into his arms. Prophet held on to her so tightly he thought he'd break her, and then he saw it: a new symbol had been branded onto her other arm; a large circle with a small starburst inside it. Eden had made and survived the second bond.

"It's all right, baby," he murmured and kissed her shoulder. "I'm here. I'm right here."

"Get me out of here," she commanded him. "Please! Get me away from here!"

THE TERROR
OF KNOWING

He woke up to her touch, as always. Lilith stood naked at the foot of the bed and then began to slither up to Kifo, lying on his back and facing the ceiling. "I've missed you, Kifo," she purred. Lilith steadied herself over him and then pressed her lips to his. The sweeping flavor of her tongue still excited him. Everything about Lilith would always excite him. She rested the weight of her beautiful curves on top of him. "I've stayed away too long," she whispered, sliding her hand down to his erection and wrapping her long slender fingers around it. He wanted so badly to be in her mouth.

She seemed to read his mind and smiled. "You've been distant, Kifo," she said softly. "I can usually sense when you need me, but . . ." She shrugged her soft shoulders. "You know that I am here for you whenever you need me. You know that I am never far away. Don't you?"

Wisps of white bangs flirted with her beautiful blue eyes, which shone like crystals, even in the dark.

"I know, Lilith," he said, still wishing she'd take him in her lovely mouth.

Lilith planted sweet kisses on his chest and flicked her tongue around his nipples.

She raised her face to him and pouted. "Then you should also know how I hate being away from you for too long."

"Really?" he asked. "Why's that?"

For the briefest of moments, she looked unprepared. But Lilith recovered quickly. "Because I love you," she said, all too naturally. "Don't be silly, Kifo," she added.

Lilith was a spy. She was Sakarabru's whorish little spy who kept tabs on all of the major players in the Demon's game to make sure that none of them slipped and fell out of this torturous spell that they were all under. The Demon had done terrible things to his body but even worse things to his mind, things that still held Kifo under his power. Kifo had done things to others all for the promise of Lilith's love and Sakarabru's acceptance.

Kifo smiled and guided the slut's face down to where he wanted her the most. "I love you too."

So much of his own life had been disrupted by the return of Sakarabru. Kifo's favorite dry cleaner and tailor had shut down shop, and now he had nowhere to get his suits cleaned. His favorite Creole restaurant was gone, and the jazz club he'd frequented at least once a week was gone now, too. He roamed through the empty streets of New Orleans, unseen, disgusted by what his beloved city had become.

Kifo stood looking through the window of the place where he used to buy his ties. A woman's reflection appeared behind him. Naturally, she couldn't see him, or . . .

She smiled at him. The woman wore a bright yellow hat with a wide brim, dark cat-eye sunglasses, reminiscent of the kind that women wore in the fifties, and a white dress covered in small yellow flowers, belted at the waist and flaring out at her knees. A small white purse looped over her dainty arm, her delicate hands covered by a pair of white gloves. On her feet she wore a white pair of pointed-toe stilettos.

"You finally understand," she said kindly to him, nodding her head approvingly.

"Understand?" he asked, still amazed by the fact that she could actually see him.

The woman reached out and touched his hand lightly with her fingertips. "My heart breaks for what he did to you," she said, her voice cracking.

Kifo carefully pulled his hand away and studied her suspiciously. "Andromeda?"

Andromeda was a legend, a myth. Even if she were real, Andromeda was not this woman. She couldn't have been. This woman was pretty and sensible. She wasn't the blubbering mess he'd heard that Andromeda was, cursed by too many visions conflicting and crashing into each other.

"You do something to me." She shrugged and chuckled. "I can't explain it, Kifo, but it is such a lovely feeling. You calm my storm, and for that I am grateful."

Was she really the Seer of the Ages? She could see him in his invisible form; not even Ancients could see the Djinn when he didn't want to be seen.

"What do you want?" he asked, still not convinced that she was who she said she was.

"To see the prophecy fulfilled," she admitted simply. "What do *you* want?"

He couldn't put his finger on it, but she did something to him, too—calmed his storm, maybe. But there was something about her that he found comfortable and comforting.

"To no longer be a slave to the Demon," he admitted out loud, and the sound of saying it shocked him.

She nodded approvingly. "That I do understand," she said warmly.

It was said that Andromeda could be in more than one place at a time. And that at any given moment, she could be living in the past, present, or future. "May fifth, 2014." He said the day's date out loud. "That's today, Andromeda. That's where I am today. Where are you?"

She shrugged. "Here."

"When are you here?"

She thought about it before answering. "Now."

"Now as in May fifth, 2014?"

Andromeda stared blankly at him. "Does it matter?"

It didn't, but . . .

Andromeda started walking. Without hesitating, he walked with her.

"Your friend dies horribly," she said dismally.

"My friend?"

"Your lover. The succubus, Lilith."

Lilith was a succubus? Of course. He should've known it.

"Not by his hand of course, but by yours."

He was stunned. "I don't think that I could ever hurt her."

She looked at him and smiled. "Love can make one do amazing things. Betrayal can make one absolutely terrifying. Not many can resist her. I applaud you for your resilience."

"But I didn't resist," he said disappointedly. "I've been under her spell for too long, Andromeda."

"Yes, but you broke free from it, Djinn. And you should be pleased."

"But I can't let her know," he said. "She'll tell Sakarabru that I'm not blind anymore to what he did to me. And as you probably know, he doesn't take well to failures."

"Ah, but you haven't failed, Kifo." She stopped and looked at him. "The terrible thing about being me is that I know what has happened, what is happening, and what will happen." She frowned. "The great thing about being me is the same thing." She smiled. "The Demon needed to come back. The Redeemer needed to be reborn, and unfortunately for you my friend, you needed to be the one who resurrected Sakarabru."

Kifo looked around the two of them, at the chaos and destruction that was a result of all of these things happening, and he was angry. "Did we need to do this, Andromeda? Did we really need to destroy these people and what has been our home since Theia fell?"

She nodded. "Yes," she said sadly.

Kifo wasn't buying it. He wasn't going to accept that the

Ancients had the right to play these types of games at the expense of others like this. "I disagree, Seer." This once-vibrant and historic neighborhood was nothing more than a ghost town now. And Kifo was as much to blame, if not more, than any of them. He had brought Sakarabru back. He had built up his army. Societies were ruined because of him, and in his heart, he knew that he'd never forgive himself for the part he'd played in this.

"This is what you see, Kifo, and it's all you see. Of course your heart is broken, as it should be. But trust me when I say that this is only a small part of a bigger picture. A painful part, but a necessary one. I created the Omens out of desperation and rage. But I underestimated the power of the ages. The Omens are necessary if we ever have any chance of defeating Sakarabru, but in my haste, I neglected to think of what they could ultimately do to her and to this universe."

"Mkombozi nearly destroyed the universe," said Kifo.

"If Khale hadn't stopped her, she would've."

"So are you saying that this reborn is going to suffer the same fate as Mkombozi? That she's going to lose control to the Omens as well, and that Khale will have to use the same spell against her? And then what, Andromeda? Does it start over, and do we relive this nightmare?"

Andromeda shook her head. "You are thinking ahead of yourself, Kifo. Too much thinking can overwhelm you. Trust me. I know."

Andromeda was a sweet and kind woman, but she was

dismissing his perception of the gravity of this situation, and it was pissing him off.

"For now, you only have to worry about one thing," she said to him.

"What, Andromeda?"

She walked over to him and looped her arm into the crook of his elbow. "Taking me back to your Demon."

THE REAL ME ON
THE SHELF

Eden had no idea where Prophet had taken her, but her blood was burning. She felt the soft grass underneath her feet when he lowered her to the ground, but then she smelled it as it singed.

"My blood is boiling," she said desperately, stepping away from him. Her skin felt as if it were on fire, and Eden couldn't stop shaking. She looked at him and she loved him, but she knew that she could hurt him, too. God! She didn't want to hurt him.

"You have to leave me here," she demanded.

He took a step toward her. "No."

He had to leave. "Go!" she shouted, hurling Prophet through the air with her thoughts as if he were a piece of paper.

It was too much. Too much—inside her. Eden fell to her knees at the weight of it, and she had no choice but to release it. Raw power, blasting from her in every direction. It was too much. And she wasn't strong enough to . . . to stop it. To control it. All rage, pure and chaotic rage, exploding from her and destroying everything around her.

In her mind she prayed, *Please let him be okay. Please let him be okay.*

She would die if he did.

"Calm the sister," she said to herself, "subdue her rage."

In her mind she stood in front of her fire—her fire, not the Demon's. He stood to challenge Eden, to claim what had once been his, but it wasn't his anymore.

"I need it," she told Sakarabru.

"I don't care. It doesn't belong to you. It's mine."

The fire began to rise with their argument. It burned hotter and out of control.

He jumped through it and over the cauldron to get to Eden. His form changed from that of a male on two legs to that of a bull on four.

"Take the fire. Kill the bull. Calm the sister," Eden said.

Eden stopped the bull a second before he would impale her with his horns. She dug into the ground with her heels, bent her knees, and held him back.

"It . . . belongs . . . to . . . me," she said, gritting her teeth.

The bull was powerful, but Eden was determined. Control of the fire would give her control over the sister Omen's rage. She could calm the sister, but only if the Demon relinquished his flame to her.

Eden took a step, pushing the bull back and away from her. She took another step and another, forcing him to retreat. The two Omens played off of each other. The first Omen was made stronger by the rage of the second. The second would be made docile by the influence of the first.

He was angered by her strength. Surprised by it. But eventually, the bull grew too tired to fight her.

"You can't win," she told him.

Defeat and, eventually, submission shone in his eyes. The bull slowly changed back into the form of the Demon and fell on the floor exhausted.

She looked back at the fire—her fire—and saw that it had calmed.

Eden opened her eyes and stared out of the window at the blue sky. Prophet lay behind her, still sleeping, with his arm draped across her. Ever the Guardian, he woke up as soon as she moved this time.

"What? What's . . . what's up?" he asked, still half asleep.

Eden had no idea what was up. One minute she was caught up in the vortex of darkness, and the next, she was lying in bed next to him as if nothing had ever happened.

"You okay?" he asked cautiously.

She thought long and hard before answering. "I don't know. Am I?"

Now it was his turn to think about it. "Probably."

"I thought I hurt you," she said, avoiding the word "killed" on purpose.

He rubbed the back of his head. "Yeah, well . . ."

"I'm sorry. I am so sorry."

"I don't need your apologies. You're here and I'm cool."

"What did I do?" she asked reluctantly. "Did I hurt any-one?"

"Just a monster of a Brood who had it coming." He shrugged. "And you may have rearranged some of the land-scaping a bit around here."

"What do you mean?"

They got up out of bed and he led her outside and showed her what he meant. Eden and Prophet stood at the edge of a crater the length of about ten football fields and as wide as a small canyon.

"I did this?"

He pulled her closer and kissed the side of her face. "The Omens in you did this," he corrected her.

To actually see with her own eyes what she was capable of was overpowering. What was she becoming? Or rather, what had she become? Her body was toxic now with the es-sence and the rage of Sakarabru. There wasn't much of her left anymore. The notion to duck and cover or to run was nothing more than a faint memory now, as Eden quietly and surprisingly embraced whatever it was that she was becom-ing. "Insecure" had been her middle name. Eden had suffered through an identity crisis her whole life. The sense of accep-tance she felt now should have alarmed her, but it didn't.

"Was it like this for Mkombozi?" she eventually asked, reflectively.

"It was tough," was all he'd say.

"When did you realize you'd lost her, Prophet?"

He got very quiet. "Not until Khale took her away from me."

Either he was lying or he was just being kind. But Eden suspected that he had known long before then that Mkombozi was lost to the power and influence of the Omens.

Eden could feel herself slipping away from him, and she knew that it was only a matter of time before the impact of the Guardian on her life and in her heart would be ineffective.

"How long can we stay here?" she asked.

He shrugged. "For a while. Long enough for you to rest."

Eden had passed that point of no return. Maybe it was in his nature to try to pad the reality of the situation with softer versions of the truth, but she knew better. This was nearly over, and she was ready for it to be, whatever that meant. If by her sacrifice she could rid this world of Sakarabru and give it a chance to repair itself, to rebuild, and to become whatever it was meant to become now, then she'd make that sacrifice. Losing him would be her only regret when the dust settled.

"Let's go back inside," he said, quietly. "I feel like making love to you."

She forced a smile. "I'll try to be gentle with you." It was a joke, sort of.

"Please do."

Neither one of them wanted this to end. He pressed her back against the wall in the shower and filled her body up with his. The two of them kissed slowly, stared into each other's eyes, and stayed locked together, barely moving until the water started to run cold. This wasn't about orgasms or even the pleasure of sex. It was about the bond between them that had lasted for more than four thousand years. It was about sealing the connection that would last as many lifetimes as either of them had or would have.

He didn't have to say he loved her. Eden felt his love inside her.

END OF THE INNOCENCE

J arrod had gotten word to them that the Ancients were gathering in New York. If it had been up to Prophet, he and Eden would have stayed hidden in that cabin in the South Carolina woods and left the rest of the world to its own devices. She needed time to rest, to adjust. But Eden had finally given in to her fate. She'd not only given in to it, but she was running straight for it, almost as if she couldn't wait to get it over with.

Prophet took his time driving up the coast from South Carolina headed back to New York City. Eden's head rested on his shoulder as she slept. The miracle of his life was that he had found her again. She had been reborn, giving him a second chance to finish loving her and to correct the mistakes he'd made with Mkombozi.

Eden's survival of this second bond was as much a blessing as it was a curse. Twice she should have died, and twice she had miraculously survived the bonds with two of the most dangerous elements ever to come from Theia. How was it possible? And what did it mean? She was Mkombozi, reborn, but she was also human. By Ancient standards, Eden was frail, helpless, and certainly not capable of going up against Sakarabru. Khale had used dark and forbidden magic to bring Mkombozi back. He couldn't help wondering how dark and how forbidden.

The second Omen had begun a transformation in Mkombozi that made her volatile and unpredictable. She was always angry and too eager to fight, even with him.

"Never make the mistake of believing that you are superior to me, Guardian," she warned him once.

Tukufu humbly bowed his head. "That thought has never crossed my mind, Beloved. Not now. Not ever."

He looked up at her and waited, hoping that she would be amused by his antics. Mkombozi's dark eyes bore holes into him and Prophet's knees suddenly became weak, until he could no longer stand and he dropped to the floor at her feet.

"Let me go, Beloved," he said through gritted teeth. He had always offered his humility to her willingly. She'd never had reason to take it from him.

"My love for you is boundless, Beloved," she responded. "But I will not suffer your teasing and taunts."

It wasn't her talking. She would never have spoken to him or treated him like this. It was the Omens, the essence of a Demon.

Mkombozi squatted down in front of him and used the handle of her kpinga to raise his face to hers. "She is mine now, Guardian. The Omen of war, the source of the Demon's strength."

"And are you hers?" he challenged, taking his life in his own hands.

Mkombozi surprised him and laughed. "Stand, Guardian." She stood up and stepped back. *"You really do need to work on your sense of humor Tukufu. Or maybe it's my humor that needs work."*

There were moments where Mkombozi seemed eager to succumb to the influence of the Omens. She was almost too easily swayed by them, too ready to submit to what they wanted her to become. Prophet couldn't help wondering how soon it would be before Eden relinquished herself to them.

Prophet pulled up and parked in front of Khale's Lower Manhattan apartment building. Ancients of every kind crowded in front of the place waiting and watched as Eden and Prophet climbed out of the car and headed for the front door.

"Please! Redeemer, don't do this to us again!"

"There are other solutions! Other ways!"

"This world doesn't need you! It deserves a chance to heal from this! We all do!"

Eden marched on in front of Prophet like a determined soldier, unflinching and unwavering. Word had spread quickly that she'd survived the second bond, and now opposition to her role as Redeemer was growing. She wasn't the heroine to the Ancients that Mkombozi had been when she was declared their Redeemer. They were afraid of Eden, terrified that she'd do to Earth what Mkombozi had ultimately done to Theia.

Isis stood at the entrance and blocked their way through the door.

"Are you so determined to see that history repeats itself, Guardian?" She looked over Eden's head and glared at Prophet.

Other Ancients continued shouting at the two of them.

"Get out of the way, Isis," he told her.

"Listen to them. They don't want this. No one wants her here, Guardian," she argued, still not acknowledging that Eden was even in the vicinity. "There are other alternatives," Isis reasoned. "We can fight the Brood. Some of us have relationships with the humans; we've talked to them and they're willing to stand alongside us in this. With their army, their air force and naval resources, we can beat them, Tukufu, and we wouldn't have to destroy a world to do it."

Eden walked up to Isis and stood within inches of the Ancient. "Move," she boldly demanded. Isis stood six inches taller than Eden and made the mistakes of staring down her nose at the reborn Redeemer. Before Isis could open her mouth to say another word, Eden reached up, wrapped her hand around Isis's throat, and forced the much taller Ancient down to the ground on her knees.

"I am so not in a good mood right now," Eden told her. "I've got an Omen in me that's itching to break something and your neck is feeling pretty damned good in my hand."

Isis gagged and stared up at Eden with bulging eyes.

Prophet glanced around at an already nervous crowd slowly backing away from the three of them. This definitely not a good PR moment for the Redeemer, but if her intent was to scare the shit out of everyone by taking down one of

Khale's fiercest and most deadly Generals, then she'd certainly succeeded.

"Maybe you should let her go?" he offered. "We really need to go inside."

It was a half-assed effort on his part, but at the moment, it was all he had.

"We'll go in when this Ancient addresses me with respect," Eden shot back. "Today. Tomorrow." Eden shrugged. "One of these days, Isis, you and I are going to share some girl time."

Eden released the grip on Isis's neck and shoved her back onto the pavement.

Isis came to her senses, stood up, and reluctantly stepped aside.

Jarrod was the first one to greet them as they entered and closed the door behind them. He approached Eden as if she were radioactive.

"How's it going?" he asked pensively.

She nodded. "I'm not gonna bite you, Jarrod."

He looked to Prophet for permission to sort of hug her. When he got close, Eden frowned and he jerked back.

She smiled. "Kidding."

"Who else is here?" Prophet asked.

Jarrod motioned toward the parlor. Khale was standing there. Prophet was surprised she'd be here, and so she shouldn't be surprised when he finished kicking her ass. He started toward her to do just that, but Eden put her hand against his chest.

"No," she murmured.

He looked into Eden's eyes. She shook her head. Eden didn't exactly soothe the savage beast, but she managed to put him back in his cage, for the time being.

"I knew you could do it," Khale said to Eden. "There's no way I would've done that if I didn't think you were strong enough to survive."

"You suspected that I *might* survive, but you weren't sure. Were you?" Eden asked.

Khale tried to smile. "I'd hoped that I was right."

"You put a fuckin' knife in her, Khale." Prophet was livid. "You can see where someone might have a problem with this. Right?"

Khale slowly approached the two of them. "She did it, Guardian." She spoke calmly.

"She might not have done it, Khale," he shot back. "And if she hadn't, then you and I would not be having this conversation right now."

"No, because you'd be dead," Khale threatened.

Prophet started to charge her, but Jarrod stepped between him and Khale. "Whoa, brother."

Prophet glared at him. "I'm not your fuckin' brother!"

The Were shrugged. "It was a figure of speech, man."

Jarrod's dumb ass must've thought he was being funny when he lightly tagged Prophet in the arm, but it was a dangerous move on his part.

Khale looked at Eden.

"Careful, Khale," Eden warned with a smirk on her face. "That knife trick is not going to work a second time."

Khale nodded. "I know, sweetheart," she said, sounding

believably sincere. "It broke my heart to have to do that to you."

Good girl. Eden didn't look like she believed the Shifter's lies any more than Prophet did.

"Once I understood where the Omen was, I knew what had to happen," Khale explained. "You had to cross over to the afterlife to get to it, Eden. I couldn't see any other way. There was no other way."

Eden studied the Shifter long and hard before she finally responded to that nonsense. "When I was small, MyRose used to ask me why I didn't seem to care for you. She'd ask me why I didn't like you." Eden paused.

Khale's warm expression turned to ice as she waited for Eden to tell her. But Eden pushed past her.

"Is there anything to eat?" Eden asked, going into the living room and then searching for the kitchen. "I'm starving."

Kale had gathered the heads of Ancient nations: Aelia, the leader of the Mer nation. Jarrod of course was the leader of the Weres. Prophet was the only Guardian in attendance. Since The Fall, the Guardians kept their distance from Prophet. It was his oath to the Redeemer that had alienated him from his brethren. Mkombozi had killed so many, including those whom other Guardians had sworn oaths to. A Guardian's Oath was his purpose, and without it, he was hollow. Isis was there to represent the masses. She spoke for the Ancients outside on the front lawn who wanted no part of this prophecy fulfillment.

"You had no right, Khale," Isis said fervently, sitting across from the Shifter, "no right to do this." She glanced at Eden.

"We can fight the Brood. We have humans on our side and together we can—"

"What will you do about the Demon, Isis?" Aelia probed. Aelia truly did have a face that resembled that of a fish. In the water she was as graceful as a dancer, but on dry land, she had to use a wheelchair to get around, shrouded from head to toe in wet coverings to keep her skin from drying out. "He poisoned our waters on Theia. He'll do the same here."

"The human Brood aren't as powerful as Theian Brood," Isis argued. "Once we know what we're dealing with, we can beat them! They're still human! Their bodies still have the same human frailties and disadvantages. Sure, they may be a bit stronger and faster, and they have the advantage of numbers on their side. If we come together with the humans, we can defeat this army, Ancients," she said passionately. Isis avoided looking at Eden. "And we won't have to rely on prophecies."

Before anyone could stop her, Eden had crossed the room, grabbed a handful of Isis's hair, and jerked back her head. "You are alive because of me, Ancient," she snarled in Isis's face. "Disrespect me again and I will tear off your fuckin' head!"

"Eden," Prophet said, gently grabbing hold of her arm and pulling her away from Isis. "You've made your point."

He led her back to her seat next to him. This was the Redeemer that everyone was afraid of. This was the evidence he'd been looking for since the second bond. The influence of the Omens was beginning to claim her and take her from him after all, the way they'd taken Mkombozi.

"And what of Sakarabru, Isis?" Khale asked, coolly acting as if nothing had happened. "Do you think that if we simply kill off his Brood Army that he'll surrender? Settle down, marry a nice woman, and retire perhaps?" she finished, sarcastically.

"Sakarabru won't retire," Eden finally said. "He won't go away quietly and live among us in peace." She stared at Isis and spoke as if she knew the Demon personally. "He will level this world if he has to, just to prove that he can. He'll crush the humans and the Ancients, add water, and get his mystics to mold them all over again into whatever he wants them to be. I used to think that Sakarabru had already turned my world into hell on Earth, but he's just getting started and if I can stop him, I will."

Without saying another word, Eden stood up and left the gathering.

"Guardian," Khale called after him as he turned to leave. "Are you as ready for this as she is?"

He left the room without answering.

MAGIC MOMENTS

Tell him you seduced me," Andromeda said, batting her
eyelashes. "Tell him that you made love to me with such
passion that I swore my unending devotion to you and
willingly agreed to follow you anywhere."

Kifo laughed.

"Tell him I'm a stalker and that you friended me on Facebook
and that I've been tracking you like a desperate nutcase that you've
had to get a restraining order against because you fear for your
safety." Andromeda had asked Kifo to bring her to Sakarabru. And she'd made him promise not to interfere.

"You will solidify his trust in you, Kifo," she explained.
"Taking me to him will endear you to him even more."

Andromeda was not at all like he'd imagined she'd be. She
was sentimental, considerate, and cunning. In the short
time he'd known her, the last thing in the world he would

want to do was to hurt her or to let anyone else hurt her. But he knew what would happen if she made him do this.

"Andromeda, he'll punish you. He'll torture you in the most horrific ways. You can't ask me to do this!"

"But I do ask this of you, Kifo, and more. I don't make this request lightly. I have been in the company of Sakarabru before and I know what he is capable of," she admitted solemnly. "I know what he will do to me, because he's done it before."

Andromeda was talking in riddles. "When? When were you with him?" he asked.

The Seer smiled. "There you go again—talking about time. Time is nothing to me, Kifo. How do you expect for me to measure here and now against then and tomorrow?" She shrugged. "I can't. Not when they are all the same to me."

Kifo was numb. She would willingly ask him to take her to the torment that Sakarabru would inflict upon her, and expect him to do nothing? It didn't make sense.

"Why, Andromeda?" he asked. "You can't expect for me to do this without telling me why."

"How else do you think she'll get the third Omen, Kifo?" Andromeda's brown eyes twinkled. "Of course she'll have to come for it. And it will be waiting for her when she needs it the most."

Andromeda had been right. Lord Sakarabru could not believe his good fortune when Kifo came to him with Andromeda as his prisoner. He laughed and praised Kifo as if he were his true champion. He promised Kifo anything he wanted and told him that all he had to do was ask. And then he had his Brood take her away.

Kifo stood in the darkest corner of the room watching in silent despair and in horror at the terrible things Sakarabru was doing to her. Andromeda's screams had long since turned to disgusting, strangled gurgles. The stench of blood and excrement permeated the room. Her pretty dress lay torn, stained, and crumpled on the floor, covered in layers of skin and saturated in blood.

The thrill in Sakarabru's eyes was undeniable. He could've had his Brood torture her. He could've tormented her with his mind and not laid a finger on her, but the Demon relished bathing in her sweat and tearing away her flesh with his bare hands. As Kifo stood there watching, memories hidden in the darkest spaces of his mind began to awaken. Andromeda's screams became Kifo's. The blood slathered on the Demon's face became Kifo's blood.

"You should tell me what it looks like, Seer," Sakarabru growled in her face. "Tell me what the Omen looks like so that I can stop searching for it."

Andromeda gurgled some unintelligible sound. Sakarabru laughed and then scraped the tip of the iron knife against exposed tendons. "Atta girl! Make me work for it!"

Before he'd brought her here to Sakarabru's torture chamber, Kifo had learned so much from her about the Omens that she'd made him promise never to speak of them with anyone.

"What are the Omens, Andromeda? What are they, exactly?"

Her delicate mannerisms and nature were old-fashioned and

charming and brought out Kifo's most gentlemanlike qualities. She insisted on walking with her arm in his, and he loved letting her.

"The first Omen is the mind of Sakarabru. It is the essence of his thoughts and his nature. It is his cunning and his fear. His control."

Kifo was surprised. "Fear? Lord Sakarabru has fears?"

She nodded. "We all do. Why should he be any different? Of course he has them, but he keeps them hidden and safely tucked away. He is good at keeping them safe."

"So when the Redeemer bonds with this first Omen, she bonds with the nature of Sakarabru?"

Andromeda became very thoughtful. "She understands him. She knows him. And yes. If she isn't careful, she can become him. Sakarabru is not all monster, Kifo. There are elements of him that can be very attractive, especially to the Redeemer, and especially when she makes the next two bonds. It is this first Omen that can control the other two. But if she's not careful, it can control her as well."

They continued strolling for a while longer before he asked the next question.

"What is the second Omen?"

"Ah! The second Omen is his rage. It's strong and chaotic. Angry and vicious. But it's that part of him that has no sympathy or empathy. It's the part of him that's the most destructive, the warrior in him, and without the first Omen, it would rip the Redeemer in two."

"The first Omen can control the second?"

"It must. For the Redeemer to survive the second bond, she has to discover this. She has to know it, or the second Omen will undoubtedly kill her."

"And what is the third Omen?"

They stopped walking, and Andromeda turned to face him. "The third Omen is his passion, Kifo."

Kifo was confused. "Passion? I don't understand. Passion seems silly, Andromeda. Sakarabru has telepathic abilities; he's got the power of influence. How would his passion serve the Redeemer in his destruction?"

"Think of it as his ego. It is the audacity of the Demon that gives him his power. Sakarabru is able to do what he does because his ego is massive. He desires to do these things and he's driven to do them because they please and satisfy his true nature. His pure nature is evil, Kifo. And that is all it is. Without this third Omen, the Redeemer is simply a very introverted girl prone to fits of destruction. The third Omen makes her believe in the powers she possesses. It gives her the confidence that she has every right to use her abilities to whatever end she sees fit. She has to be poised to understand the depth of her powers and that it is her right to destroy the Demon and her privilege."

Kifo thought for a moment. "In this case, the end she should see is the end of Sakarabru."

Andromeda winked. "That's the plan."

"But . . . why her? Why couldn't any one of us make these bonds with the Omens to defeat Sakarabru? I could've made them. Knowing what I know now, I would've. Mkombozi was just a royal. This reborn is just a human. My mystical powers are unmatched, Andromeda. Someone like me could've ended this long ago."

Andromeda pressed a warm hand to his face. "But you are not his child, Kifo. You are not his flesh and blood. Mkombozi, and now Eden, are natural extensions of Sakarabru. Imagine that *they are all pieces of the same puzzle. Of course they fit. The Re-deemer is and has always been an extension of her father. And they will fit until the very end, until not only the destruction of the Demon is complete but the destruction of the Omens as well."*

"What do you mean?"

She smiled, looped her arm in his, and began walking again. "I mean that Sakarabru's destruction is only a part of a much bigger adventure. And your role in it has just begun."

Andromeda lay in a heap on the floor looking nothing like the pretty woman he'd brought here. She wasn't moving. Sakarabru motioned for someone to bring him a drink, which he guzzled greedily. He looked over at Kifo and raised his glass in a toast, then nodded at the pile that was Andromeda.

"She never ceases to amaze me," he said, breathless. "Sometimes, I get the feeling that she enjoys our visits as much as I do."

Kifo felt like vomiting. "Did she tell you where to find the Omen?" he struggled to ask.

Sakarabru laughed. "Weren't you paying attention, Djinn?" Sakarabru finished what was left of his drink. "She *is* the Omen."

He came over to Kifo and towered over him. Kifo noticed that the Demon didn't stand as tall as he had when he was first brought back. Sakarabru's stamina wasn't very impressive either. He tired easily, and the weight of this atmosphere was starting to affect him the way it had affected all of them when they'd first come to this world.

"I think we have just found our advantage, my friend." Sakarabru placed a bloody hand on Kifo's stark white sports jacket. "If the Redeemer wants to make her bond, then she'll have to come here to do it," he said menacingly. "You're the only one I trust, Kifo. Bring me my little reborn. Convince her that you know where the third Omen is."

Kifo looked stunned. "She won't believe me, Sakarabru."

"Make her." He thought for a moment and then suddenly came up with what seemed like a more reasonable idea. "Tell Khale where it is," Sakarabru finally said. "She'll see to it that the reborn comes for it."

"Here? You expect Khale to come here?" Kifo asked. "She'll suspect a trap."

Sakarabru considered what Kifo had said. "Yankee Stadium," he finally said, looking at Kifo and grinning. "Tell her that the Omen is in Yankee Stadium."

Kifo nodded. "Yankee Stadium."

TROUBLE ON THE WAY

There was something strangely melancholy about coming to an end of a thing. Sakarabru had been living on the edge of a precipice for far longer than he should have been. He had been born for one purpose, and that was to rule, his way, in his world. But fate obviously had other plans for him, and Sakarabru was here now, in this new world, but the one constant remained. To rule was his destiny.

This place disgusted him. Sakarabru's shoes were covered in the debris of disobedience and failure. Paul Chapman had proven to embody both. What was left of the Brood lay shredded on the floor at Sakarabru's feet. He had failed to stop the reborn from bonding with the other Omens and let her live for the opportunity to make the final connection.

Sakarabru squatted to look into what used to be Paul Chapman's face and shook his head, disappointed. "I had such high hopes for you, Brood. You were to have been my greatest general. But you failed me."

The beast wallowed in his own piss and weakness and the Demon desperately needed a shower.

"I should wash your back." Lilith appeared as if by magic in the shower behind Sakarabru.

The succubus had always been there for him, in whatever way he needed her. And she'd waited here for his return, all these many years later. She and Kifo had been loyal to him, unwavering and unquestioning.

He sighed as she slathered soap over his back, down his arms and legs, across his buttocks. Naturally, she paid special attention to his balls and cock. Lilith was an impossible habit for any creature to break once he or she had had a sample of her. She was the nectar where he was the thorn. She was the prize at the end of a long and agonizing journey. Lilith could be whatever an individual wished her to be. To Sakarabru, she was Khale née Khale in her natural and perfect state.

Her flawless sky blue skin reflected the light beautifully. A long flowing stream ran down her back, and she had round hips that lengthened into strong toned legs. Her eyes! He could never tire of gazing into her beautiful eyes, the color of violet, wide and bright. They had caught him and held him captive. Khale parted her lips slightly, raised them to his, and swept her delicious tongue against his. Ample breasts offered erect, ripe nipples primed for suckling. Sakarabru dropped to his knees and took one in his mouth and then the other.

He parted her soft thighs with his hand and eased his long finger into the delectable folds of her most precious self. Khale raised one leg and draped it over his shoulder. Sakarabru lowered his head and drove his tongue deep into the recesses of her flicking it against her thickening clit.

"Yesssss," she hissed. "Oh . . . yessss!"

He fucked her with his tongue, the way he'd remembered she'd loved it. But he would not let her come. Sakarabru pushed her back against the wall, stood up, reached around her thighs, and raised her off the ground, then lowered her on his throbbing shaft.

Khale cried out. Her violet eyes bore into his as she thrust her hips against him, pounding him with the same force that he pushed into her. He was going to explode inside her! He was going to hurt her in the most fantastic way! He was going to own her, make her his, and dare any male to even try to enter her after he'd finished with her. Khale would want no other! She would need no other. And she would only ever crave him with the same passion that he craved her.

She cried out and bucked wildly against him. Sakarabru grunted deep in the back of his throat, closed his eyes, and flexed from his shoulders to his feet, as he released himself inside her. She was his. Khale née Khale would always be his.

It would all be over soon and there would be nothing standing in the way of him and the domination of this world. He glanced back at Lilith sleeping in his bed, still disguised as Khale. She was a tool with which he could live out a fantasy, a memory, or maybe even his own version of a prophecy. He might kill all of the other Ancients, but not her, not willingly. Khale had been the most beautiful creature he'd ever seen, and his love for her had been true. But she'd used him to create the abomination that was Mkombozi, and now this reborn.

He couldn't help smiling in his admiration of her. She had been as cunning and as conniving as a Demon, and yet she had managed to pass herself off as one of them—one of the Ancients. Maybe in her heart, that's what she had hoped she was, but deep down, she hated him because he recognized herself in him.

Kifo could be convincing. He was a good liar. He had even lied to Sakarabru by saying that he'd seduced Andromeda, tricked and captured her. The Seer could not be captured. She could only surrender, and for whatever reason, she had surrendered to Kifo. And he had gone along with it. Maybe Andromeda was the one setting the trap. She was certainly cunning. Sakarabru had peeled her like fruit and found nothing that would cause him concern. How many times had he taken the Seer apart in the past? And how many of those times had she stolen from him and used her prize to create her Omens? Had she stolen from him tonight?

It was a mangled mess of "what-ifs" tangled in his mind. Sakarabru was tired, and maybe he was overthinking things. He had always been suspicious of everyone around him, but it had saved his life on many occasions. It was exhausting being so solitary, but necessary. But if he ever did discover that Kifo had betrayed him, the Djinn would pay dearly for

that betrayal at the end of Sakarabru's most brutal and sa-
distic wrath. And as for Andromeda, he was through playing her games. She'd survived and escaped him so many
times before. He'd like to see her escape after he took her
head.

"Sakarabru," Khale moaned seductively.

A beautiful hardened nipple pressed invitingly against the
bedsheet.

"Yes, my love," he responded.

"Come to bed," she begged. "I'm getting cold."

Tomorrow he would kill a seer and a reborn. Tonight he
would fuck Khale until she begged for him to stop.

FIGHT THE POWER

Eden had grown more sullen and moody with each passing day. And of course the Guardian was never far from her side, watching over her as if he were waiting for something to happen. They were no closer to finding the third Omen now than they had been three days ago, when Eden and Prophet had come back to lower Manhattan.

"Eden, concentrate," Khale gently coaxed her. "The first two Omens should lead you to the last one. That's how it worked before. The first two led Mkombozi to the final one. The Omens need to be complete. They need each other."

Eden pressed her lips together in frustration; they were well beyond the point of coddling her. Khale studied her, wondering if she weren't somehow blocking any messages that the other two Omens might send to her out of spite to get back at Khale for what she'd done to her at the house of the Seer twins. But surely she wouldn't be so petty. Eden had come so far, and she had to understand the gravity of this situation, especially now.

"Maybe you aren't recognizing what they're telling you," Khale continued. "Do you see a place in your mind that seems random? Is there a word that keeps repeating to you, or a song? Anything?"

"Nothing," she said resentfully. "I'm getting nothing, Khale."

"Try harder," Khale urged.

"I don't have time for this," Jarrod said irritably, getting up to leave. "I've got my own kind to check up on, Shifter," he said, gathering his things to leave. "You know where to find me if you need me."

"Since you're so into fates and prophesies, Khale, maybe you should take this as a sign," Isis said indifferently. "The fact that Eden doesn't know might mean that this isn't meant to be."

"We're not alone," Aelia said suddenly, sitting up straight in her wheelchair. "Someone's here."

Prophet sensed it too and immediately stood up and prepared himself for whatever might materialize in that room.

"Show yourself," Khale commanded.

In one corner of the room, Kifo gradually revealed himself. They all knew him. He was the chief mystic to Sakarabru, and he had been the one to build this new army. Prophet lunged at him and immediately took to shoving his elbow into Kifo's neck and slamming him back against the wall. Isis pulled out a Colt .45 and pointed it at his head. Out of water, Aelia was pretty much useless.

Khale approached him. "Sakarabru's taken to sending spies, I see."

Kifo tried shoving the Guardian's arm from across his throat, but of course it wouldn't budge. So he did what came naturally. Kifo disappeared and then reappeared on the other side of the room.

"Fuckin' Djinn," Prophet muttered.

He adjusted his shirt and tie. "I'm not a spy," he retorted.

"Yeah. You'll understand if we don't believe you," Isis said sarcastically.

"What else would you be doing here if not spying, Djinn?" Khale probed.

Kifo looked at each one of them around the room, until his gaze finally landed and lingered on her. No one had to tell him who she was. Kifo was looking at the reborn. Andromeda had told him that the reborn had survived the bonds with the first two Omens. Being this close to her now, he could feel the familiar essence of Sakarabru emanating from her aura. Kifo could see the Demon's dark nature reflecting back at him in her eyes.

"It's you I came to talk to, Khale," he said finally, forcing his attention back to the Shifter.

She stared back at him suspiciously. "Me? Why?"

"Alone," he insisted.

Khale hesitated for a few moments, considering his request. Kifo was obviously here on Sakarabru's orders. She needed to hear what he had to say. "Leave us," she told everyone.

The two of them waited until everyone in the room left.

As Eden passed by him, she gazed up at him with a familiar scowl in her eyes, so reminiscent of Sakarabru.

Khale had tried to reason with Kifo weeks ago, and he'd chosen to ignore her. Now, of course, she was fascinated and curious to know what he had to say to her.

"Talk," she said simply.

The proud and obedient Kifo almost seemed to melt before her eyes. He stiffly walked away from her and stood looking at the crowd gathered outside of the window. "They'd have torn me to shreds had they seen me walking among them," he said absently.

"Deservedly so."

"You told me that Sakarabru had tortured me."

Khale watched him closely. The Djinn was a master mystic, and with a wave of his hand or the murmur of a word he could cast a spell on her, making her susceptible to whatever trap he was trying to set for her.

"You accused me of lying, if I remember correctly," she said.

He turned to her. "You were the enemy, Khale. What did you expect me to say?"

"Were? I *am* the enemy, Kifo," she reminded him.

Unexpected vulnerability appeared in his expression. "Sakarabru is the enemy of us all."

She stared suspiciously at him. "Why did you really come here, Djinn?"

"Have you found the third Omen?" he asked, pulling back his shoulders.

Khale couldn't help finding his question funny. "As if

I'd tell you. Go, Kifo." She motioned toward the door. "You are wasting my time."

"I know where the third Omen is," he volunteered.

The hair on the back of her neck stood up. Kifo had just said a mouthful, but the problem was, it was either a lie or a trap or both. Khale was exhausted. She'd spent the last few days trying to coax the location of the Omen from Eden, and she hadn't slept for staying up all night long worrying about what their next move would be.

"Really, Kifo," she said wearily. "You can't possibly think that you can come in here and drop a bomb like that on me and expect me to take the bait. Do you?"

He nodded. "Yes."

Khale shook her head in disbelief and walked over to the sofa and sat down. "Go," she demanded, waving her hand toward the door.

"You should hear what I have to say."

"Just . . . get out of here, Kifo, before—"

"You told me that he tortured me," he said quietly.

"I told you the truth and you dismissed it."

He looked thoughtful all of a sudden, and vulnerable. Kifo hesitantly took a seat in the Queen Anne chair across from Khale.

"I didn't believe it because I . . . didn't remember it," he admitted.

She watched carefully as he gradually unfolded his lie. She was beginning to admire his acting skills. Kifo was quite impressive. The Djinn was the enemy, and the enemy had to die, but for a moment she had conceded that fact. Kifo was a victim of Sakarabru. As much of a victim as she had been, as much of a victim as the human Brood Army had been.

Kifo took a deep breath. "I was so young, Khale," he said, introspectively. "Equivalent to a human boy of fifteen, maybe sixteen."

She had heard that Sakarabru had found a young Djinn, a master mystic, and had held him captive for longer than anyone. The child had survived ten of Earth's years in Sakarabru's torture room. Kifo didn't seem to know it, but when Sakarabru had found him, he was closer to a boy of six.

Kale watched him shrink under the heavy weight of sadness and discovery. "It's hard sometimes, but I try not to linger on the details," he offered. "They come to me, though, more and more in little packets, mostly when I'm sleeping," he admitted.

"Why are you telling me this, Kifo?" she asked suspiciously.

"The Djinn masters who took care of me were spiritual beings, peaceful and accepting. I have dishonored their memories by things I've done. I've committed terrible acts of cruelty believing that what I was doing was right." He looked meaningfully back at her. "I've destroyed an entire race of people, Khale. Because of me, this world will never be the same, and I can't forgive myself for that. I don't deserve forgiveness."

She wanted to believe him. Hell, Khale needed to believe him, because right now, if he truly did know where the third Omen was, he was the closest thing they had to salvation. But again, Kifo was the enemy and he had been for a very long time. Sakarabru had taken that little Djinn and molded him into exactly what he'd wanted him to be. It had taken so much pain and darkness. She wanted to believe that Kifo had changed, but trusting him would be foolish.

"Did Sakarabru send you?" she asked, point-blank.

He nodded. "Yes. He did. But he believes that it was his idea. He believes that he sent me here to set a trap for the reborn."

"He believes it?" she asked cautiously. "So what's the truth?"

He took a deep breath. "Andromeda sent me," he confessed. "And she said that you probably wouldn't believe me."

"I don't. Why would she send you?"

He shrugged. "You'd have to ask her. But she told me your secret, Khale."

Khale sat up straight in her chair. "What secret, Djinn?"

"She told me the reason that Mkombozi was chosen as the Redeemer. She told me why Mkombozi was the only Ancient capable of bonding with the Omens," he explained cautiously.

Sakarabru could've told him this. The Djinn was as much of a liar as the Demon ever was.

Kifo seemed to read her mind. "I would never speak of this to anyone, Khale."

The dragon in her began to stir awake. The Djinn's eyes grew wide at the subtle transformation he saw in her eyes. Kifo would not live to see the outside of this house.

"What if I am telling the truth, Khale?" he said quickly. "What if I am truly repentant for my transgressions and

Andromeda really did send me here with this message? Are you really willing to risk the salvation of this world and the opportunity to destroy Sakarabru once and for all over what I have told you?"

"He sent you here to set this trap."

"He has Andromeda, Khale," he said, choking up. It seemed too authentic to be faked. "He wanted me to convince you to bring the reborn to Yankee Stadium tomorrow and to tell you that I had seen Andromeda hide it there. But that's a lie. Andromeda *is* the third Omen. He has her in New Orleans. And if the reborn is going to claim it and bond with it, she'll need to get to the Seer."

It was far too elaborate and well thought out to be a lie, and Kifo had either put on an Oscar-worthy performance or he was telling the truth. Either way, Khale had to be prepared for both. And she had to decide what to do next. Eden would have to decide. Ultimately, Eden was going to have to rise to to occasion of her destiny and make that final bond. If Kifo was lying, she pitied him.

RIVER DEEP, MOUNTAIN HIGH

Eden paced nervously back and forth in one of the bedrooms upstairs. "This is weird," she kept muttering to herself, wringing her hands together. "I know him, but I don't know him," she said out loud.

She had never seen that dude before, but there was something eerily familiar about him. "How can I know him?" She was talking to herself more than she was to Prophet. She had a sense of déjà vu with the guy who had appeared out of thin air in Khale's living room, but Eden couldn't make the connection in her mind. Then it dawned on her that the feelings reeling inside her weren't hers. They were Sakarabru's.

Eden stopped pacing and headed for the door. "I need to talk to him."

Prophet got up to come with her, but she didn't want that. "No."

"What?"

She didn't need him hovering over her all the time. Eden didn't want him shadowing her every move. Prophet was smothering her. She understood that it was his job to be her Guardian and to look after her, but lately she was starting to think she couldn't even take a piss without him standing close enough to wipe her ass. It was an unexpectedly ugly thought. Eden just needed some space.

"I'll just be downstairs," she said, attempting to ease the tension.

She closed the door behind her when she left.

Kifo. Khale had called him Kifo. They both froze when they saw Eden coming down the stairs.

"Eden, you should be resting," Khale said, but Eden ignored her and walked over to this Kifo and stood directly in front of him.

He had dark beautiful skin and was clean shaven. The irises of his eyes weren't brown. They were black. She didn't trust him. He seemed to tense in her presence. Kifo was afraid of her.

"Why did you really come here?" Eden challenged.

He noticeably swallowed and worked doubly hard to maintain his solid and polished composure. The illusion of dignity was important to him because he'd lost it long ago.

"I came to tell Khale that I know where the last Omen is," he admitted.

The thought came to her about Kifo. He'd been hurt before so badly, and he'd suffered so long, until she wondered if he'd actually enjoyed it. Did he savor his suffering and relish these moments the way that she . . . These weren't her memories. They were residual memories of the first Omen, of Sakarabru.

"Why should I believe you?" Eden sneered. The longer he was in her presence, the angrier she was becoming.

Kifo seemed to sense this rage swelling inside her, and he took a step back. Eden immediately filled in the space he'd tried to put between the two of them. She was the dominant, the one he answered to, the one he owed his allegiance to. Kifo had no choice but to be obedient.

"Convince me that you know where my Omen is!" she commanded.

Khale's voice came from some faraway place. "Eden! Stop it!"

The shifter had no place in this. Kifo, her little Djinn, Eden's little magician, would answer to her.

"Convince me that you can be trusted, Djinn! Convince me that I was right in choosing to let you live!"

This wasn't her! It didn't even sound like her! Eden craved the sounds of his screams! She salivated at the thought of spilling his blood. Kifo could not be trusted! He could not . . .

"Eden!"

The sound of Prophet's voice brought her back inside this room. Pictures had fallen off the walls, vases had been broken. Kifo stood there looking as if he had seen a ghost, or worse. She was so close to losing what was left of herself.

"Where is the third Omen?" she asked softly.

She needed to know where it was. Eden needed to get this shit over with. Her end was here. It was right here in front of her.

"Where is it, Kifo?" she asked again, looking into his hooded black eyes.

"The Omen is the Seer Andromeda," he told her.

Eden shook her head, confused. "I don't . . . I don't get it. The Omen is *in* Andromeda or it *is* Andromeda?"

"It *is* her."

How the hell was she supposed to make sense of that? The first Omen had been a thing, an object passed from that crazy old man to Eden. He passed it to her by touching her. The second Omen was a . . . a spirit, the spirit of Sakarabru's rage. Eden had to literally die to go into the afterlife to get that one. And now he was telling her that the last Omen was a person?

She looked at him as if he were out of his mind. "I'm supposed to bond with Andromeda?"

He raised his chin defiantly. "Yes."

Eden was dumbfounded. "How?"

Kifo's blank expression pretty much answered her question. He had no idea.

Eden slowly turned away from him. She'd come too far to go back. It would be impossible to unbond with the first two Omens. She couldn't change her mind and say, "That's it. I'm stopping right here. No more bonding, and to hell what happens to all you Ancients and the rest of the world. Y'all can kiss my ass."

Eden looked at Khale. "You're the genius," she said sarcastically. "Any ideas on how I'm supposed to bond with the Seer of the Ages that doesn't involve you cutting my throat?"

"None."

Eden turned to leave the room. "I need my Guardian."

She sat cross-legged on the bed while he paced slowly back and forth.

"He's setting us up," Prophet eventually said, stating the obvious.

Even if he hadn't said it, she knew the moment she laid eyes on the guy talking to Khale that he had come here under false pretenses. Eden knew him but not directly. He was familiar to her because Sakarabru knew him, intimately, and he wasn't to be trusted.

"We've got nothing else, Prophet," she said.

He stopped and stared at her. "Do you hear yourself?"

"What?" She shrugged.

"Three months ago I couldn't get you to stop crying, and now you want to go rushing off to New Orleans on the chance that you can make this last bond."

So what was he saying? "I mean, what else am I supposed to do? I need all three to defeat Sakarabru, and I've only got two. This dude may be lying or he may be telling at least a part of the truth, and we've got nothing else."

"You sound almost anxious to do this, Eden." He was studying her, looking at her almost as if he didn't recognize her.

"You're right," she admitted reluctantly. "It's incomplete, Prophet. I'm incomplete."

She felt like some junkie in need of a fix. As terrifying as it had been to make these first two bonds, Eden felt off balance without that last one. There was a void inside her that desperately needed to be filled.

He sat down next to her. Eden could see the worry in his eyes. "I can't lose you again. I won't."

"Then don't," she said, pressing her hand to his face. "This is hard for both of us, Prophet. But I'm in this now and I can't turn back even if I wanted to. All I can do is finish this and then hope that I can hold on to some semblance of myself when it's over—if I live through it."

For the first time since she'd known him, Eden sensed his doubt and uncertainty. Prophet had been strong for her. He had been encouraging her and taking care of her, making sure that she was okay. Now he was the one that needed reassurance, and she owed it to him to give him that.

Eden crawled onto his lap. "I am fighting this," she told him, staring into his eyes. "Every second of every day, I am fighting for me and you because I don't want to lose you either."

He was strong and steadfast, and he loved her in a way Eden never dreamed she could be loved. Prophet was ready to lay down his life for her if it came to that. Of course he was worth fighting for.

"I'm not leaving you, either," she assured him. But the reality of the situation loomed between them. "If things don't work out, though"—she choked back tears, at the thought of dying—"you'll come with me?"

"I'll follow you anywhere. I told you that. I meant it."

That's what she was afraid of, even more than bonding with that last damned Omen.

Eden was awake and staring out of the bedroom window long after Prophet had fallen asleep. The Djinn appeared as if by magic, standing in the corner of the room.

"A month ago, you might've scared the shit out of me," she admitted softly.

Kifo surprised her, and maybe even himself, with a smile. "I owe you an apology," he said sincerely. "I was not strong enough to resist the influence of Lord Sakarabru. I bought him back," he confessed. "I rebuilt his army, and I ruined what was once a pretty decent world."

This was his idea of atonement?

"So what do you want me to say? That's it's okay? That we all make mistakes?" she said sarcastically. "That on behalf of humankind, I forgive you?" She could tell that Kifo was seriously kicking his own ass for what he'd done. Eden needed to be a bigger person and not continue to add insult to injury. "Tell me that Andromeda really is the final Omen, Kifo. And that once I bond with her, that'll be that, and that whatever's going to happen is going to happen, and that you're not setting me up."

"I'm not setting you up."

She stared at him. "Even if you are, does it really matter?"

Kifo shook his head. "Exactly."

"Sakarabru wanted me to lead you to Yankee Stadium," he admitted. "Away from Andromeda and directly to him."

The two of them locked gazes in a moment of silence. Eden had evolved into a destiny she never wanted and into a creature she never wanted to be. Kifo was probably leading her to her death but if he was, then he was probably doing her a favor.

"When do we leave?" she asked him.

"As soon are you're ready."

USE SOMEBODY

Picking up the pieces from a moment like this was never easy, but it was possible, because at this same moment, Andromeda was strolling along a white sand beach, with the sun shining down on her face and the Mediterranean air caressing her skin. At this very moment she was eating a bowl of her favorite ice cream at a bistro in San Francisco. And right now, in another place, Andromeda was about to make her lover scream her name to the heavens and swear his love to her for all eternity. This sacrifice had been necessary and even welcomed because it was selfless, and the selfless moments were always the sweetest.

Her wounds were healing nicely. Sakarabru had taken such pleasure in tormenting the Seer. The sadist in him loved to watch her suffer. But what he failed to understand about the closeness of these encounters they shared was that they always left parts of him open and vulnerable to someone who

knew what to look for. Andromeda had always prided herself on her insightfulness and intuition. She understood the
nature of a thing pretty quickly, and she had grown to
understand the nature of Sakarabru intimately.

She picked up what was left of her pretty dress, disappointed that she'd soiled it. It had been one of her favorites,
but she'd never be able to wear it again. She'd gotten it from
Bolen's Department Store in Louisville, Kentucky, back in the
year 1957. To her, 1957 was just a number, but humans had
this obsessive compulsion to measure things, time being one
of them. Maybe one day she'd go back to Bolen's and try to
find another dress just like this one. For now, she was naked.
She was finished here. Andromeda had done what she had
come to do. The third and final Omen was now where it was
meant to be, placed there by the incomprehensible babblings
and cries of a tortured Seer who had finally spat the foul
taste of the Demon out of her mouth and back onto him.

"Tell me where my Omen is, Seer!" he yelled, driving his
dagger slowly into the raw flesh of her belly. "End your suffering, Andromeda."

His face was mere inches from hers. The pain was unbearable, but bear it she did. Instinct and reflex took over
where intent left off.

"Ptuah!" she spat in his face.

Of course he was furious. And of course, he would make
her pay for her transgression. Andromeda turned her face to
where she knew Kifo stood. Tears of desperation filled her
eyes, her lips trembled as he twisted his blade in wide circles inside her. Andromeda wanted to smile. Kifo kept his

promise and she knew that it was killing him to do so, but it was also necessary. He materialized long enough for her to see him. And Andromeda winked. The rest was up to Kifo and the Redeemer. Andromeda could only hope that Kifo was as observant and as diligent a mystic as she believed him to be.

"Don't do this to me, Prophet," Eden said as the two of them stood outside the SUV.

Kifo and Khale were inside.

He stood there as defiant as ever. "I can't believe we're even having this conversation."

"You're a distraction that I don't need," she said earnestly. "It's over and you know it. And if I'm going to do this, then I don't need you in the mix."

"I'm insulted," he protested mildly.

"I'm not trying to insult you."

"You have." Prophet reached for the handle on the passenger door, pulled it open, and waited for her to climb inside. Eden sat sulking as he made his way around to the driver's side and climbed in behind the wheel.

The mood in the vehicle was tense and heavy. In a matter of hours, Eden would come face-to-face with the Demon. Questions started to come to mind. Eden wondered why she hadn't thought to ask them before.

"What's he look like, Kifo?"

"Taller than normal," he said from the backseat. "Sakarabru was resurrected with his former Theian form. We were taller then. Evolution has changed us. He's . . . good-looking, I guess. Time and the transition to this world has turned his hair white. His eyes are blue?"

"Green," Khale absently interjected. "His eyes are green."

"How much does he know about me?" Eden continued probing.

"Very little," Kifo said. "Sakarabru knows of a reborn Redeemer. His only point of reference is Mkombozi."

"Is he afraid of me?" The question surprised even her.

"Yes," Kifo said quickly.

Eden wanted to find solace in that answer, but there was none. Mkombozi had gained the strength to defeat Sakarabru, but she'd lost her soul to the Omens. Eden could feel her own spirit slipping away already. And she had no doubt that the last bond would seal the deal. The idea of going head-to-head against one of the most powerful creatures in the universe was too unbelievable to grasp. And the fact that she was the one who was supposed to take him down—well, that was just crazy. What would the bond with Andromeda give her? She had the connection to the mind and strength of the Demon. What was left? Andromeda was the Seer of the Ages, which meant that she could travel through time, or something like that. Maybe that's what she'd get from the bond. The ability to time-travel. Or maybe she'd just grow taller.

"Oh shit!" The Guardian growled, slamming his foot so hard on the brake that he pushed a hole through the floor of the vehicle.

The bull burst through a thick cloud of black smoke forming out of nothing in the middle of the highway, his head lowered, and charged directly at the vehicle.

"No!" Khale shouted at the sight of the Demon. She shifted into an eagle upon impact and flew out with the shattered glass from the backseat window.

Sakarabru met the car head-on and drove enormous golden horns into the front end of the vehicle. The razor-sharp tips of them projected through the dashboard, one of them just inches away from stabbing into Eden's chest where she sat in the passenger seat.

Prophet jerked her toward him just in time and held her against him. The bull Demon raised the entire car off the ground on his horns, held it over his head, and then he released an Earth-quaking yell into the atmosphere as he flung the vehicle through the air, across a ravine, and crashing into an open field. He charged into the trench and waited as the vehicle rolled violently until it stopped and landed on its hood.

"I know she's somewhere inside that piece of shit!" He growled, starting to charge at them again.

The Demon was caught. A fifty-five-foot anaconda wrapped herself around both legs, squeezed him around the waist, his neck, face, and finally both horns. Khale was suffocating him. She glanced over at the wreckage in time to see the Guardian pulling Eden out of the car and leading her toward the forest. A wave of pain suddenly tortured Khale. She looked down and saw that the demon had taken a bite out of her.

He spat out the meat. "Get the fuck off me, bitch!"

She constricted even more. "Kiss my ass!" she hissed.

A thousand hands seemed to start pulling at her all at once, tearing into her, biting and . . . The Demon's Brood had come out of nowhere and converged on the two of them like a colony of bees. They were shredding her into pieces, and she had no choice but to change. Barely escaping with her life, the hawk had just enough strength to barely keep herself beyond the reach of the arms of the Brood. She held on long enough to get to the forest, where Eden had disappeared, and found a branch high enough that she couldn't be reached.

She was covered in blood; chunks of flesh were literally gone. Pain engulfed the Shifter as she desperately scanned the forest floor for Eden. "Eden!" she called out. "Keep running!" Khale pleaded, hoping that she could hear her. "Whatever you do! Keep running!"

SET THE WORLD ON FIRE

Thirty Brood stood between Prophet and his target. Thirty motherfuckers that meant about as much to him as mosquitoes. He swatted against them with forearms as thick as pythons. Prophet snapped necks like toothpicks, snatched off arms as easily as pulling the wings off flies. His focus on the Demon was unwavering; their bites, their knives plunging into his rib cage meant nothing to him. He felt numb and determined, crushing their bodies under his feet as he trampled over them. The Demon stood there waiting for him, their gazes locked on each other. The adrenaline surging through the Guardian's veins took him back to a time when war was everything and killing his enemy made his mouth water.

The last Brood standing between Prophet and Sakarabru had the misfortune of stumbling and falling. Prophet felt its skull crush under his heel. He lowered his head and lunged for the Demon, but before he could barrel into him, Sakarabru caught him by the hair, raised his knee, and planted it solidly under the Guardian's chin. Blood sprayed from Prophet's mouth.

"Where is she?" the Demon growled in his face.

Prophet spun free. It was a foolish question to ask a Guardian. Prophet smiled leaded back, and kicked, driving the heel of his boot into Sakarabru's knee. Prophet planted his feet, drew back his massive arm, and drove his fist full force up into the Demon's diaphragm. *Opportunity! Take it!* Prophet commanded himself. He took advantage of the Demon's exposed neck, grabbed hold of the back of it, and drove his knee hard into the Demon's throat. At least now they were even, and neither one of them could breathe.

Eden had been running away from the wreckage through the forest parallel to the highway. She had to put as much distance between Sakarabru and herself as possible. She had to somehow get to Andromeda and make the bond with the last Omen. God! It was impossible! It was all so impossible! Prophet! She thought he was behind her. Oh God! He had stayed behind to . . .

"No! Prophet!" she cried out. Eden couldn't let him do this. She started to run back to him! Sakarabru would kill him.

"He's killing him!" Kifo cried out.

Eden followed the sound of his voice. "Kifo? Kifo!"

He appeared as if out of nowhere. A wave of mistrust washed over her. Kifo was a liar. Kifo couldn't be trusted. He had betrayed her.

"You set us up! You fuckin' betrayed me, Djinn!"

Eden blinked and suddenly saw the Djinn kneeling at her feet. Blood seeped through the fibers of his stark white suit. "He's killing the Guardian, Eden," he said. "Sakarabru is too strong for him. He's too powerful."

"I need Andromeda!" she said, panicked. "I can't do this without her! I need the last Omen!"

Kifo struggled to his feet.

"Where's the Seer?" she shouted.

He helplessly shook his head. "I don't know."

Eden couldn't do this without the last Omen. "She's at the . . ." Kifo was magic. He could disappear and reappear like magic. "Take me to her," she commanded. Eden rushed over to him and wrapped her arms around him. "Magic, Kifo!" she said, squeezing her eyes shut. "Make your magic!"

Prophet's agonizing cries snapped Eden out of her desperation.

"No!" Eden couldn't let this happen. To hell with the third Omen. She couldn't let Sakarabru kill Prophet. She ran back toward the wreckage.

Her mind was racing. To beat the Demon she needed the third Omen! But Andromeda was the third Omen, and she was nowhere near. They didn't have time for her to make the bond. Prophet's life was on the line.

Eden had doubled back and kept out of sight of the Demon, making her way to find the only weapon she had in the wreckage of the SUV. She kept low and watched as Sakarabru impaled Prophet through his chest with his horn, raised him off the ground, and slung him through the air.

She watched in horror as the Demon stumbled back. The Guardian lay motionless a hundred yards away. She heard the Demon laugh all of a sudden.

"Welcome back, little Redeemer!" he called out, turning around in circles looking for her. His gaze finally rested on the wrecked car. Eden crouched low and dug through pieces of metal and broken glass until she found it. She hadn't used it since she was attacked by the Brood after she'd made the second bond. Prophet called it a *kpinga,* and even now, it felt like a natural extension of her.

"There you are." His tone grated against her skin.

Think, Eden! He was coming toward her. The air pressed in on her with each step he took. Sometimes she could make things happen by thinking about them. Eden had to concentrate. *Quicksand! Thick. Deep. Step. Step. Thick.* She saw his next step, saw him sink deep into the ground, thick like molasses, holding him there. She saw him struggling to pull his leg free, but there were hands in the quicksand, holding on to him, grabbing him, and trying to pull him deeper into the growing hole.

"You're going to have to do better than that, sweetheart," he threatened, forcing himself free and still coming toward her.

She only had two Omens. There was no way she could defeat with just two. They'd told her that. Everyone knew that she couldn't beat him with just two.

Eden saw his head spin around. She forced it to turn until she could hear the snapping of bone.

The Demon laughed. "That fuckin' hurt."

"Come on," she murmured. "Kill him, Eden! Think!" She envisioned a tree branch flying through the air like a spear aimed at his head. She saw it pierce his skull and come out on the other side. Sakarabru stumbled again, glanced at the branch lying on the ground on the other side of him, spat blood, and kept coming.

If she couldn't kill him then she had to focus on making herself stronger. His mind was her mind. She knew what he was going to do, but maybe he knew what she was going to do too. Eden stayed low and crept back away from the wreckage. He was so close. He saw her traps as soon as she did. But even if he didn't see them coming, he knew how to break free of them. Eden concentrated on herself and saw herself stronger than she ever thought possible. She saw herself faster than the Human Torch from *The Avengers*. She wasn't afraid. She saw her fist filled with the power of lightning, and she saw herself charge him, without fear or hesitation, slicing him across the neck with the blade of her weapon, slicing open his throat, decapitating him and finally putting an end to all this.

"You can't do it, reborn," he said catching her in midair, dangling her above ground by her throat. He had her! The Demon finally had her! Sakarabru held her suspended in the air. Intense emerald eyes burned into hers. Terror filled Eden at her core. She couldn't scream! She couldn't fight! She was frozen with fear. *Wake up, Eden! Please, wake the hell up!* But this was no nightmare and he was no bogeyman! He was the Demon of Theia and of this world! "My little Redeemer," he said almost admiringly.

One by one, Eden felt the vertebrae along the base of her neck snapping and popping. Her arms and legs dangled helplessly at her sides. Her *kpinga* lay at her feet, and tears slid down her cheeks. He would be the last thing she ever saw of this world. Her last memory.

"Now Eden!" she heard someone call out to her—

"Now! Make the bond! Make the bond! He's the third Omen!"

It was Kifo's voice.

The Demon. He was the third Omen! Sakarabru is the Omen and not Andromeda?

"She tricked us, Eden!" Kifo shouted. "Andromeda tricked all of us!"

Eden grabbed hold of his wrist with both hands. She stopped fighting him. He was the third Omen. Yes! She knew it. She could feel it. The nature of Sakarabru. The heart of the Demon surged through her body like a bolt of lightning.

"No!" she heard him yell.

He released his grip around her neck, but she didn't let go of him. He shook his hand, trying to fling her off of him, but Eden held on, letting the surge coming from him fill her to capacity. Eden closed her eyes and saw his beauty. Sakarabru had stared back at her in a stance of entitlement and privilege. He was breathtaking and proud. He was ego.

"You do not deserve me," he said, smugly. "You are not good enough."

His ego was the third Omen and it taunted her, but it was no fighter. She watched in fascination as he tugged at the cuffs of his sleeves, swept his hair from his face, doted on all of the beautiful things about himself.

Eden walked over to him and stopped. He looked down his nose at her, and laughed. She drew back her arm and slapped him hard across the face. He raised his chin, adjusted his collar, and licked at the trickle of blood pulled in the corner of his mouth.

"You do not deserve me," he said defiantly.

But she did deserve him.

"Three for three. Bring me. Redeem me. Or die the lamb."

Eden had earned the right to him. She had fought, and died, and lived. She had survived because she was the Redeemer and to destroy him was her destiny.

Eden slapped him again, and then grabbed him by hair, and pulled his face to hers until they were close enough to kiss. "Bitch," she said, gritting her teeth, "I own you!" She let him go when she was ready. Eden dropped to her feet and stood facing him.

Agonizing and torturous pain starting at the soles of his feet crept up his ankles, his legs.

His life was hers for the taking. His pain was hers to give. His suffering would be her pleasure.

"I didn't finish it the last time, Demon." Eden stepped toward him.

She knew him. Sakarabru couldn't have a thought without her knowing what it was. She anticipated every move he made and countered his blows with slices across his face, neck, and arms. She stabbed him in his midsection, moving too fast for him to see. Eden gouged his eyes and ears. Sakara-bru screamed in agony. She had made and survived all three bonds with all three Omens. Eden was a different kind of monster. He had no idea who he was fuckin' with.

Blood dripped down his face where horns had been and pooled in his eye sockets. "You are nothing to me," she said, stalking circles around him. A memory. History. A remnant, she never felt so whole and full and endless—without boundaries.

In her mind, Eden saw Khale, embedded and held in place in the bark of a tree. The Shifter struggled to free herself, but only Eden could free her.

The ground beneath Eden's feet began to rumble. The Earth split in a circle around the perimeter of the clearing and across the highway. Dark and menacing storm clouds quickly formed in the sky, shooting lightning into the air all around them.

"Eden! No!" She heard Khale's voice, but it sounded so far away.

The Demon had been cut down to his knees, mottled flesh and blood pooled all around him. A desperate and powerful rage burst from his mouth, shooting flames toward her. Eden yelled at the top of her lungs, forcing the blaze back toward him and down his throat, burning him from the inside out.

A fire began to rage through the forests surrounding them. She watched the demon writhing in pain, and she relished it. Is this what freedom felt like? She was complete in and of herself. Eden needed no one and nothing.

"Eden! Eden!"

Prophet was standing, but barely. He held out his arms to her. "Stop," he warned. "Eden! Listen to me! You've got to stop!"

Stop? No. She didn't want to stop. She was finally liberated. The excitement of the Demon twisting and turning as she wrenched his life from his body gave her such joy.

The Demon cursed her in the Ancient tongue, as more and more of him dissolved into the ground. She should stop! No. No. Not yet. Not now. And why should she stop? Why should she ever fuckin' stop?

"Too much," Prophet yelled. "He's done, Eden!" He stumbled toward her.

Eden couldn't stop. She didn't want to. It needed to be over. She was ready for it to end. Eden never saw Khale. She never heard her cry out to her, warning her that she was going too far, reminding her of what happened to Mkombozi when she went too far. She didn't hear Khale begin chanting the spell that sent Mkombozi to the afterlife on Ara.

"I want it over. I want to end him." And everything. Everyone. The Demon. The Ancients. Eden could do it. She needed to because who else could put and end to this chaos. Sound caved in on itself as did light. Peace. It was dark and quiet and warm. Arms wrapped around her. A voice? His voice. Prophet's voice. "Then end him," he told her. "Where you go, I go, Eden. End it, so that it can finally be over, for both of us."

He would let her do it. Prophet would never leave her. Not again. He would follow her anywhere.

HOLDING ON TO YOU

Andromeda had found another dress just like the one she's soiled in Sakarabru's torture room, only this one had pink flowers on it, and she loved it even more.

"You look lovely, Andromeda," Kifo told her, holding out his arm for her to take.

He had promised to take her for a nice stroll along the River Walk in San Antonio.

"Thank you, Kifo." She blushed.

She had made up her mind to let him love her if he chose to do so. He seemed interested in a courtship.

It had been a week since the Demon's destruction. This was the first opportunity that the two of them had had to talk about it.

"I was worried that you hadn't paid attention," she said in earnest.

"It was hard to. I wanted to kill him for hurting you. All I could think about was that I'd given you my word that I wouldn't interfere."

"I wanted to tell you everything," she said sincerely. "But I knew that if I did, he'd know. Without meaning to, you'd give him some clue to what I'd done, and everything would've fallen apart."

"Well, I understand that now," he said quickly.

The Seer had led Sakarabru to believe that she was the Omen on purpose. She had planted that thought in his mind while he was torturing her. What sounded like anguished babble to Kifo was actually one of Theia's lost languages from before. To Sakarabru it sounded like a confession.

"I—am—the—third—Omen!"

She had planted the words in such a way that he believed he had come up with the conclusion on his own. The truth was, Andromeda had made *him* the third Omen. Kifo had all but missed the exchange, but in the chaos surrounding the confrontation with Sakarabru in that clearing, it came to him. It was so subtle. Kifo had been sick to his stomach watching what the Demon had been doing to Andromeda. She coughed in an instant when Sakarabru had gotten too close. Blood and spit sprayed in his face, and he beat her brutally for it. When he finished, she had looked at Kifo and winked. Winks were the universal language in any world for, "Pay attention or you'll miss something wonderful."

Eden loved the house in Vermont. Even in the midst of the storm constantly raging inside her, she could find peace here, at least for now. The Guardian, her Guardian, had saved her. He'd stopped typhoon Eden dead in her tracks with something as simple as holding her in his strong arms. It sounded corny, but corny or not, it had worked. Beauty had indeed soothed the savage beast, and she loved him even more because of it.

She watched from the porch as Prophet circled overhead and finally landed, carrying a catch of half a dozen fish up to the porch.

"I'm going to need you to gut and cook this," he said, holding up dinner.

Eden grimaced and made the universal sign for "gag."

"Does that mean . . . no?"

Prophet cleaned and gutted the fish and cooked them outside over an open flame. Eden had hardly said two words in days. She hadn't slept or eaten. She hadn't so much as had a drink of water. She had fulfilled the prophecy. Eden had destroyed the Demon, but she was still bonded to the Omens, which were a part of him. Sakarabru was gone, but not really.

In the back of her mind, she'd sort of hoped that killing him was indicative of a new beginning, and it was, but now she wondered what it was a beginning to. Somehow she'd managed to survive the bonds and live with these things still inside her. The last Omen left its mark, a circle with three smaller circles inside it, in the middle of her back between her shoulder blades.

The Omens together had turned Mkombozi into another kind of creature, one that no one could contain and control. The Ancient had destroyed the Demon and very nearly every single Ancient in their world, had it not been for Khale stepping in at the last minute. So if those damn things had made an Ancient lose herself, what, ultimately, would they do to Eden?

"I cooked," he said, finishing up his meal. "You do the dishes."

He treated her the same. Like she was still Eden. It was hard not to love him for that. She wished she were that girl again.

He put his plate down on the deck. "Come here," he said, holding out his hand to her. Eden put her plate down, too, went to him, and climbed on top of him.

"We have survived a Demon, twice, one and a half world destructions, six bonds with Omens, and about three attempts of Khale trying to kill us."

Eden gazed into those heavenly eyes of his and smiled.

"I think we're going to be all right."

"Well"—she shrugged—"today we're all right and I'm good with that."